THE KING'S MAGE

ELIZABETH BAXTER

VINCI
BOOKS

By Elizabeth Baxter

The Songmaker

The Last Priestess
The King's Mage
The Traitor's Song

Vinci Books

vinci-books.com

Published by Vinci Books Ltd in 2026

1

The publisher and the author have made every effort to obtain permissions for any third party material used in this book and to comply with copyright law. Any queries in this respect should be brought to the attention of the publisher and any omissions will be corrected in future editions.

A CIP catalogue record for this book is available from the British Library.

Paperback ISBN: 9781036708474

The EU GPSR authorised representative is Logos Europe, 9 rue Nicolas Poussion, 17000 La Rochelle, France

contact@logoseurope.eu

Chapter One

Rovann woke with a start. Searing agony throbbed in his right arm, sending spears of fire vibrating through his body, threatening to tip him back into unconsciousness. For a moment, it consumed him. He couldn't think straight. He couldn't see. He couldn't hear.

But worse than all of this was a terrifying realization that he couldn't breathe. His lungs strained for air but it wouldn't come. Something warm pressed against his lips, blocking his airways. Then his sight cleared to reveal a woman's face close to his. Green eyes burned from a face covered in dirt and grime.

Maegwin.

And her hand was clamped tight over his mouth, suffocating him.

The day's events flashed through his mind. He and Maegwin confronting Lord Cedric Hounsey only to discover he was already dead, a revenant held in thrall to the Songmaker's will. The betrayal in Maegwin's eyes as he, Rovann, denied her revenge against Hounsey and then invaded her mind to seize her power to enable them to escape.

More images flickered. The storming of Carrow Crossing by Hounsey troops. His vain attempt to hold them off while Captain Tyan, Mage Syrie and the soldiers escaped. The enemy arrow that exploded through his right forearm.

Then finally the words Maegwin had whispered to him as he fell into unconsciousness.

It's just you and me now, Rovann. And you're all mine.

And here she was, a crazed look in her eyes, trying to smother him. A sliver of ice-cold fear stabbed through his abdomen. There was no recognition in Maegwin's eyes. Only a raw emotion that Rovann couldn't quite place. Covered in the blood and filth of battle, she looked like some wild she-devil dredged from an old saga.

She was going to kill him. After all they'd been through he was going to die at Maegwin's hands. His supposed ally. His friend.

No! I will not!

Summoning his ebbing strength, he reached for his sorcery only to find it gone. Where the burning core of his power should be, there was...nothing. Emptiness.

He'd spent too much of his strength in the citadel's defense. *Idiot*, he chided himself as his lungs burned and his consciousness began to fade. *Now your quest is over before it's begun.*

A small, traitorous part of him was relieved. It was over. Let someone else face the Songmaker. But another, stronger part shouted in outrage that it should end like this.

I won't allow it! he raged. *I will not!*

He thrashed in Maegwin's grip, determined to break her hold.

"How many more times?" she hissed. "Be quiet, curse you! Do you want to give us away? Hush!"

Comprehension dawned. He went as limp as a doll. She watched him warily as she slowly withdrew her hand and Rovann drew in a rasping breath.

"What are you—"

She pressed a finger to his lips. "Hush! They're close."

For the first time, Rovann noticed his surroundings. He was lying propped against a tree. A thick tangle of undergrowth surrounded him through which he could hear the murmur of the river. Over the growl of the water came something else: movement in the bushes, the sound of stealthy footsteps and low voices. Close.

Rovann froze. He held his breath. Slowly Maegwin drew her dagger.

Not more than five paces to Rovann's left a cry went up. "There! What's that? Is it a boat? It is! After them, you fools! And get archers to the riverbank! Move!"

Crashing sounded, uncomfortably close. After a moment it moved away from them, gradually dwindling into the distance. All was still. Rovann's heart thundered in his ears.

Maegwin crouched like a beast ready for flight. After several tense minutes she closed her eyes and sighed in relief, her shoulders sagging with released tension. Then she climbed to her feet.

"I'm going to have a look around. Wait here. I won't be long." Before he could protest she melted into the trees.

Rovann was left alone. The summer sun was halfway to the horizon, sending slivers of light to cast a patchwork pattern on the ground by Rovann's outstretched feet. Bees droned in and out of a bunch of purple foxgloves to his right and birds chattered in the branches above.

Rovann breathed deeply, trying to clear his head and find his bearings. Judging by the position of the sun, he guessed it was late afternoon, several hours since he and Maegwin had escaped from Carrow Crossing. A few hours? It felt like a heartbeat. Rovann could still hear the roaring of fighting, smell the stench of fear and taste the iron tang of blood. He could still see Lord Cedric Hounsey's grinning face.

He raised his hand to wipe sweat from his forehead but gasped as stinging pain ran up his arm and into his shoulder, making him dizzy. Gritting his teeth, he looked down. His right wrist was a mangled, swollen mass of torn flesh and encrusted blood. Where the arrow had penetrated, Rovann saw the white of broken bones and his fingers looked like thick, useless sausages. Slowly he raised the arm, grimacing against the pain.

"Don't."

Maegwin stepped into the clearing and crouched in front of him.

"Don't touch it."

Rovann sank back, laying his head against the tree trunk and resting the injured arm in his lap.

"Did you find anything?"

Maegwin inspected his injury and frowned at what she saw. "A party of Hounsey soldiers. The woods are full of them. We are being tracked. I suppose it was too much to hope that we got away without being seen."

"How far from the citadel are we?"

"Not as far as I'd like," she growled, straightening. "But as far as the river will allow. There's a waterfall ahead so I had to put in and get you ashore. I set the boat adrift hoping they might spot it and follow."

"It won't take them long to realize it's a decoy,"

Rovann said, glancing around their hideout as if expecting soldiers to come crashing through the trees any moment. "Then they'll retrace their steps. We can't hope to stay hidden."

"Don't you think I realize that?" she snapped. "We can't even get across the river. The far bank is a cliff with nowhere to land the boat."

This was not what Rovann wanted to hear. He needed time. Time to recover his strength. Time to treat his wounds. Time to think of a way out of this and form a plan to find the Songmaker. But he didn't have any.

"What of Captain Tyan, Syrie and the rest?" he asked. "Did they escape?"

Maegwin shrugged. "I don't know. I think so. You collapsed after you fired the bridge and I rowed us away as fast as I could. Soldiers were firing at us from the bank. I had to get us out of there."

Rovann studied her face. Although she was caked in crusted blood, none of it seemed to be her own. She seemed unharmed but exhausted. His earlier distrust suddenly shamed him. She'd saved his life. Again. And in return he'd suspected her of trying to kill him.

On impulse he reached out and laid his uninjured hand over hers. She startled, lifting her eyes to meet his.

"I'm grateful for your help, Maegwin."

And I'm sorry for what I did to you at Carrow Crossing. Although he didn't speak the words aloud, he hoped she understood his unspoken apology.

She stared at him for a moment before suddenly snatching her hand away. "I gave you my word, didn't I? I'm doing this to save Leo. And to avenge my sisters."

Not for you. I owe you nothing.

Rovann heard the message behind her unspoken words.

He nodded. It was as much as he could hope for. "Then we'd better get moving."

"How do you propose to do that? The woods are crawling with Hounsey soldiers. And you are in no fit state for travel."

Rovann shifted his weight, testing his injuries. Lances of agony tore through his hand and arm. Maegwin was right. In this condition, he would be easy pickings for Hounsey.

Maegwin watched him impassively. There was a cold, remote expression on her face as Rovann struggled to his knees, cradling his injured arm against his chest. Every muscle in his body screamed in protest and little dots of light danced in front of his eyes.

Get up! he shouted at himself. *Get moving!*

But his battered body wouldn't obey. Waves of pain and dizziness threatened to make him black out.

Maegwin watched him for a moment then seemed to reach a decision. "Stay still. You need food, water and treatment before we go anywhere."

"There isn't time. We could be caught any moment."

"If we're discovered with you in this state we're finished no matter. Now sit there and stay quiet!"

She disappeared into the trees, returning a few moments later carrying a package under one arm and a bunch of dangling green plants in the other. Folding onto her knees, she laid her wares on the ground. "Syrie provisioned the boat," she said by way of explanation.

Opening the package she revealed a canteen of water, some tough strips of dried meat and hard bread. Handing over the water bottle she said, "Here; drink."

Rovann took the bottle with his good hand and set it to his cracked lips, drinking greedily. When he'd taken his fill he accepted some of the bread and dried meat from

Maegwin and began chewing mechanically. The movement tore his already damaged lips but his body reacted to the sustenance. The dizziness passed. Solidity returned to his muscles.

Maegwin ate in silence, watching him. When she was satisfied that he'd eaten enough she fetched two stones from the river's edge and began pounding the green plants into a sticky paste.

"What are you doing?"

"Making a salve," she replied without looking up. "These are rosewort. Good at keeping out infection and by the looks of your hand, you're going to need it. It's already festering. I think the arrow may have been poisoned."

Rovann didn't argue. From the sickly reek and yellow pus oozing from the wound, he knew infection was already starting to set in. Rovann had seen such wounds on the battlefield many times. As often as not they led to gangrene, amputation and death. He looked away, determined not to entertain such notions. He would be damned if he would fall to a stray Hounsey arrow.

As Maegwin worked, Rovann thought. They needed help. Shelter. Rest. Food. Horses. But where to find it? The countryside on this side of the river was in rebel hands. All the safe havens lay on the far side of the river. He knew of no settlements that might offer them what they required. Except…

He sat up straighter. "There is a place, perhaps a day's walk west of here. If we can reach it, I think the people there might help us."

She glanced at him but didn't stop working. "What place?"

"A small town, more of a village really. Stoneshowe."

"I've never heard of it."

No, not many have, he thought. *And only the desperate would willingly seek the place out. Yet, we have no choice.*

Maegwin straightened and held up the mashed rosewort to sniff it. "It will have to do. Normally I'd add comfrey or yarrow to the salve but I can't find any nearby and daren't go far into the woods to look. Hold out your hand."

Grimacing against the pain, Rovann slid his right hand down his thigh toward her. Maegwin leaned over, inspecting the wound and then shook her head.

"This is going to hurt."

"Yes, I thought it might."

Pursing her lips, Maegwin scraped the mashed weed onto the end of her finger and quickly smeared it over Rovann's injury.

Despite himself, Rovann yelped in pain and laid his head against the tree trunk as blinding white agony consumed his body. It lasted for perhaps three heartbeats before a cool, soothing sensation began tingling from his elbow to his fingers.

Maegwin ripped some strips from the hem of her tunic. "Hold still."

She lightly wrapped the material around Rovann's injured arm, immobilizing the fingers and thumb. When it was done, he found that the pain had lessened and he was able to stagger to his feet without the danger of passing out. He leaned his good hand on the tree and stood with his head hanging as the waves of scalding dizziness passed. Finally, he lifted his head.

"Here," Maegwin handed him a stout branch to use as a walking stick. He accepted it gratefully, acutely aware of how reliant he was on Maegwin. He didn't like it one little bit.

"Thanks."

She shrugged. "Lead the way."

Rovann turned in a slow circle, trying to get his bearings. After a moment, he fixed on what he hoped was the right direction. Shuffling like an old man, Rovann led them west.

Maegwin stared at Rovann's back as they marched. He hobbled along maybe five paces ahead of her. His pain was evident in the hitched and hesitant gait of his walk. Gone was the powerful King's Mage. Instead he was just an injured man who needed her help. Maegwin wasn't sure how she felt about that. In fact, she wasn't sure how she felt about anything.

She ought to feel angry. At Rovann, at Hounsey. But she didn't. She felt… nothing.

Thoughts whirled in her head, a never-ending cycle that brought her no relief. Rovann had betrayed her. He'd promised her revenge against Lord Cedric Hounsey, the man who had burned down her temple, murdered her sister priestesses and turned Maegwin into a friendless refugee. Killing him had become the burning goal of Maegwin's life, the thing she clung to. But when the time had come and she'd had Hounsey within her grasp, Rovann had let Hounsey go.

Her hands clenched into fists and her gaze fixed on Rovann's back as though she meant to burn holes into it. How could he do that to her? How could he? Hadn't she kept her word, done everything he asked of her? So why had he done it?

She ducked under a low branch and then halted as Rovann paused, looking from left to right. After a moment he set off once more and Maegwin followed, keeping a few steps behind him.

Perhaps she ought to be watching for Hounsey soldiers —Rovann was in no condition to do it—but she couldn't bring herself to make the effort. If they were attacked she would fight and do her best to kill her enemies. At the moment her plans went no further than that. She had no idea where this place was he was taking them or what they'd find there. If she asked she doubted he'd tell her. Another one of his damned secrets. Let him keep them. She didn't care.

They struggled on at a pace that made her grind her teeth in frustration. Finally, she pushed ahead of Rovann. "We're heading west, yes? I'll find a path for us. You just follow."

She didn't stop to check whether he had obeyed her command but strode ahead into the forest. The terrain was different from the forest that had surrounded her temple. There, the trees had been huge and old, with vast spaces beneath their trunks in which herds of deer would often be seen grazing. This forest was dense and tightly packed with tangled undergrowth that made it difficult to find her way. Evening would soon be upon them and they'd need a place to camp for the night. She intended to be well clear of the Hounsey soldiers by then.

She wove in and out of the trees, listening to any sounds that might indicate an ambush. All she heard was the chirping of birds and the moan of the breeze. Rovann was already out of sight behind her but she knew he would be able to follow her trail.

She reached a dry gully choked with last year's leaves and hesitated. The ditch was deep, with high sides that Rovann would struggle to climb with his injury so

Maegwin turned left and followed the channel's meandering course, looking for an easier place to cross. Her attention focused on her path, she didn't see the tripwire until it was too late.

Her ankles caught and she went sprawling to the ground, palms scraping painfully against sharp stones embedded in the mulch of the forest floor. She twisted in time to see armed men bursting from the undergrowth. They wore the greens and browns of woodsmen but Maegwin saw from their weapons that they were Hounsey soldiers.

Maegwin scrabbled at the dirt, trying to gain her feet but one of the men backhanded her across the face hard enough to send her sprawling onto her back. His hands tangled in her hair and a blade suddenly pressed itself against her throat.

"Move and I'll kill you," the man said. "Understand?"

"Yes," she murmured as the icy cold edge of the blade bit her flesh.

The man leaned close, peering at her with narrowed eyes. His stink reached her nostrils: stale sweat, damp leather, unwashed skin. She wrinkled her nose.

"I reckon this is the one," he said to his men. "She matches the description the captain gave us." Turning back to Maegwin, he demanded, "Where's your friend?"

Maegwin pressed her lips into a flat line.

The man raised an eyebrow. "Oh, defiance is it? I like that in a woman, makes them more of a challenge. Doesn't matter anyway, little lady. We'll find your companion soon enough." He turned and bellowed orders to his men. "Follow her trail and find the other one. Hanlon you go as well and be on your guard. By all accounts this man is dangerous."

"Yes, sarge." Two soldiers and a robed man who might have been a mage nodded and disappeared into the woods.

Maegwin watched her captor. His eyes were fixed on his departing men but as soon as she began moving her hand toward her dagger, his eyes snapped to her. He increased pressure on the blade and hot blood trickled down her neck.

"Oh no you don't, little lady," he said, pulling out her knife and tossing it away. "I'm going to let you up now but if you so much as breathe in a way I don't like I'll cut your throat. Understand?"

"Yes," she murmured.

He stared at her for a moment more before removing the blade and rising to his feet. Maegwin's hand flew to her throat where a small nick had opened. She swallowed a few times, steeling her courage, and then rose to her feet.

"What are you going to do with me?" she demanded.

The sergeant leered around at his men before answering. "That's the question, little lady, isn't it? You see, our orders were to capture your companion. He's the one our boss is interested in which means you are surplus to requirements." He gestured at her with his blade. "However, there could be other ways you might prove useful."

She narrowed her eyes. "What do you mean?"

He sauntered over and lifted her chin with his index finger. "Oh, I'm sure you can use your imagination." His hand went to her breast and squeezed, hard.

She slapped him across the face, snapping his head to one side, and then backed away. "Keep your filthy paws off me."

He slowly straightened. A line of blood dripped from his nostril. "Oh dear," he said. "A fighter. Still," he shrugged. "I've always enjoyed a challenge."

He moved like lightning. She barely had time to register

his approach before his fist caught her on the cheek and sent her sprawling into the dirt. He dropped his weight on top of her, pinning her to the ground. She punched and scratched at him but he grabbed her wrists with one hand and yanked her arms over her head. With his free hand he began untying his trousers.

Maegwin screamed in rage and frustration. She writhed, trying to bring her knees up but he was too heavy for her.

"My, my, you really are a fighter," he murmured. "Hold her down," he growled at his men.

Maegwin shrieked as the soldiers grabbed her ankles, pulling her legs wide and holding her there, spread-eagled on the ground.

"Try to enjoy it," the sergeant said in her ear. His hand traced a line up the inside of her thigh and then began fumbling at the lacings on her doe-skin leggings. "The more you struggle, the more it'll hurt."

But suddenly the pressure on her legs eased and Maegwin thrashed, trying to kick him away.

"What are you doing, curse you!" the sergeant bellowed at his men. "I told you to hold her down!" He glanced over his shoulder and his eyes widened. In the next instant he scrambled to his feet, quickly tying his trousers and yanking his sword from its scabbard.

Maegwin sat up and scooted backward, coming to rest against a broad tree trunk where she sat slightly dazed, trying to get her bearings. The soldiers had spread out and taken a ready stance with swords drawn, facing away from her. A figure emerged from the trees and halted ten paces from the line of soldiers.

Rovann.

"I believe this is yours."

He tossed something to the ground and Maegwin realized it was the robe the Hounsey mage had been wearing. On top of it Rovann dropped the two swords the Hounsey soldiers who'd gone looking for him had been carrying.

Rovann stood straight, feet shoulder-width apart and chin lifted defiantly. There was no trace of the injury he carried. The soldiers shifted uncomfortably. The sergeant motioned with one hand and his men moved out silently to surround Rovann.

"Don't be a fool now," the sergeant said. "You might have overcome Hanlon and the others but there are ten of us. Our orders are to take you back to Carrow Crossing. If you come quietly, you'll not be harmed."

Rovann cocked his head as if considering the sergeant's offer. "Very generous. And my friend?"

The sergeant glanced to where Maegwin sat against the tree. He shrugged. "Of course. We'll take her back as well."

"Is that before or after you rape her?"

Rovann's voice had gone deadly quiet and the threat in it made Maegwin's hair stand on end. She climbed to her feet and stood, warily trying to watch everyone at once. The sergeant seemed oblivious to the menace in Rovann's tone. Perhaps he still believed he held the upper hand. Fool.

"Spoils of war, my friend," he said, grinning. "Spoils of war."

The sergeant flicked his wrist and his men attacked in a flurry of bellowed curses and swinging swords. Rovann didn't stand a chance. They rushed him from all sides, giving him no time to respond.

Yet he seemed to melt away from their attack only to reappear behind them. In his hand he grasped a sword with a blade of silver light. The tiniest flick of the weapon and a man's head went flying from his shoulders. Turning in silence, Rovann opened another man from chest to abdomen. The man watched his entrails pour onto the floor before collapsing face-down on top of them. A third man swung in low, aiming for Rovann's calves but he merely threw out his hand, palm facing his attacker and the man was thrown through the air to collide with a tree trunk with a thump.

The rest of the soldiers backed away. Rovann went still, sword tip dangling into the soft mulch of the forest floor. He watched them in silence.

The sergeant ran a hand over his sweaty brow and then gestured at Rovann. "Now, we don't have to go letting this get ugly do we? How's about we let you go and tell our boss we never found you? How does that sound?"

Rovann said nothing. He dropped his sword by his feet where it hissed and disappeared. He raised his hands out to either side as though he would bestow a blessing on the soldiers. Around him, the wind whipped up in a churning whirlwind. Dead leaves and plant matter swirled around his feet. The pressure in the glade intensified, almost pushing Maegwin flat.

The sergeant and his men threw down their weapons and turned to flee but with a word, Rovann froze them to the spot. They turned wide fearful eyes on him.

"Wait!" cried the sergeant. "We was only following orders! We was only doing our job."

"I know," Rovann said and Maegwin thought she detected a hint of sadness in his voice. "And I'm only doing mine."

The pressure increased again and Maegwin clamped her hands to her ears at a sudden sharp pain. Rovann lowered his arms and a wave of power went rippling outwards. It ripped into the Hounsey soldiers. Maegwin gagged as they were torn into pulpy lumps of meat.

Silence fell. Rovann slowly collapsed onto his knees amid the carnage. Maegwin didn't move. Bile churned in her stomach and her pulse hammered in her ears.

Flee! A voice whispered inside. *Go now, while he's helpless!*

She took two steps away from him and then halted. He'd saved her from rape. He'd saved her from the noose in Mallyn. *So? You don't owe him anything! Flee now!*

But she didn't. She closed her eyes, pulled in a steadying breath. Counted her heartbeat: one, two, three, and then opened her eyes. Turning on her heel, she strode to Rovann and went to her knees in front of him.

He seemed barely conscious, eyes closed, breath shallow and rattling. She laid a hand on his shoulders and his eyelids fluttered open. His blue gaze found hers and she saw the barest recognition.

"Maegwin, are you all right? Did they hurt you?"

She shook her head. "No, I'm fine."

"Good. I'm glad." His eyes slid closed and he sank forward.

Maegwin caught him, supporting his weight on her shoulder. "Rovann, you have to wake up. We have to get moving."

No response.

She grabbed his shoulders and shook him. "King's Mage! On your feet! On your feet now!"

His head snapped up, eyes flicking open. She stuck her hands under his armpits and hauled him to his feet. He scrabbled, getting his feet under him and then stood leaning on her heavily.

"I have no strength left, Maegwin. I don't know if I can make it."

"You can and you will," she growled. She pulled one of his arms over her shoulder and slung her arm around his waist. "Stoneshowe isn't it? You guide me, and I'll get us there"

"West, head west."

"Right. Come on."

They limped off into the forest.

Several tense hours later they made camp between two huge boulders that had fallen from a granite cliff that bisected the woods. Maegwin dared not light a fire so she spent a restless and uncomfortable night staring out into the dark whilst Rovann shivered and moaned in his sleep, caught in fever dreams.

Maegwin roused him before first light, forced him to eat, redressed his wound and then helped him stagger into the west once more. The forest soon retreated and they began to climb to higher ground where heather replaced the trees and the wind moaned ceaselessly.

She didn't like this exposed terrain. If caught here they would be easy pickings for Hounsey's soldiers. But they labored on into the afternoon and saw no sign of pursuit. Toward evening they began to descend into a land of broken canyons and stunted trees. They passed from beneath the boughs of a gloomy copse and found themselves standing on a rutted track.

Maegwin motioned for them to cross it and take cover in the trees on the other side but Rovann halted.

"No, we turn south here and follow this trail."

She glanced around. "Are you out of your mind? We have no idea where Hounsey's soldiers might be. We should stay off the roads."

Rovann smiled thinly. His skin had taken on a sickly

gray pallor and dark rings circled his eyes. "It's unlikely we'll meet soldiers on this road. This is the way to Stoneshowe."

Maegwin frowned but didn't argue. Taking Rovann's weight once more they began hobbling up the trail.

Steep canyons soon grew to either side of the track, so high that the path was cast into almost perpetual twilight. The skin between Maegwin's shoulder blades itched. This was the perfect place for an ambush. In the darkness every sound seemed amplified: Rovann's ragged breathing, the trickle of water somewhere nearby, the rush of stones falling from the canyon wall. Maegwin's head whipped round at every noise until she was as tense as a bowstring.

"I don't like this," she murmured. "This place is dangerous."

"Yes," Rovann agreed. "We're being watched. No, don't turn around. Just keep walking."

Maegwin fixed her eyes on the bright spot that marked the end of the canyon. They reached it unmolested and Maegwin walked out gratefully into the evening sunshine. Beyond, a wide valley opened out and in this valley nestled a squalid town. Maegwin saw rows of huts, corrals full of skinny goats and slat-ribbed dogs nosing through the muddy streets.

Rovann raised his head and looked around. "Stoneshowe," he breathed. He didn't sound particularly glad to have reached their destination.

"What is this place?" Maegwin asked. "It doesn't strike me as the kind of place where we'll find help."

Rovann snorted. "No it doesn't. But appearances can be deceptive. Come on."

They made their way into the town proper and Rovann guided them to what appeared to be the center of the settlement: a wide cobbled square surrounded by long stone buildings that Maegwin guessed might be shops or other businesses. The square was crowded and the noise of arguing and haggling was almost deafening after the silence of the wilderness.

"Over there," Rovann said, pointing.

They crossed the square and settled onto a wide stone bench next to a cracked fountain.

"What now?" she asked impatiently.

Rovann shrugged. "Now we wait."

Maegwin looked around. To an untrained eye it might appear that they were being ignored but she noticed many furtive glances flick their way and knew their arrival had been marked. She tensed. Almost every person carried a weapon of some kind, be it a knife, a bow or a curled piece of wire hanging at the waist which Maegwin assumed to be a garrote.

"You still haven't told me what this place is," she said quietly. "Why won't Hounsey soldiers come here? Is Stoneshowe loyal to the king?"

Rovann snorted. "Hardly. Soldiers won't come here because I doubt they know of it. Stoneshowe appears on no map. Officially this place does not exist just as the people who live here do not exist."

"What do you mean?"

He turned to look at her. "Stoneshowe is a criminal settlement, peopled by those who've been banished by King William or have fled his justice."

"What? And you thought—" her words trailed off as she realized that someone had moved to stand in front of them.

Her eyes traveled up from the man's muddy boots, to his broad chest and scarred face. In one hand he carried a double-headed ax.

Maegwin began to rise from the bench but Rovann put out a hand to stop her.

"He'll see me?" he said to the man.

The man grunted. "Follow me."

Without waiting for an answer he turned and strode away. Rovann lurched to his feet and hobbled after. Maegwin paused for a moment, cursed under her breath, and threw up her hands in frustration. She hurried after Rovann and together they followed the man from the square and through a series of dark alleys to a nondescript door.

The man thumped on the door three times and then ushered them inside as it creaked open. They found themselves in a bare room with only two wooden chairs and a battered old table.

"Sit." The man said before disappearing through an inner door.

Maegwin slid into a seat beside Rovann and glanced around at their sparse surroundings. The room smelt of mildew and the only light came from a grimy window looking out into the alley.

After what seemed an age the inner door opened and another man strode through and stood looking down at them with his hands on his hips. The man wore knee-length leather boots, a black tunic and had two morningstars tucked into the belt at his waist. He was so tall his head almost brushed the ceiling and a wild mop of unruly dark hair curled to his shoulders.

The man scowled. "Singer burn my eyes!" he cursed in a deep, powerful voice. "I never thought to see your sorry face again, Rovann. You've got a nerve coming here you traitorous mage-born scum!"

Rovann looked up at the man. "Hello, Thaldan."

"Who's he?" Maegwin whispered.

The mage turned a wry smile on her. "He's my brother-in-law."

Rovann watched the expression on Thaldan's face twist into one of fury and a sinking feeling filled the pit of his stomach. What had he expected? A welcome? After all that had passed between them?

He shifted his weight, wincing at the sudden pain. It was becoming increasingly difficult to concentrate. "Thaldan, listen to me," he said, placing his good hand flat on the table. "I've come to you for help. I need medicine and supplies for a long journey."

Thaldan raised an eyebrow in a gesture so reminiscent of his sister. "Oh, is that all you need? Why didn't you say so? I'll have it ready in just one moment." The tall man leaned forward, placing his hands on the table. His dark eyes looked Rovann up and down, taking in his injured arm and bedraggled state. "Look at you," he said, shaking his head. "The vaunted King's Mage brought so low. You know, I spent years dreaming of this meeting, dreaming of how I'd take my revenge against you. And here you are, come crawling to my door like some beggar. Why would I help you, King's Mage? After everything you've done to me?"

"I did what I had to," Rovann replied. "You left me no choice." He glanced around at the small, dark room. "And it looks as if you haven't changed, Thaldan. This one of your secret meeting rooms? Still in the trade I see."

The tall man went still as if sensing a trap. "Is that why you're here? Have you brought the king's army to Stoneshowe? Have you broken your word yet again?"

No," Rovann replied. "You're safe, I promise. You have nothing to fear from me."

Thaldan crossed his arms over his chest. "That's what you told my sister."

"That's not fair."

"Isn't it? She'd still be alive if not for you. I lost count of the number of times I warned her against going south with you. Mages care nothing for others. It doesn't matter who gets caught in the crossfire. Istra was just another of your victims, wasn't she, Slayer?"

Rage surged through Rovann's veins, pumping energy into his tired limbs. He lurched to his feet, sending the table flying.

"Shut your mouth!"

In a flash, Thaldan pulled the morningstars from his belt and held them up threateningly. "Go on then, King's Mage," he said in a low dangerous voice. "Try me."

Rovann open his mouth to retort but Maegwin was suddenly pulling him back and interposing herself between him and Thaldan.

"Stop it!" she snapped at the two men. "Stop your stupid, boyish posturing." She turned to Thaldan. "Rovann is hurt and needs help. If you're not willing to offer that help just say so and we'll be on our way."

The tall man frowned at her. "And you are?"

She lifted her chin. "Maegwin de Romily."

"A mage?"

"No. I'm a priestess of Sho-La."

His eyes narrowed. "Why would a priestess be traveling with the King's Mage of Amaury?"

"That's my business."

"And now it's mine," Thaldan growled. "Answer my question or neither of you will leave this room alive."

22

Maegwin glanced briefly at Rovann before answering. "We are on a rescue mission. A friend was kidnapped by the Songmaker. We intend to free him."

Thaldan shifted, a strange expression flashing across his features. "If he's been taken by the Songmaker then he's already dead."

"How do you know that? Rovann asked. "What do you know of the Songmaker?"

Instead of answering Thaldan thumped on the inner door and three armed men filed into the room. One of them trained a crossbow on Maegwin.

"Try any of your trickery, King's Mage," Thaldan said, "and your friend will end up being a pincushion. I don't want to hurt anyone so don't force my hand."

"What are you going to do with us?" Rovann growled.

"For now? Nothing. I don't trust you. You say you've brought no other mages but I think I'll send my men to look around before I take your word for that. In the meantime you'll be our guests."

He gestured and two of his men moved forward to bind Rovann and Maegwin's hands. The third man kept his crossbow trained on Maegwin's chest. Rovann grunted in pain as the man wound rope around his injured wrist. For a second black dots danced in front of his eyes and he thought he might faint. After a moment it passed and he straightened to find Thaldan watching him with an appraising look in his eyes as though trying to gage the extent of Rovann's weakness.

Rovann stared right back.

The tall man waved his hand. "Take them away."

They were led through the inner door and into what Rovann realized was a warren of small rooms and tight, dark corridors. All the doors were shut but from behind some he heard muted conversation and from somewhere up ahead wafted the aroma of cooking. The three men ushered them unceremoniously into a small room that was more like a cell and then slammed the heavy door behind them. Keys rattled as the door was locked.

"What are you doing?" Maegwin yelled. "Let us out! We've done nothing wrong!"

"Save your breath," Rovann said sliding down the wall to sit with his knees hunched to his chest. "They won't come until Thaldan's ready."

She scowled but then seated herself in a corner. "Thaldan really doesn't like you, does he?"

"You noticed?"

"So what happened between you two? Why such venom?"

Rovann laid his head against the wall and closed his eyes. Seeing Thaldan again had triggered memories that he'd thought long buried. Memories of Clan Tamarand, of his brother-in-law's enmity, but most of all of Istra. He'd forgotten how much she resembled her brother. "Thaldan is a criminal, and a major one. For years he was the head of a smuggling network that brought illegal weaponry into Amaury across the western border. I had him arrested and put on trial."

"You arrested your own brother-in-law?" Her voice was incredulous.

He looked at her. "What was I to do? Turn a blind eye because he's family? I have a duty, Maegwin."

"I know," she said. "But banishing him? It seems a little…harsh."

"Harsh?" he grated. "He should have hanged! It's only because I pleaded with the king on his behalf that he still has his miserable life. I thought perhaps he might remember

24

that and help us." He leaned his head back once more. "Seems I was wrong."

"What will he do?"

"I don't know."

She was silent for a time and Rovann could feel her eyes on him. She seemed to be working herself up to something. At last she said, "Rovann?"

"Yes?"

"Thank you. For saving me from those soldiers, I mean."

He raised his head to find her staring at him intently. "You're welcome."

She glanced away, began picking at the hem of her tunic. "What you did in the forest, could you do it again? Get us out of here?

He shook his head. "I've got nothing left, Maegwin. And besides, even if I could get us away from Thaldan's men, how would we get out of Stoneshowe alive? Thaldan will have alerted the town to our presence and if we tried to leave without the proper escort, we'd be hunted down."

"Great. Just great."

The door creaked open and two armed men entered. One covered Maegwin with the crossbow whilst the other placed two trays on the floor.

"Courtesy of the boss," the man said before they both turned and left, locking the door behind them once more.

Maegwin scooted over to the trays and whistled under her breath. "These men might be criminals but they eat fit for a king." She pushed one of the trays across the floor to Rovann and then pulled one to herself and began shoveling pieces of food into her mouth.

Rovann glanced down. In a large clay bowl thick slabs of meat sat in a dark sauce. Tender green vegetables were piled on the side. On a smaller plate sat a loaf of golden bread and a pot of what looked like honey. A pottery beaker was filled to the brim with wine.

Rovann's mouth watered at the scent of the food. With his good hand he picked up a fork and shoveled pieces of meat into his mouth, chewing greedily. After the weeks of soldier rations the juiciness of the meat threatened to make his taste buds explode. When the meat was finished he picked up the dish and slurped down the rest of the sauce. Then he ripped up the bread, smeared the slices with honey and wolfed them down. Finally he set the beaker to his lips and drank noisily. When he'd finished he wiped the back of his hand across his mouth and sat back as sustenance flowed into his battered body.

"If we're prisoners," Maegwin said with her mouth full. "Why are they feeding us like this?"

"It's a message I'd wager," Rovann replied. "Thaldan wants me to know how well he's doing despite my attempts to ruin him." He shrugged. "But if he wants to carry on proving his point, that's fine by me."

Maegwin snorted. "Agreed."

They sat in silence for a while and Rovann began to doze. Then suddenly Maegwin spoke. "Are you going to tell me what's going on?"

He opened his eyes, blinking to clear his thoughts. "What?"

She pulled her knees up to her chest and hugged them. "I brought you to Stoneshowe and asked no questions. But if I'm to help you on this quest I need to know the plan. Where are we going? Where do you think we will find the Songmaker?"

He didn't answer for a long time as though weighing up how much he could say. Finally, he sighed. "Do you remember what Hounsey kept saying in the tent? He kept mentioning 'the twins'. He claimed that's where Leo and Prince Owen had been taken."

Maegwin looked at him blankly. He wasn't surprised she didn't remember. She'd been so intent on killing Hounsey he doubted she'd heard a word that was said.

"Hounsey couldn't resist goading me but I think he may have inadvertently revealed the Songmaker's hideout."

"Go on," she prompted.

"There have always been rumors that the Songmaker's base is outside Amaury, somewhere in the lands beyond the western border. I think the rumors are true. There is a legend that says Tyrlindon once had a twin city, one that has long been lost. I think that's what Hounsey was alluding to, Tyrvanan, Tyrlindon's twin. I think that's where we'll find Prince Owen, Leo and the Songmaker."

Maegwin frowned. "So you're basing this whole mission on rumor, legend and a few hints dropped by a revenant? That's not much to go on, King's Mage."

"I know," he said, leaning his head against the wall. "But it's all we have. And it feels right. I can't explain it any more than that."

"So if there were rumors of this other city, why didn't you send someone to investigate? You could have captured the Songmaker a long time ago."

He looked at her and smiled wryly. "Ah. There we have it. It was a rumor only, Maegwin, one of many. We couldn't act on so slim a possibility when the dangers would be so high. You see, the legend says that Tyrvanan lies beyond Roamsford Edge."

Maegwin's eyes widened slowly as comprehension dawned. "You mean—? We have to cross it? Roamsford Edge?"

He nodded.

"Have you lost your mind? Even in the temple we knew of the Edge. It has a dark reputation, Rovann. Nobody enters it. The forest does not suffer people to pass."

"I know," he said. "But we will find a way. We must."

She stared at him for a long time. Then, shaking her head and muttering to herself, she lay down and turned her back on him.

Rovann settled down onto the hard stone floor and fell into an uneasy sleep. The throbbing pain in his arm woke him at regular intervals meaning his rest was fractured and not refreshing. He shivered uncontrollably even though his skin burned. The infection was spreading. He didn't have much time.

Sometime later he was awoken by someone kicking his leg. He jerked upright and squinted against the glare of a torch. Thaldan stood looking down at him with a troubled expression on his face.

Rovann ran his tongue around his cracked lips before speaking. "Your men found nothing I assume?"

"No," he replied.

"So you believe me?"

Thaldan waved his hand irritably. "Yes, I believe you. But that's not important now."

Rovann frowned, detecting an undercurrent in the man's words. "Then what is?"

The smuggler stared at him for a long moment. Rovann could almost see the thoughts turning behind his eyes. "You will see. Come."

Thaldan's men dragged him and Maegwin to their feet and led them from the cell and back through the maze of rooms and corridors. After only a moment, Rovann was totally lost and had no idea in which direction they were heading. They reached a set of stone steps that led down into darkness. Thaldan raised his torch and set it in a bracket on the wall then led the way down the stairs.

Rovann found himself in a low stone cellar. The floor was nothing but bare earth and the place stank of mold. A large white sheet covered what looked to Rovann to be three dead bodies. Thaldan turned to face him.

"My men didn't find any of your mages when they scouted around Stoneshowe. But they did find these."

He crouched and pulled back the sheet to reveal three dead men. Their skin was almost white, bloodless, as though they'd been drained. The men were naked and on their chests had been carved a broken circle with the letter S in the center.

Rovann crouched unsteadily next to Thaldan. "Who are these men?"

"Three of my own. They were on a job on the western border but they never made their rendezvous with my supplier. Seems like they ran into some trouble."

Rovann reached out his good hand and held it several inches above the chest of the nearest man. Lingering sorcery tickled against his palm. "You've seen this before, haven't you?"

Thaldan straightened and rubbed his chin. "Yes. For over a year now I've had a rival on the western border. It started with shipments going missing, suppliers missing their rendezvous, things like that. Then it got nasty. Instead of just shipments disappearing, my men started vanishing only to turn up days or weeks later with this carved into their chest."

Rovann slowly climbed to his feet and stood leaning against the wall. His head was pounding and his legs had gone weak. He really needed to lie down. "You recognize the symbol?"

Thaldan frowned. "I wish to the Singer that I didn't. The last thing I need is to get caught up in your cursed mage war. It's him, isn't it? The Songmaker."

"Yes, I'm afraid it is," Rovann said, eyes roving over the bloody symbols. "This is his mark. Your men aren't the first to turn up dead with it carved into them. And they won't be the last. It seems you've inadvertently solved a mystery, Thaldan. The Songmaker has been gathering an army in secret in the borderlands for months. We wondered how he'd supplied his troops without us finding out. Seems now we know. He's been smuggling weapons and materials over the western border. Looks like you've been getting in his way, Thaldan."

A snarl curled the man's lips. "Bastard. I'll have his cursed hide for this!"

"No you won't," Rovann replied. "If you tried he'd destroy you. You can't take him on, Thaldan. The only way to stop this is to help me."

Thaldan hooked his fingers into his belt and glared. "Every time I see you, King's Mage, I get dragged into your mess. You're like a carrion crow—never far from death and destruction."

"This isn't my 'mess', Thaldan. The Songmaker is a threat to the whole of Amaury. Whilst I'm sure your concerns extend no further than yourself, I'm trying to stop this man destroying the kingdom! Now are you going to help us or not?"

The dark-haired man rubbed his chin. "You think you can stop him?"

"I don't know. I'm going to try."

Thaldan watched him in silence. His eyes darted to the

three dead men then back to Rovann. At last he seemed to reach a decision. "Then you'll have my help."

This time he and Maegwin were led back into the complex but taken to different rooms. Rovann found himself being ushered into a large bedroom. Thick rugs covered the floor and a bed stood in one corner. A window overlooking the street filled the room with light.

Two middle-aged women entered and bade Rovann lie down on the bed. He did as they asked. One of the women set a hessian bag down on the floor, from which she pulled a host of medical supplies that she set out on a bedside table. She peeled back the dressings covering Rovann's wound and hissed through her teeth.

"Blind my eyes! This won't do, this won't do at all! You'll be lucky if you keep your hand, young man."

Rovann ground his teeth against the aching pain. It had grown so bad he no longer cared if he kept his hand as long as the pain stopped. "Do what you can."

The two women conferred in hushed tones. One of them stripped off his clothes and then washed him down as gently as she could. The other began mixing powders and liquids into a flask which sent an acrid odor stealing through the room. She carried the concoction over to Rovann.

"We'll need to clean the wound, set those broken bones and sear the infection from your blood. It will hurt. It's best if you're asleep when we do it. Here, drink this."

Rovann eyed the flask warily. "What is it?"

"Something that will send you into a deep sleep. Now drink it!"

Rovann took it in his good hand and set it to his lips. The concoction was so strong it made his eyes water. Steeling himself, he tipped the flask back and gulped the contents in one long swallow.

Almost immediately something seemed to grab his consciousness and drag him under. As he faded into sleep his last thought was, *I hope Thaldan hasn't decided to poison me.*

———————

Rovann woke slowly. His bare toes brushed against smooth warm sheets and the comforting weight of a soft blanket covered his torso. The muted conversation of people passing on the street wafted to him and the scent of baking bread came from somewhere in the house. He opened his eyes. Dawn sunlight streamed through the window and dust motes danced in the shafts.

It took a moment for him to realize that the pain had receded. He felt... good. Rested. Whole. He turned his head slowly to the side and saw that Maegwin was dozing in a chair by his bedside. Experimentally, he pushed himself into a sitting position and was pleasantly surprised when the expected waves of dizziness and pain did not come.

His injured arm was bound tightly in clean white bandages and although it was tender when he poked it, it was the tenderness of healing rather than the agony of an infected wound.

Maegwin shifted in her chair. Her eyes snapped open. "Morning," she said, leaning forward to peer at him. "How do you feel?"

"Better. Much better. How long have I been asleep?"

"Almost two days."

"Two days!" he cried, throwing off the covers. "We have to go!"

"Get back into bed!" she commanded, flinging the blankets back over him. "Shilma will have my hide if I let you up before she's ready. She and Melnay worked on your wound for almost a whole day. You had gangrene and they thought you'd lose your hand for a while."

Just then the door creaked open and the women in question bustled into the room.

"I thought I heard voices in here," said the eldest of the two, coming to stand by Rovann's bedside. "It's good to see you awake. Are you having any pain? Dizziness? Nausea?"

Rovann shook his head. "You are Shilma? I owe you my thanks."

She waved his gratitude away, pulled back the covers and inspected the bandage on his hand. Taking a small sharp blade from the table beside Rovann's bed, she said, "Hold still while I take this off. Let's see how well the wound underneath is healing."

She deftly set the tiny blade to the bandages and began to slice it. Only then did he realize that rather than bandages it was some kind of hard cast designed to keep his hand immobile. When she'd sliced it down the middle Shilma carefully pried it away from Rovann's arm and then lifted it off.

He examined his injury with some trepidation. Bruising blackened his arm from his knuckles to his elbow but the skin was unbroken and the bruises were already starting to turn yellow in places. Where the arrow had pierced his arm was only a tiny white scar. Slowly Rovann clenched and unclenched his fingers, marveling at how they obeyed his command with only the slightest ache to show the bones had ever been broken.

Shilma nodded, a look of satisfaction on her face. "Good. It's better than I dared to hope."

"Better than any normal healer would expect," Rovann agreed. He caught the woman's gaze. "You're a mage, aren't you?"

She seemed about to deny it but then changed her mind and nodded. "I have some small skill with Fire. Enough to heal a few wounds but not much else."

"A most valuable gift, Shilma. Thank you."

She smiled. "I'll tell Thaldan that you're ready to travel."

She and her companion turned and left the room. Rovann swung his legs over the edge of the bed just as the door opened and Thaldan strode in.

"Good. About time," he said without preamble. "Get dressed. There will be a meal waiting for you downstairs. Then you can be on your way."

Rovann forced himself to meet the smuggler's hostile gaze. He bowed his head to his brother-in-law. "I know there may never be peace between us, Thaldan, but you have my thanks."

"Stop the Songmaker from killing my men, that's all the thanks I require." He rubbed his chin. "I'll have two horses saddled and provisioned. My people will make sure you're not followed from Stoneshowe. Now hurry up and get out of my house."

Chapter Two

Rovann swung up onto the roan gelding and gathered the reins. Thaldan held his gaze for a long moment, his dark eyes probing. *Remember your promise.*

"This is Brye," the smuggler said, looking away. "A good horse. Take care of him."

Rovann nodded. "Thank you, Thaldan. I won't forget your generosity."

Then he kicked his mount into motion. As he rode away he did not look back.

He and Maegwin stole quickly through the waking town, thick cowls pulled up to hide their features. As they moved from shadow to shadow, Rovann felt like a fugitive, a wary denizen of the dark, eager to escape notice. But there were always eyes watching, he knew, and he found himself peering at the faces they passed, wondering if he was looking at a renegade spy.

Is this what we've come to? he wondered. *Convinced every friend is an enemy?*

They didn't speak and reached the outskirts of the town as the sun was poking its head above the trees. Kicking their mounts into a trot, they followed the north road for several miles before finally pulling to a halt at a nondescript crossroads.

Twisting in his seat, Rovann gazed back the way they'd come. The road snaked like a silver ribbon behind them. Nothing moved upon it.

"What is it?" Maegwin asked.

"I'm not sure. But I feel..."

Swinging one leg over the saddle, Rovann dropped to the ground and placed his hand on the road's hard-packed surface. He opened his senses and sent them ranging outwards. The golden web of life engulfed him immediately but after a moment he began to detect the individual lives of the world. Somewhere on the road a farmer was pulling an unruly donkey to market, further north a chattering family was on its way to an early morning fishing trip.

"I don't think we've been followed."

"Then Thaldan has been true to his word." She looked around, gazing at the empty countryside. "What now?"

"We continue due west until we reach Roamsford Edge. Then we'll need to find a way through the forest. We should find Tyrvanan on the other side."

"And you're sure that's where we'll find Leo and Prince Owen?"

Rovann nodded and remounted his horse. Maegwin was a stony, glowering presence at Rovann's side. Her expression didn't invite conversation and Rovann could feel the annoyance radiating from her. He opened his mouth to speak but then thought better of it. He didn't have any words to say that would ease her mood.

They halted around midday and as Rovann cooked a meal, Maegwin watched him from across the fire.

"What are you running from?" she asked suddenly.

Startled, he looked up. "Running? Is that what you think I'm doing? Surely we're moving *toward* danger rather than away from it?"

"Not for you, I think. Seems to me you'd rather consort with criminals in Stoneshowe than stay in Tyrlindon. I heard what Thaldan said to you. You can't escape memories, Rovann. They'll follow you wherever you go."

He glanced at her sharply. She spoke as though from bitter experience and her gaze was unfocused, far away, as though images were playing through her head. "They change you. Make you into something new, whether you like it or not." Her voice was barely above a whisper.

"Maegwin?"

Her gaze snapped up. "Nothing. Never mind."

Rovann dished out a thin broth and handed Maegwin a bowl. They ate in silence, interrupted only by the raucous bickering of a pair of crows perched in a tree above. The day had become cool and blustery. The wind rattled the branches and kicked up streamers of dust along the path. To the north, a bank of dark clouds was gathering, promising rain later.

Rovann looked at the sky and sighed.

When they had eaten Maegwin gathered the dishes and took them to a stream. Rovann was relieved to be alone. He didn't like the feelings Maegwin's question had stirred up. Running away? Was that the truth? Was he shirking his responsibilities? Should he have returned to Tyrlindon?

Istra's voice echoed in his head. *Duty again, Rovann? Will you always worry about what you should do? Will you never be free of it?*

"I will never be free of it," he whispered.

The crows 'karked' loudly and flew off, their ponderous wing beats slapping at the air. Rovann doused the fire then went to check on the horses. At Rovann's approach the roan swung up his head, snorted, then returned to ripping up tufts of grass. Rovann patted him on the neck.

"Time to go."

They took a route that cut across country and Rovann set a pace that would eat up the miles without exhausting their mounts. At first they stayed off the path, forging a way through undergrowth and using animal trails but late in the afternoon they swung slightly north and came out onto a little-used road.

Forest closed in on either side creating a gloomy, oppressive atmosphere with thick shadows beneath the trunks of the pines. The cloud-bank sealed the sky in a gray blanket but the rain held off.

Maegwin seemed lost in thought, staring as if seeing things that he couldn't. Rovann scanned the woods, alert for danger but the shadows between the boles were impenetrable as though they held secrets they refused to give up.

"I'm sorry," Maegwin said suddenly.

"What?" he replied, startled.

"I didn't mean to make you sound a coward. You're not that, Rovann. Never that."

Rovann stared at her for a long moment, unsure how to respond. He cleared his throat and looked away, desperately casting around for something to say. "It's a rare thing to be called into the service of a goddess," he blurted. "How did you become a priestess of Sho-La?

Maegwin pursed her lips in thought. "My earliest memories are of working in one of the tanneries of Mallyn with other street children. The master of the tannery was a cruel man. When I was seven he beat me so bad I ran away. I wandered the woods for days, slowly starving. But a woman came to me. She had silver skin and hair as blue as midnight. She led me through the forest until I found a temple. The sisters took me in. Sho-La had called me. It was my destiny to serve Her. What do you know of Sho-La, Rovann?"

"Not much," he admitted with a shrug.

"Ah, She is the light of the universe. She teaches compassion, kindness and a love that transcends all creation. With Her, I am never alone." She pulled her horse to a halt suddenly and stared into the shadows beneath the trees. Her voice became low and hesitant. "But there's another side to Her. Darkness, anger, retribution… sometimes I feel…" She shook her head. "It doesn't matter."

Rovann watched her, suddenly wary.

It's just you and me now, Rovann. And you're all mine.

"Your turn," she said, shaking off her sullen reverie. "How did you become a mage?"

Rovann clucked at his mount, urging him on. "Throughout my childhood I did strange things without knowing how: predicting the weather, sensing danger, that sort of thing. But when I was eleven I burned down my father's barn just by picturing a flame in my mind. After that I was packed off to the college in Tyrlindon."

Maegwin laughed, a sound like the tinkling of a stream. She flashed Rovann a brilliant smile and his stomach lurched. When Maegwin smiled her beauty was breathtaking. Suddenly uncomfortable, he nudged his horse ahead of hers and focused his attention on the road.

Throughout the day the landscape gradually changed. The brooding trees fell back to be replaced by stubby hills and rough gullies. Great moss-covered boulders stood out of the ground as though the bones of the earth were pushing through its skin. The road wound inexorably around these obstacles, up short slopes and then down again into shallow valleys. As a result, the going became tougher and Rovann was forced to ease the pace.

Rovann consulted the map Thaldan had given him. According to the faint, hand-written labels, they were passing into a region known as Turandor, a sparsely populated land of rocky soil. The few villages that existed in Turandor were spaced far apart and so as night approached, Rovann led them off the trail and into a grassy clearing.

Whilst Maegwin cooked supper, Rovann busied himself brushing down the horses. His roan suddenly raised his head, ears pricked forward, snorting and stamping. On Rovann's other side Maegwin's horse tossed her head nervously.

Maegwin came silently to her feet, dagger in hand. "Something's out there."

Rovann held out a hand to stall her, closed his eyes, and sent his senses questing out. He found it almost immediately: a presence moving toward them along the little-used path they had traveled most of the day. Biting back a curse, he crept through the scrub to the top of a rise that looked down on the road. Kneeling in the thick grass, he and Maegwin peered through a gorse bush.

Rovann cursed himself for a fool. He'd been so sure they'd not been followed. Damn Thaldan and his empty promises.

They waited for what seemed an age, silent, motionless. Faint sounds wafted to Rovann on the breeze.

Voices. Low, whispered.

Two figures emerged from the darkness, walking side by

side. Then something large lumbered into view behind them and Rovann squinted, trying to make it out. The thing moved smoothly, making an odd creaking noise and the stomp and snuffle of horses carried on the night air. A caravan.

"Gypsies!" Rovann breathed.

Giddy relief washed through him. Thaldan had not betrayed him after all. Without thinking, he stood. The people on the road saw him silhouetted against the sky and broke into panic. Shouts rang through the night. Figures darted around. Horses whinnied in fear.

Rovann ran to the edge of the rise. "Wait! I'm sorry, I didn't mean to scare you!"

A deep voice called from the darkness, "Who are you?"

"I'm Rovann, my companion is Maegwin. We mean you no harm."

There was a whispered conversation and then the voice demanded, "Why were you watching us?"

"We heard noises. Travelers are seldom seen on this road."

Silence for a moment.

"Aye, that's true. If you're not bandits, you'll come down and make our acquaintance. But move slowly now, and bring no weapons."

"What are you doing?" Maegwin hissed, grabbing Rovann's arm as he made to walk away. "We're supposed to be traveling in secret!"

Rovann shook free of her grip. "We need information, Maegwin. They might be able to give us that."

"You have no idea if they can be trusted and you've just given them our names!" In the darkness Maegwin's eyes glinted with anger.

"Maegwin, gypsies travel all over the land and hear

gossip. I need to know what is happening in Tyrlindon. I have to take the risk."

Without waiting for an answer he stalked off.

He approached the group of gypsies who eyed him warily. The two who had been walking in front of the wagon were tall young men carrying knives strapped to their waists. In the caravan a gaggle of children peeked shyly out of the opening, watched over by an elderly lady with her hair tied in a multitude of thin gray braids. At the head of the group waited a grizzled bear of a man with ruddy cheeks and a mop of brown hair, hands planted on hips and wearing a scowl. Beside him stood a slim, regal woman who regarded Rovann and Maegwin steadily.

"Aye, well you don't look like wights or bandits to me," said the man. "And you certainly ain't gypsies. What brings you out here?"

Rovann thought quickly, remembering what he'd seen on Thaldan's map. "We're traveling to Yatarn to visit my mother."

The man regarded them silently, as though trying to find the lie. Eventually he stuck out his hand which Rovann shook. "The name's Garn and this is my wife Etta." He nodded toward the caravan. "That there is Etta's ma, Reya, and the rest of those scallywags are our troupe. Acrobats and entertainers of the highest order, that's us! We're heading to Silverport."

Rovann sensed the opportunity for gathering information. "Silverport is a long way from here. Surely Tyrlindon would be easier to reach?"

Garn rubbed his chin and frowned. "Aye, it would. It's not safe round the capital right now though."

"Not safe?" Rovann asked, feigning ignorance. "Why not?"

Garn eyed him as though wondering how much to say. "You country folk ought to be safe enough I reckon, but if you want my advice you'll stay away from the capital. There's war brewing. A great big army marching on Tyrlindon is what I hear."

Rovann's stomach twisted. Had Hounsey found a way to cross the river after all? Maegwin stirred beside him, shooting him a worried look. "An army? Approaching Tyrlindon? Why?"

"Stone me, have you not heard the news? The land's at war, lad! The Songmaker's rebels are bent on ousting King William."

Rovann pursed his lips, putting on a thoughtful expression. "Well, news takes a long time to get out here. The rest of the land seems to forget we exist."

"Let's hope it stays that way and the war doesn't reach this far. If I had my way we wouldn't be traveling at all but earnings have turned pretty grim in this region ever since —" Etta gave him a sharp glance and he abruptly changed the subject. "Anyways, we won't be going any farther today."

"Maegwin and I have made camp over there. It's a good flat spot sheltered from the wind. Why don't you join us?" said Rovann.

Garn nodded. "Much obliged."

The troupe fell into the chore of making camp with practiced ease. The two older lads drove the wagon into the dell, unhitched the horses and began rubbing them down for the night. The children jumped from the cart and scurried to their tasks: collecting firewood, assembling tents, unpacking supplies, peeling vegetables, setting up a chair for the elderly Reya. Garn and Etta supervised the operation and soon there was a merry fire crackling in the glade with a pot gently heating over it.

They took seats around the fire and Garn passed around mugs of a hot, sweet liquid that smelled slightly of aniseed.

"Companions of the road," he proposed a toast.

Rovann raised his mug and took a swig. The sharp taste stung his throat and made his eyes water. It was all he could do not to cough it up.

Garn broke into a broad grin that showed all his enormous square teeth. "A bit robust for you is it?"

He chuckled and emptied his mug in one long draft just to show how it should be done. Following his example, Maegwin set her mug to her lips and drained it. She did not even flinch.

Garn stared for a moment than let out a bellowing laugh. "Well met! That'll teach me to brag eh?"

Maegwin raised her mug in salute.

Garn turned to Rovann. "You're traveling to Yatarn you say? Do you and your wife carry weapons?"

Maegwin looked up at Garn's assumption and met Rovann's eyes. Two spots of color formed on her cheeks. He shrugged slightly. Let the gypsies assume they were married. It hardly mattered.

"Weapons? Why would we need them?"

Garn glanced into the darkness then at Rovann. Firelight danced in his eyes. "The country up west is restless. Strange goings-on. Rumors of—"

"Monsters!" cried one of the children suddenly, a girl of five or six. "Monsters in the woods! They come at night and pull your eyes out!"

"Hush, Ryn," Etta breathed. Pulling the girl into her lap, she stroked her hair until she calmed.

Garn and Etta shared a troubled glance. The elderly

Reya shook her head, making her braids clack and muttered something like a prayer under her breath.

Into the heavy silence Rovann said, "Garn? What is it?"

He rubbed at the side of his face. "Ah, I'd hoped the little uns hadn't heard the chatter. Does no good to go frightening children."

"Tell them," Etta said quietly, nodding toward Rovann and Maegwin.

Garn hunched forward and spoke in a low voice. "There are rumors that wights are abroad in the west country."

Rovann blinked. "Wights?"

"Aye, terrible things not from this world. Some say the barriers between the Realms are breaking and demons are coming through. If you are traveling west, be sure you can defend yourselves."

Rovann studied Garn's face. Fear rode behind his eyes. These people were fleeing something. But wights? He'd never heard of them encroaching so close to the haunts of people.

"We can defend ourselves," Maegwin declared suddenly.

Garn regarded her, nodded. "Aye, perhaps you can. But enough of such talk, it withers the soul. Saran, is that soup ready yet?" He pulled himself to his feet and lumbered over to the cooking pot.

But Etta and Reya's dark eyes regarded Rovann, suggesting they knew far more than they let on.

Garn ladled out the soup and two of the youngest girls brought a bowl over to Maegwin and Rovann, faces grave as though they undertook a solemn duty.

Rovann accepted his bowl and inclined his head, "Thank you, my lady."

The girl smiled shyly and then got embarrassed and ran away to hide behind her mother.

As they ate, Rovann did his best to steer the conversation to safer subjects. "So, what made you decide on Silverport?"

Garn gestured with his spoon. "Where better? We've spent the last few years touring the southern towns, mainly Mallyn and the areas around. But it's time we moved on. There's too many troupes in the south now and people aren't willing to pay as much. I've heard it told that in Silverport a troupe can earn a year's wages in a month!"

"Garn!" Etta scolded. "Don't go filling the children's heads with such fanciful ideas."

Garn shrugged. "Anyway, we left the south about a month ago and after hearing the rumors of war around Tyrlindon, thought it best if we took the north-west road and skirted Tyrlindon to the north. We hoped to ply our trade in the western provinces but…well things didn't quite work out that way."

When they had finished their meal Garn gathered the children around him for a bedtime story whilst Etta gathered up the dishes.

"Rovann will you help me with these?" she asked.

Rovann climbed to his feet and followed the dark-haired woman to the back of the caravan where a tub of soapy water waited.

Etta began scrubbing the crockery in silence. Rovann sensed there was something on her mind so he remained silent, giving her the space to collect her thoughts. She rinsed out a plate and passed it to him. Rovann dried it with a piece of cloth and placed it back in the tiny cupboard built into the back of the caravan.

"Your wife is very quiet tonight."

"Er, yes," Rovann floundered, "she's a little shy."

Etta's dark eyes flicked up to his and then back to the wash tub. At last she said, "What do you know of my people?"

Rovann took a dish and wiped it dry. "That you are wanderers, going wherever the fancy takes you. Queen Sophia granted your people freedom of the roads."

Etta nodded. "It was not always so. Long ago, my people lived in the Vale of the Blackwood, which has now been swallowed by Roamsford Edge. We kept watch on Amaury's border and grew to know the wights of the Edge. As a result, we became learned in the ways of the Realms. When Roamsford Edge devoured our home, we decided to become nomads. Queen Sophia granted us freedom of the roads in payment for our long service."

She looked at Rovann and her gaze was intense, pinning him to the spot. "Be careful," she whispered, grabbing Rovann's arm in fingers like pincers. "My husband spoke the truth. Something roams the wilderness in the west. It is hunting something. Or someone. And it stinks of Chaos." She released his arm and Rovann realized she had placed something around his wrist: a bracelet of intertwined willow twigs with tiny feathers tied along its length.

"Wear this. It will help to keep you safe."

Rovann stared at the charm, sensing how it vibrated with Eorthic power.

"Thank you," he muttered.

Etta smiled. "I think we are done here."

Maegwin stretched her toes out toward the fire, enjoying how the warmth eased the ache from her tired muscles.

Rovann returned from cleaning the dishes, following Etta back into the circle around the campfire and Maegwin watched him, wondering what had passed between the King's Mage and the gypsy woman. She thought about asking him but decided against it. She doubted he'd tell her anyway.

Around the fire her companions talked in low voices but she had no desire to join the conversation. Her nerves jangled. Restlessness filled her veins. Somewhere ahead lay the Songmaker, Leo, and her vengeance. They needed to get moving.

"Where are you two from then?" A voice said suddenly, startling her.

She turned to see Etta's elderly mother, Reya, leaning forward in her chair, staring at Maegwin intently. "Sorry? What?"

The woman waved her hand, making the bangles that marched up each arm, rattle. "Where you from? Your man and you?"

Maegwin blinked, flustered. Rovann glanced up but didn't speak. "Um, Stoneshowe," she mumbled. "We're from Stoneshowe."

The old woman pursed her lips as if she was sucking on a lemon. "Hmm. You, maybe. But your man has the coloring of the northlands."

"Um, that's right," Maegwin answered, thinking quickly. "Rovann is originally from Mandrake but left many years ago for Stoneshowe."

"And that's where you met?"

Rovann leaned over and smoothly cut in. "Yes. I'm a stonemason and moved south to find work. Once I met Maegwin, there seemed no reason to leave." He smiled and laid a hand on Maegwin's knee.

She did her best to keep her face neutral. Lying seemed to come naturally to the King's Mage. *That's politics for you*, she thought sourly.

After a moment, she turned back to the fire, hoping the old woman was satisfied with their answers. But Reya, it seemed, wasn't done yet. The crone grinned, showing her gums, and then nudged Maegwin with an elbow.

"He's a handsome one, ain't he? You did well there, gal." Her expression turned wistful. "Ah, how I miss my husband. He's been gone twenty years or more. Got thrown from his horse. Broke his neck. Now there was a man easy on the eye. And more than satisfying between the sheets—if you take my meaning!"

"Mother!" Etta scolded. "You're embarrassing them. And you shouldn't talk like that in front of the children."

Etta waved away her daughter's concern. "Pah!" She looked Rovann up and down, appraising him as though he was a prize bull at market. Then she nudged Maegwin and said in a whisper loud enough to carry to everyone. "I bet he keeps you nice and warm on winter nights, eh? I wouldn't mind crawling under the sheets with that one!"

"Mother!" Etta cried.

But Reya only threw back her head and cackled.

Rovann, Maegwin saw, had fallen uncomfortably silent. His cheeks had flushed and he studiously looked in the opposite direction. Despite herself, she felt a grin pulling at the corners of her mouth. He might easily face soldiers in battle or fight mages with terrifying sorcery, but under the attentions of this irreverent old woman, he was defenseless.

"Oh, he has his uses," Maegwin said, copying Reya's gesture of looking him up and down. "Fetching and carrying. Cleaning. That sort of thing. But I have to supervise him of course."

"Ha!" Reya snorted. "A gal who knows her own mind! That's what I like! What do you say to that then, young man? Eh?" She shook a finger in Rovann's direction.

The King's Mage looked from Reya to Maegwin and back again. "I, um, I…"

Garn cleared his throat, coming to Rovann's rescue. "I'd give up, friend. It's no use trying to argue with them." He glanced at Maegwin, Reya, then his wife. "We're dangerously outnumbered."

Reya snorted a laugh and after a moment Maegwin found herself joining in. Tension leaked out of her like a burst drum. How long had it been since she'd experienced this easy companionship? It seemed forever.

"Come on, you lot," Garn said, getting to his feet and addressing the sleepy children. "Time for bed."

He shepherded the children into the caravan then Etta helped Reya to her feet. The old woman gave Maegwin an exaggerated wink before she shuffled off to her bed. Maegwin and Rovann were left alone by the fire.

"What was all that about?" Rovann demanded.

She looked at him with wide-eyed innocence. "Whatever do you mean?"

He frowned. "You know exactly what I'm talking about."

She crossed her arms over her chest and frowned back at him. "Just playing my part. Didn't want them to get suspicious, did we?" A smile quirked her lips. "And besides, we wouldn't want to deny an elderly lady her bit of fun, would we?"

Rovann shook his head in bewilderment. "I thought she was going to eat me alive." He glanced at her, wry amusement shining from his eyes. "Give me a renegade mage any day."

She nodded. "Yep, much easier to deal with."

He laughed, a bright, clear sound that filled the night. Maegwin grinned in response.

Rovann climbed to his feet. "It's an early start tomorrow. We should get some sleep. Good night, Maegwin."

"Good night, King's Mage."

Chapter Three

Light seeping through the soft canvas of the tent wall woke Rovann the next morning. As he roused from sleep he noticed something warm pressing against his back. Groggily, he opened his eyes and turned over, only to realize the warmth was coming from Maegwin who'd curled up beside him.

Hesitantly, he sat up. Maegwin shifted in her sleep, protesting the sudden lack of heat so Rovann pulled the blankets over her shoulders and scrambled through the flap.

The sun had just risen above the horizon, a tight yellow ball that promised a sweltering day. Streamers of mist lay strung out along the ground. The gypsies were beginning to stir.

"What's for breakfast?" Garn bellowed as he emerged from his tent, stretching his arms overhead.

"Fresh air and grass if it was left to you!" Etta replied irritably, pulling a brush through her dark hair.

"I'll take care of it," Maegwin spoke from behind Rovann. He hadn't heard her emerge from the tent. Sleep still clouded her eyes and her red-gold hair lay in tangles on her shoulders. "It's the least we can do after your hospitality."

As Maegwin prepared breakfast Rovann packed away the tent and readied the horses. When that was finished he seated himself by the campfire and took out his whittling knife. He'd found a suitable log on the forest floor and now he set the knife-edge to the wood and began whittling. Soon shavings were flying off in all directions.

Maegwin served everyone fried bread and eggs for breakfast.

"Looks as though it's gonna be a warm one today," said Garn, gesturing at the sky with his fork. "I love summer days. It's what makes being a wanderer so special. Long evenings, quiet mornings. There ain't nothing like it." His face turned solemn and he fixed Rovann with a stern gaze. "You still planning on traveling west?"

Rovann glanced up from his carving and nodded.

Garn stroked his chin in thought. "I'll not try to talk you out of it. You look as though you know what you're doing but if you happen across any gypsies on the road, mention my name and they'll give you what aid they can."

Rovann bowed his head. "Thank you, Garn."

He and Maegwin watched in silence as the gypsies climbed into the caravan and prepared to leave. Etta said nothing, but gave Rovann a probing glance that made him uneasy. Reya grinned her toothless smile at the pair of them.

Once the troupe were aboard Garn shook the reins and the caravan lumbered off, creaking and shaking down the road. Garn peered over his shoulder and bellowed, "If you're ever in Silverport, look us up! We might even give you a free performance!"

"Can they be trusted?" Maegwin asked as she stared after the departed gypsies.

"I hope so," he replied. "Because if they can't, we're all in trouble."

They mounted their horses and resumed their trek.

True to Garn's prediction, the day turned hot. The early mist soon burned away, the sky becoming an uninterrupted arch of blue. The bright sunlight picked out everything in startling detail: the veins in a leaf, minute striations of the pebbles on the road, the delicate hairs on the stem of a daisy.

It was a beautiful morning and normally Rovann would have taken pleasure in it. But not today. As the breeze brushed against his skin, something dark and alien touched his consciousness. It had no odor or taste but behind the glory of the day, he sensed something was wrong.

Etta's warning came back to him. *Something roams the wilderness in the west. It is hunting something. Or someone.*

Absently, he traced his thumb across the bracelet she'd given him. Its woven links felt rough against his skin but it vibrated with a primitive power that reminded him of Thaldan's mage.

Rovann closed his eyes. His breathing slowed. In a heartbeat he shed his body and went soaring up into the sky. Below him shimmered the rich tapestry of life. Everything seemed to be in its proper place: the deep green auras of vegetation, the silver flashes of animals within it. He returned to his body with a jolt to find Maegwin staring at him, a frown pinching the skin between her eyebrows.

"What is it?" she asked.

Rovann shook his head and they rode on in silence.

They met no other travelers. In places the road became little more than a dirt track, often overgrown by vegetation and rutted with cracks and pits. It meant they moved slower than Rovann would have liked. At midday they stopped to rest the horses and grab a quick meal. As she was filling her horse's nosebag Maegwin raised her head, nostrils going wide.

"What's that?"

Rovann strode to her side. A strange odor carried on the wind. The scent had no place in the clean summer's day. It was a wrongness he could not explain. It spoke to him of killing and lust and darkness.

"I don't know," he breathed. "Perhaps it has something to do with the gypsies' warning. It's far from here. No threat." He tried to speak with conviction but his doubts were plain in his voice.

Maegwin looked around uneasily. "I don't like it. Is this another trick of Hounsey's? Has he managed to track us after all?"

"I don't know. Come on."

With every mile the sense of wrong increased. By mid-afternoon, it had become so strong that even the horses seemed to sense it. They laid their ears flat and rolled their eyes nervously.

The road passed through a small woodland. Last year's leaf litter lay thick on the ground, making a springy carpet that swallowed all sound.

Then, as they rounded the bend, Rovann spotted something lying in the middle of the road.

Hairs rose on the back of his neck. The air suddenly felt close, oppressive, as though a thunderstorm was approaching. Brye shied and stamped his hooves, reluctant to go nearer. Instinctively, Maegwin clutched the dagger strapped to her waist.

They dismounted and tied the horses to a tree.

Cautiously, Maegwin at his side, Rovann edged down the road. The object was dark, roughly man-sized, and showed no signs of movement. As they got near enough to make out the object's features, Rovann's breath hissed between his teeth.

It was a stag. The creature lay on its side, splayed across the road as if to block it.

"Dead since last night I'd guess," Maegwin observed.

Slowly, they sidled around to the other side and Rovann realized that they'd found the source of the wrongness.

A pool of blood had gathered around the stag's head where its antlers had been savagely torn off, leaving stringy pink flesh dangling from the wound. Yet that hadn't killed the beast. With a rising sense of horror, Rovann realized that after being ripped from its head, someone had stuffed its antlers down its throat, piercing its jugular, choking it to death.

The stag's sightless eyes were wide with terror and sweat had dried into white deposits of salt on its coat. The hard-packed mud around the stag was gouged and pitted with hoof-prints. It had fought to the end.

Rovann scrubbed a hand through his hair, thoughts churning in frightening circles. Something with immense strength had held the stag down as it was killed, destroying it with the very symbol of its power and majesty. The brutality of the killing left him cold.

"Who would do such a thing?" Maegwin asked hoarsely.

Rovann looked around, scanning the undergrowth in case something hid within.

"I don't know. But it feels like a warning."

"To who? Us?"

"To any who come this way. Whatever did this wants us to know they're around."

"Hounsey?"

Rovann shook his head. "I don't know. I don't think so. This feels...different."

"What should we do with the carcass?"

"Leave it."

Maegwin's mouth tightened but she made no comment. Instead, she knelt and held her hand over the stag's heart. Tears shone in her eyes as she whispered, "May you find your way to the gardens of Sho-La, Great Heart. Be at peace."

They hurried on. Rovann guessed that Maegwin's assessment was right: the stag had been killed sometime yesterday evening. The killer could be miles away by now. Or it might be nearby, waiting.

Maegwin said nothing all day and Rovann found his thoughts turning to Tyrlindon. Had the attack begun yet? Was the king safe? A hundred unanswered questions crowded in on him. Where was the Songmaker? Was Prince Owen still alive? Was Leo?

Suddenly a pheasant burst from a bush and scrambled awkwardly into the sky, cawing in outrage. Brye startled, shied to the left, and Rovann was forced to saw on the reins to bring him under control. The beasts had been skittish since they had found the stag. Maegwin's horse, normally as placid a mare as anyone could wish for, rolled her eyes at the slightest sound.

Rovann didn't like it. This whole situation felt wrong. There was something important he had overlooked or misunderstood. But try as he might, he couldn't think what it could be. He was the First of the Council, the strongest mage in Amaury yet he felt vulnerable, as though he wore a blindfold.

As evening rolled toward them, they finally began to encounter signs of civilization. The fields were demarcated by dry-stone walls and barns stored hay and fodder for animals. Herds of sheep covered the hillsides. High up on one side of the valley they saw a drover's hut.

Soon houses started to appear, small white-washed cottages with thatched roofs. But they still didn't see a soul. A mile or so further on, they spotted a dilapidated sign which read, *Threeways: one league.*

Rovann exchanged a look with Maegwin. The village might have an inn. Although he wanted to move with stealth, he was uneasy about spending another night camping by the side of the road. His mind made up, he kicked Brye into a canter and the roan was happy to comply, as if he could already smell the stable.

They reached Threeways as dusk was settling. Rovann was not sure it deserved the title of 'village'. Five or six thatched cottages clustered around a crossroads. A wide road ran off to the prosperous regions to the north. The inn was the only two-story building in the settlement. It stood guard at the crossroads as if to keep a watch for weary travelers. The building boasted a slate roof instead of thatch, and had a sizeable stable yard at the rear.

The village seemed deserted. Nobody moved through the streets, no dogs barked, no geese honked. Tying the horses to a post outside, Rovann pushed through the door into the inn.

They walked into a wall of noise. It looked as though the whole village was clustered round the battered tables filling the small common room. The scent of pipes and cooking filled the air and the space near the ceiling was filled with hazy smoke. Although the night wasn't cold, a fire blazed in the hearth with bunches of protective herbs hanging above.

The creak of the door made heads turn. Conversation suddenly died to be replaced by a sullen, unfriendly silence.

The innkeeper, a scrawny man with one ear missing, placed his hands on the bar and leaned forward. "What can I do for you, strangers?"

Rovann couldn't mistake the wariness in the man's tone. Carefully he answered, "My wife and I have been traveling all day and would like a room for the night."

The innkeeper looked them over, his keen eyes assessing. "Is that so? And where would you be going?"

"Yatarn. My mother is ill. We're going to visit her."

The man's eyes narrowed with suspicion. "Yatarn is in gypsy country. You don't look like gypsies to me."

Rovann did his best to smile disarmingly. "No. We've lived in the south for many years."

"Lies!" a woman shouted suddenly. "We haven't had travelers through here for weeks! Nobody would risk the Yatarn road with the way things are."

The woman's words brought a rumble of agreement and the atmosphere went up a notch. Behind him, Maegwin tensed, and Rovann willed her to remain quiet.

Casting a look over the crowd, he said, "I assure you, we're not lying. We'll be gone in the morning."

The innkeeper stared at them for a long time. At last he said, "Perhaps you're telling the truth. No way to be sure. Times have been troubled around here lately. Strange goings-on. Things going missing. Slaughtered cattle. Odd symbols drawn at the side of the road. So you'll forgive us if we are a bit wary of strangers."

These were country folk, brought up on folklore and

superstition and Rovann read fear in their eyes. "We've been warned. On the road earlier we came across something strange: a stag had been choked to death on its own antlers."

A whisper of alarm raced around the room. Angry muttering began.

"How do we know they're not responsible?" the woman asked. "How else would they know of our problems?"

Rovann held out placating hands. "We met a family of gypsies led by Garn and Etta. They warned us of the peril in the countryside but we chose to risk it for the sake of my sick mother. Garn also told us that if we ever needed aid we were to speak his name. Well, I ask for that aid now, in Garn's name. We mean no harm. We just want a bed for the night."

A burly woman seated by the fire pulled herself to her feet. She had her hair pulled back by a brightly woven scarf in the gypsy fashion. She looked Rovann over with open hostility. Then her eyes alighted on the charm tied around Rovann's wrist and her expression relaxed.

"Garn is my cousin," she announced. "And this man wears one of Etta's charms. Give them a bed, Tattin. Or you'll answer to me."

The innkeeper waved his hand at the woman. "Fine, Tarla." He looked at Rovann. "Do you want food?"

Rovann nodded. "My thanks. It's been a long day."

"I'll see what the cook can rustle up. Find yourselves a seat and I'll bring it over. My boy, Fenno, will care for your horses."

Carefully, Rovann and Maegwin picked their way through the room and found a vacant table at the back. The crowd returned to normal. Conversation resumed. Maegwin eyed the villagers suspiciously.

The innkeeper came over, expertly balancing two steaming plates in the crooks of his arms whilst carrying a tankard in each hand. He placed his burdens on the table and said, "My lad has taken your horses to the stable. They'll be brushed down and fed. I've had a room on the top floor made ready for you, away from the noise down here. You can go up whenever you wish."

Rovann smiled graciously. He pulled out two coins: one silver, one gold and tossed them to the innkeeper. "Many thanks."

The innkeeper caught them and tucked them into a pocket of his apron. "Enjoy your supper."

The stew looked as though it had been sitting in a pan since lunchtime: a thin layer of grease covered the top and the lumps of meat looked gray and stringy. Nevertheless, Rovann picked up his spoon and ate ravenously. Maegwin followed his example. The beer was excellent and helped to wash away the slightly rancid taste of the meal.

As he ate, Rovann surreptitiously listened to the conversations around him, hoping to pick up any useful information.

"So what do you reckon then?" one man asked his fellow. "Is it a prank of some sort, somebody's idea of a joke?"

The other man snorted. "You'd have to be one sick bleeder to do these sorts of things, wouldn't ya? No, this is something a whole lot worse, I tell you. My ma's got gypsy blood and they knows more than most folk about weird goings-on. She reckons it's a demon what's stalking them woods and it's only been killing cattle until it's worked up enough of a hunger to come after real prey: us."

The first man laughed, a valiant effort to scoff at his

friend's pronouncement, but the laugh came out a little too shrilly, with an edge of hysteria in it.

A woman, hunched over a table by the fire, was speaking in a low voice to her two companions. Rovann had to strain to pick up the words.

"Did you hear what happened to Lorn? He has a small-holding on the hill. One of his pregnant ewes was killed during the night. But listen to this: whatever did it ripped the ewe's belly open, took out the lambs and dumped them on the ground by their mother. What would do such a thing?"

"Wolves?" suggested one of her companions hopefully.

The woman scowled. "Wolves? You serious? When do wolves make a kill and then take nothing to eat? Besides, we haven't had wolves round here since the winter, they'll all be up on the higher slopes at this time of year."

Her two companions nodded in sullen agreement.

Rumors. Tales.

Rovann needed more. On impulse he slewed round in his chair and faced the woman by the fire.

"Has anyone seen this thing?"

She looked up in surprise. Her fellows stared into their mugs, uncomfortable with his query but the woman stared at Rovann as if assessing what she could tell him.

"That's what makes it so bad," she said at last. "Nobody *has* seen it. Perhaps if we had, we'd have a better idea of what we're dealing with. But it comes in the night, when nobody's around. Some have even stood guard over their flocks just to find, come the morning, they've been slaughtered right under their noses. If you're traveling to Yatarn you need to be careful."

Rovann turned back to his table. Maegwin had finished her meal and was staring avidly at the woman Rovann had just addressed. There was a faraway look in her eyes and the fingers of her left hand drummed on the table absently.

"Maegwin?"

She startled and began to rise from her seat before realizing who'd spoken. "Yes?"

"Are you well?"

Maegwin looked around, scowling as if troubled. "I'm fine." But her fingers went back to their drumming.

At the end of the room, the fire popped and crackled. By the door, someone laughed at a ribald joke. At a table, a heated discussion broke out over a game of cards. The warm hum of conversation and companionship filled the air. But at Rovann and Maegwin's table silence reigned.

Without glancing up from her contemplation of the table top, Maegwin reached out one hand and grabbed a tankard. The other hand continued its drumming.

Behind Maegwin, a red-faced man who looked to be well into his cups began weaving through the throng toward a table near the fire, carefully holding two frothing tankards in each hand. As he passed their table, the man stumbled, sent his elbow crashing into Maegwin's shoulder, spilling sticky brown ale down her back.

Maegwin's reaction was instantaneous. She surged to her feet and spun, sweeping the tankards from the man's hands where they crashed to the floor in an explosion of ale and pot shards. Grabbing the man by the shirt, she threw him across the room sending him crashing into a table, its occupants diving out of the way with bellowed curses. The table broke under the man's weight and he sprawled on the floor amid the wreckage.

Everything seemed to happen in an instant. Rovann watched Maegwin's face contort in fury, saw her stride after the man, saw her whip the dagger from its scabbard at her side, saw her bend down and grab the man's hair, saw her raise the weapon above her head.

He launched himself. As the blade began its downward swing he grabbed her wrist in both hands and yanked savagely.

Maegwin fought Rovann's grip. They struggled briefly before Rovann wrenched the dagger from her hand and tossed it to the floor where it bounced with a metallic ring.

Rovann grabbed Maegwin and bundled her unceremoniously out the door and into the night. He didn't stop to let her protest, but dragged her past the crossroads, down the road until they were out of sight of the inn. There he pulled her into a tree-shrouded clearing. The moon was full. It lit the glade in brilliant silver.

"What was that?" he roared, unable to control the rage in his voice. "Have you lost your mind? You would have killed that man! Killed him!"

Maegwin backed away until she was hidden by shadow. The moon cast light only on her face and in her visage Rovann saw a terrifying mix of fury, sadness, pain and confusion. Her eyes were unfocused but her hands curled into tense balls at her sides.

She opened her mouth to speak but a sudden gust of wind snatched her words away. The wind blasted through the glade, shaking the trees and whipping up dust from the hard-baked earth. On the wind came a stench so overpowering it nearly forced Rovann to his knees. Around the clearing the shadows ran like pooling ink. Fear swirled in his stomach as he realized what that meant.

The stalker had found them.

Chapter Four

Maegwin's heart thundered against her ribs. Blood roared in her ears. Adrenaline pumped through her system, making her breath come in ragged gasps. Thought seemed to have stopped entirely, to be replaced by a burning, animal hunger. Somewhere, buried deep, she realized she had lost control and that scared her, but not enough to over-come the desperate, overwhelming need for violence that coursed through her veins.

Through the fabric of the Realms, she thought she heard a goddess laughing.

She crouched, facing Rovann. Fury rolled off him in waves. She glimpsed his power like a bonfire raging. Good. He would be a worthy opponent. Her hands curled into fists and she rocked onto the balls of her feet, ready to fling herself at him.

Then a gust of wind blasted through the clearing, driving her back. With it came a terrifying stench. Death. Rot. The pervasive odor of hatred.

Maegwin shook her head and her thoughts slowly

cleared. Her heartbeat slowed and she straightened, scanning the clearing for signs of the threat.

Around her, shadows began to move. The darkness started to run like rivers of ink and pooled in the center of the clearing.

In sudden fear Maegwin backed away, moving to stand beside Rovann.

Then suddenly the inky darkness coalesced and rose up, up, to form a shape in the clearing's heart: a tall, black figure. The creature seemed to have no arms or legs, only a shadowy body like a darker piece of the night. Atop its body sat a white, bulbous head that hung grotesquely at an angle. The apparition seemed to suck all warmth and light from the world. Even the moonlight became muted.

The head turned slowly in their direction, its neck popping and cracking. From its mouth came a long sigh that carried the stench of a crypt.

"Ah. You smell so sweet. Ripe. Come to me so I may devour you."

The creature's echoing voice held a strange, hypnotic quality and, to her horror, Maegwin found her body obeying its compulsion. She took a step toward it. And another.

Rovann spoke softly. "No."

The compulsion evaporated and Maegwin halted, pulse hammering with cold fear. How had it mastered her so easily? Was she so weak?

Quiet laughter. It bubbled like blood through a wound.

"So. You have passed my first test. No matter. Still I will consume you."

Rovann grasped Maegwin's arm and pushed her behind him. Slowly, he edged toward the creature. "You're far from home, Unforgiven One. Why are you here? You hold no power in the Realm of Earth."

The entity flickered and seemed to grow taller. It shook its head slowly, the crunch and crack of bones loud in the night. "Rather it is the Realm of Earth that has no power against me. Ah, I smell your strength! Come to me so I may chew you."

Anger flared in Maegwin's chest. Pushing past Rovann, she leapt, aiming a kick at the creature's head. But as she reached the space it occupied it vanished and then reappeared a few feet away.

Maegwin spun to face it just as something exploded against her abdomen and flung her across the clearing like a doll. The ground rushed up to meet her and she landed on her back with an impact that left her winded and gasping. A rivulet of blood ran down the side of her head into her ear.

The thing was on her in an instant. Its heavy body pushed her down, filling her nostrils with its carrion stench. The gaping mouth descended toward her face, making sucking noises, eager to taste her lifeblood.

Maegwin screamed in horror. Then there was a flash of light and the creature disappeared.

Rovann crouched by her side. "Are you hurt?"

Maegwin tested her legs and was surprised when they moved. Holding out her hand, she allowed Rovann to pull her to her feet. The cut on her temple leaked blood into her eyes. Irritably, she wiped it away. She could not afford distractions.

It was standing silently on the other side of the clearing, regarding them with its head cocked to one side. Maegwin took a step, but Rovann held out a hand. Glancing in his direction, she caught the meaning of the look he gave her.

Do nothing.

Rovann addressed the creature. "I ask again, Unforgiven One. How have you managed to leave the Outer Darkness?"

It remained still, staring at them with an interest that sent chills along Maegwin's skin. She wanted to run, to get as far away from this monster as possible.

At last, its mouth opened and words slithered out. "You know that answer, Realm Walker. The ancient barriers are failing. The time of reckoning is coming." It made a noise like a dog sniffing the air. "Ah! Freedom smells so sweet!"

Rovann shifted uneasily. "Did the Songmaker send you?"

A ghastly smile split the white face. "Let me lick your blood."

Without warning, Rovann jabbed out his hands. A sheet of brilliant silver sprang into existence, wrapping itself around the creature. But with a hiss, it flickered out of existence and reappeared in front of him.

An unseen force exploded into Rovann, flinging him across the clearing. With a thud he crashed into a tree and slid to the ground.

The head turned slowly to regard Maegwin. It smiled.

Crouching low, she dodged around the apparition and flung herself across the clearing to Rovann's side where she skidded to her knees, throwing up leaf-litter. The mage's eyes were closed, his face pale. She grabbed Rovann by the shoulders and pulled his head onto her lap.

"Wake up!" she cried in desperation. "Rovann!"

His eyes fluttered and opened, focusing on her anxious gaze. In the next moment, he rolled onto his front and then staggered to his feet.

The creature hadn't moved. It watched the King's Mage with a grin on its face. Rovann spread his hands wide and chanted in a low, earthy language. Maegwin recognized the sound of the Eorthe, the same power Syrie had used to get them to Carrow Crossing.

A spear of white light appeared in Rovann's hand. He pulled his arm back and sent it flying through the air.

The grin disappeared from the creature's pallid face. It stepped back, preparing to defend itself. But, Maegwin realized suddenly, the spear was not designed as an attack. It thudded into the ground two paces from where the thing stood, standing upright like a blazing sentinel. As soon as it touched the bare earth, the bar of light multiplied: became five, six, seven that circled the creature, imprisoning it within a glowing cage.

The thing yowled in fury. Its head spun crazily, seeking a means of escape.

"Well done!" it cried. "Eorthic power, eh? You're better than I thought. But I am Chaos. The Eorthe cannot hold me."

"Why are you here?" Rovann panted raggedly. "Who sent you?"

In answer, the creature grinned. The rictus smile spread across its face, becoming wider and wider, bisecting its head until the top half fell back, opening out like some fetid flower. Darkness poured out.

Maegwin stepped back as the wave flowed across the ground toward her. She recognized instinctively this was not darkness as she knew it. Rather, it was *nothing*. Absence, non-existence. Chaos.

She looked up, seeking Rovann, only to see that the flow of darkness was pushing him back too, across the clearing, away from her.

"Rovann!"

"Maegwin!" he bellowed. "Don't let it touch you!"

With a strangled cry, she turned and ran. She had gone maybe five paces when something as cold as frozen metal touched the back of her leg. Her strength flooded away as if her veins had been opened. Glancing down, she saw a black tendril of darkness curled around her ankle.

A second later, another tendril caught her other ankle and she crashed to her knees. Desperately, she scrabbled in the dirt, throwing up clods of soil and dead leaves, trying to crawl away from the horror that held her.

But there was no escape.

The smoky fingers moved up her legs, twisted round her abdomen, stretched up toward her face, spreading icy cold through her body that robbed her strength. A finger caressed her cheek and Maegwin heard the creature's voice in her mind.

"I see your thoughts, torn one. You are more like us than you think. Ah, I smell our kinship! Embrace the truth of your nature! Look!"

The tendril of Chaos forced her lips apart and pushed into her mouth. The darkness filled her, stealing her breath until she was sure she would drown. She wanted to scream, to thrash and wail in terror, but her body was held fast.

The Chaos tore through her mind and Maegwin screamed in pain, clasping her forehead in both hands. She felt it take hold of her, blast away everything she'd been taught in the temple of Sho-La, leaving behind only the anger that had become her almost constant companion. It stoked the fires of her rage until nothing remained. Only fury. Only violence.

Then she rose in one fluid movement. Her thoughts had become strangely crystalline in their clarity and they focused on one thing only. Vengeance.

Maegwin ran from the clearing. She pelted through the

woods and back to the village where she strode to the inn and burst inside.

The patrons looked up in sudden alarm as the door banged against the frame. By the bar the man she'd attacked earlier was being comforted by two women. Good. Time to finish what she'd started.

In four strides she crossed the common room, grabbed the man's dagger from its sheath and ripped it across his jugular. The man's eyes widened in shock, his hands going to his throat which spurted bright red arterial blood all over Maegwin, filling her mouth with a salty tang.

As the patrons screamed she turned to one of the women, stabbed the knife into her stomach and smiled as the woman collapsed to the floor.

The innkeeper rushed at her, a club clasped over his head. Maegwin spun, ripped the weapon from his grasp and then smashed it into the innkeeper's surprised face. He crashed to the ground and lay moaning. Maegwin hefted the cudgel and smacked it into the innkeeper's head over and over, until there was nothing left of him but a pulpy mess and bits of fractured bone.

But inside she was screaming.

Help me!

Something crashed into her cheek, sending her sprawling against the hard wood of the inn floor. She scrambled to her feet to find a man facing her. He had wavy blond hair and bright blue eyes. She knew this man. Didn't she?

"Maegwin!" he bellowed. "You are a priestess of Sho-La! This is illusion! Remember yourself!"

His words touched something deep inside.

Sho-La? she asked silently. *Mistress?*

A voice answered. A kind voice that echoed across the

span of years. *Arise, Priestess Maegwin. Be welcomed into my service.*

Maegwin shook her head. "This is illusion. It's not what I am."

And suddenly she was back in the dark clearing.

The entity studied her from behind the bars of its cage. The darkness that had poured from its head was gone.

Rovann knelt by her side in the thick mulch.

"It wasn't real?" she gasped, clutching his arm.

"No," he replied, taking hold of her shoulders and forcing her to look at him. "All lies. It can't harm you now."

"Lies?" asked the creature. "Are you sure? Don't you see the darkness within her, Realm Walker?"

Rovann straightened. "One final chance. Why are you here?"

It grinned. "Let me slurp your liver."

A flood of revulsion washed through Maegwin. Pulling in a steadying breath she scrambled up to stand on shaky legs.

The creature cocked its head, sending the sound of cracking bones into the night. "Tyrlindon is doomed. Will you leave them to die?"

"How do you know of Tyrlindon?"

"Let me eat your innards."

Rovann's mouth twisted. He raised his hands and called forth power that crackled like lightning around his fingers.

But suddenly a new voice cut through the night.

"Rovann."

He spun. A woman stepped out from the shadow of the trees. Rovann's eyes widened, his power dying.

"Istra?"

The woman was short, slightly built and Maegwin recognized her. This was the woman Cedric Hounsey had conjured in his tent at Carrow Crossing, the woman he'd used to taunt the King's Mage. Rovann's dead wife. But this time she was not alone. Other figures stepped out of the night, gathering behind Istra. Maegwin saw women, old men, toothless crones. They stared at Rovann with cold, emotionless eyes.

Rovann recoiled as if he'd been struck. "What is this?" he gasped. "What are you doing?"

A moan went up from the gathered figures and it set Maegwin's hair on end.

"We are your dead, beloved," Istra said, stepping forward with her arms outstretched. "You killed all of us. Will you not embrace us?"

The crowd surged forward, arms reaching for Rovann who scrambled back. "No. No," he mumbled.

The horde of people seemed endless, disappearing into the darkness of the forest. Maegwin saw that they all bore wounds: burns, torn limbs, the marks of sorcery.

"Embrace us, beloved," Istra said. "We are your victims. Embrace us. Set us free."

Rovann turned to stare at the creature. "You bastard," he rasped. "I'll kill you for this. You and your master. I'll kill you both."

A blade of golden force materialized in his hand. With a wordless howl, Rovann sprang forward and sank it into Istra's chest. In an instant the apparitions disappeared and Rovann stood with his head hanging. He looked like a man defeated.

Movement caught Maegwin's eye. Before she could shout a warning, the shining bars of the thing's prison shattered like glass and a wave of force threw her across the clearing. She landed on her shoulder and yelped as pain flared through her upper chest.

Rovann whirled and sent a spear of light hurtling for the creature but it simply melted away and reappeared a few feet away.

Scrambling to her feet, Maegwin ran and jumped high into the air, kicking out viciously at the creature's neck. As her foot connected, its head snapped to the side, the bones cracking horribly. For a moment, it staggered before its featureless face turned to her with a mocking grin.

"I'll chew out your tongue."

Rovann grabbed her wrists suddenly and spun her to face him. "I must fight it on the astral. Can you guard my body?"

"Yes!" she answered. "Go!"

Rovann nodded and folded onto his knees. A soft sigh escaped his lips as his eyes slid closed. A second later, the monster disappeared.

Maegwin dropped into a fighting crouch, scanning the dark wood. Her fingers twitched, curling into balls and back again. Stooping, she picked up a stout branch and held it out in front of her like a cudgel. Somewhere in the distance an owl hooted. The moon came from behind a cloud, bathing the glade in eerie illumination. There was no sign of the creature. Glancing at Rovann's body she knew he still fought, but far away, where she couldn't follow.

Why could she not see? Why were her senses so closed? She tapped the stick against her leg in frustration.

She thought back to her teachings at the temple. It was said that the high priestess had been able to Walk the Realms although Maegwin had never taken the time to learn the meditation techniques required. But she thought she could remember the basics. She took long, deliberate breaths until her breathing slowed and her pulse steadied. Then, in her mind's eye, she pictured the glade: the sky, the moon-light, the trees, the grass underfoot. She wove every little detail of her surroundings together, creating a likeness of the world around her. When the image was perfect she opened her senses and tried to feel the world's vibrations. She felt herself sinking, drifting down into the depths of her soul. As she did so, the life around began to give up its secrets.

Rovann shone with a startling golden light, and from his wrist ran a cord that traveled up and disappeared into the dark sky. In wonderment, she glanced down at herself and realized she was no longer within her body. Instead, she floated a few inches above her crouched form and she too glowed with light.

With a cry of triumph she soared into the air, following the path of Rovann's life-cord.

Looking around, she saw that the countryside below blazed with myriad different auras: green for the trees, silver for the animals that lived within it, blue for the living streams and rivers. Above her, she made out a shimmering arc of light that marked the boundary of the Realm of Earth.

Maegwin flew toward that border where she found Rovann. On this plane he had no substantial form. Instead, he appeared like a golden wraith, vaguely man-shaped, flickering and insubstantial.

And he was not alone. Bound tight in strips of swirling light floated the creature of Chaos.

They faced each other across the astral. Both were silent, as still as sculptures.

Rovann spoke. "I'm getting tired of asking this question. Why have you come to the Realm of Earth?"

There was a crackling noise, like dry twigs snapping,

and Maegwin realized with a shudder that the creature was laughing. "You fool! I have already found her! Look!"

It pointed in her direction. Seeing her, Rovann's eyes widened in surprise.

A cackle escaped the slit of a mouth. "She will serve us in the end!"

"Enough," Rovann said quietly.

Suddenly he threw up his arms and power blazed forth.

"Let me eat your liver before you kill me," the creature rasped.

Rovann plunged one astral hand deep into its core and sketched sigils in the air with his other hand. A gate flared into existence, burning with strange symbols. Rovann dragged the thing through the door and disappeared.

Chapter Five

Rovann stepped through the shining gate that appeared at his command, feeling the sharp tug as he left one plane of existence and entered another. He found himself in the Realm of Fire. The gate closed behind him with a snap and his ephemeral astral form was immediately buffeted by the wild, violent energies of Fire. Swirling gales ripped through the upper atmosphere, threatening to tear him to shreds.

Wrapping his strength around himself like a shield, Rovann dragged the bound entity deeper into the Realm. He'd planned to take the creature all the way to the Outer Darkness but realized it was too much of a risk. Was he strong enough to withstand the rift in the wall of Chaos? He wasn't sure.

And besides, if he encountered Istra there he might lose control completely.

Istra.

Her image played across his memory like a dream, threatening to shatter his concentration.

As they moved deeper into Fire, the creature of Chaos

howled. It writhed and squirmed, contorting its body like some terrible snake. Gritting his teeth, Rovann clung on.

Scalding winds tore at him. Clouds of noxious gas swirled. A rain of molten metal pattered around him. He wouldn't last much longer in this volatile Realm. He came to a halt high above a lake of lava and sent a mental summons spiraling out into the Realm.

Creatures of Fire, I need your help!

After a moment, he sensed a vast intelligence stir in answer to his call. An enormous beast winged its way toward him through the raging sky. With a start, Rovann recognized the dragon, Tanyaka.

She hung in the air before Rovann, regarding him with solemn eyes. "You have called, young one. How may I aid you?"

Rovann bowed to the great dragon. "Your fears were proven correct, Old Heart. One of the Unforgiven Dead broke into the Realm of Earth."

"I see it." There was unmasked contempt in the dragon's voice as her eyes narrowed on the struggling creature. "Give it to me. It has been an age since I drank a demon's essence."

Rovann perceived the dragon's spirit shimmering golden inside her body. It was a force of pure elemental energy, powerful and deadly. Tanyaka reached out a claw, hooked the creature and drew it toward her. The thing thrashed and screamed but to no avail. Tanyaka lifted it into her mouth and swallowed.

The dragon's life-force engulfed the creature, as though it was a burning coal thrown into a vat of water. The entity flickered for a second, and then began to disintegrate, torn apart by the elemental force of the dragon's soul. In seconds it was destroyed.

Rovann sighed, tension flowing out from his astral form. "My thanks, Old Heart."

Tanyaka showed her gums in the dragon imitation of a smile. "You are welcome, Warrior of the Realms. Remember, I am ever your ally."

Rovann nodded. Bidding her farewell, he formed a door and stepped back into the Realm of Earth. He felt the tug of his tired body and knew he ought to return but the creature's words plagued him.

Tyrlindon is doomed. Will you leave them to die?

The creatures of the Outer Darkness were liars and he had no reason to believe it. Yet some instinct whispered that it told the truth. He had to know.

Ignoring the growing instability of his astral form, Rovann sped through the upper reaches of the astral plane until he spied the Carrow River sparkling below.

Dropping lower, he followed the line of its meandering until he spotted the remnants of Carrow Crossing. The sight left him cold.

The huge iron and timber bridge that had spanned the river was a ruin. Little had survived the torrent of Fire Rovann had unleashed. The iron supports were twisted and blackened, the wood charred and crumbling, leaving the bridge a burnt-out husk.

But this hadn't stopped Lord Cedric Hounsey.

A floating contraption now crossed the swirling Carrow River, several paces downstream from the ruined bridge. It bobbed and bucked in the current but would provide ample crossing for determined soldiers.

Rovann cursed Hounsey's engineers. They were better than he'd expected. How long had it taken them to build that floating bridge? How far behind Captain Tyan and his soldiers was Hounsey's army?

Raising his eyes to the brooding gray mass of the citadel, Rovann saw that Hounsey's flag, a silver bear's head on a red background, now flew from the highest tower, fluttering and snapping in the night wind. And, he realized suddenly, a second flag flapped beside it. This one bore a yellow sunburst behind a silver harp.

The standard of the Songmaker.

Rovann gritted his teeth. The Songmaker now dared fly his colors openly. His allies flaunted their allegiance. It spoke of the confidence of the renegade mage and his followers. His strength was growing.

Rovann turned away and crossed the river, picking up the road as it left the bridge and sped along it, eyes scanning the road for signs of movement or of Hounsey's camp. At the same time, he kept an eager eye on the astral, mindful that Hounsey's mages might be patrolling. Luck was with him and he moved undetected through the countryside until he spied a cloud of dust rising against the lesser darkness of the night sky. As he crossed a hill and looked down onto a plain that marked the border of Tyrlinshire he finally spotted Hounsey's forces.

He stuttered to a halt, cold dread thudding through his astral form. It was enormous. As far as the eye could see, soldiers marched in tight formation, like some terrible, undulating beast. Armor and weapons glinted in the moonlight and the tramp of so many feet rumbled like thunder. They had marched through the night, driven by the Songmaker's will.

They numbered in the thousands. Tens of thousands. How had Hounsey and the Songmaker raised such a force? How could Tyrlindon answer it?

He drifted closer, moving high above the army to avoid any wards Hounsey's mages might have set. He took it all in, making a mental note of numbers and disposition. Spinning in a slow circle, he searched for Hounsey and his mages but saw no sign of the lord. Then something caught his eye. A shimmering disturbance rippled on the astral right above the center of the host. To Rovann's eyes it looked like heat haze rising from a bonfire, but within the ripples ran oily streaks. Chaos.

So, Hounsey was here after all.

Satisfied, Rovann moved away, speeding ahead of Hounsey's army high on the astral. He passed the vanguard, a unit of light cavalry lead by a tall woman dressed as a mage, and into open countryside. He saw deserted villages and empty fields where the country folk had fled before Hounsey's might.

Finally, another, smaller dust cloud appeared on the horizon and this time he spotted the standard of King William flying above the column. Dropping low he was relieved to spot soldiers he recognized. They'd found horses from somewhere, perhaps requisitioned from a farm on route, and now moved at an urgent pace. At the head of the force rode Captain Tyan, and beside him, Syrie. The soldiers looked tired, haggard, and they carried the stains of the battle at Carrow Crossing.

Unease squirmed through Rovann. Why were they still on the road? Several days had passed since the siege. They should have reached Tyrlindon by now. What had delayed them?

"Halt!" Tyan called suddenly. "About and weapons ready!"

The company reined in, swinging their mounts around to form a line across the road. The thunder of hooves sounded behind and two mounted figures came galloping toward them.

Tyan drew his sword but as the riders came closer, the captain let out a sigh and slammed his weapon back into its scabbard. Rising in his stirrups, he shouted, "About time! What took you so long?"

The riders sawed on the reins, pulling their lathered mounts to a halt where they stood stamping and snorting. Rovann spotted a woman with dark hair piled in ringlets on her head and a man with an enormous, drooping mustache. He recognized the riders: Lady and Tallo.

Lady threw a salute at Tyan. "Sorry, captain. Tallo ran into a spot of bother."

Tallo's tunic, Rovann saw, was smoldering slightly. And was it his imagination or were the ends of his mustache singed?

"Yes, and who's bloody fault was that?" the soldier snapped. "I told you to wait until I gave the signal. You knew I was leaning over the charges but you lit them anyway. You did it on bloody purpose!"

Lady's eyes went wide with shock. "Did not!"

"Did so!"

"Soldiers!" barked Tyan. "Did you complete the task?"

Lady grinned. "Aye, sir. It should be going up right about now."

The group stared down the road, expectation heavy in the air. When nothing happened, Syrie nudged her mount to Tallo's side.

"Well?" she demanded.

Private Tallo tugged on his mustache. "I don't understand it. I was sure we—"

His words cut off as a sound like thunder rumbled through the air. In the distance a ball of fire suddenly shot into the sky, as high as a barn and burning in a long line, straight across the road. It lit the night like a beacon.

"Ha!" cried Tallo, punching the air. "Got you, you bastard!"

The rest of the soldiers let out whoops of triumph but Tyan's harsh command cut through their jubilation.

"That won't hold them for long. Come on, if we reach Stowmeade by dawn we can fire the bridges there as well. Then the bastard will be delayed by another day at least."

Yes, Rovann thought. *That's why you haven't yet reached the capital. You're risking your lives to delay the army. Why? Is Tyrlindon unprepared?*

Rising quickly into the upper levels of the astral, Rovann sped across the countryside. Finally, he spied the massive, tangled web of life-force that was Tyrlindon.

He immediately saw that something was wrong. The ward the Council of Mages had placed above the city still held. On the astral plane it appeared as a shimmering bubble that cocooned the buildings below. But it was failing.

Its surface flared in a dozen places as the power within crackled and fizzed, becoming increasingly unstable. Dropping closer, Rovann drew the correct symbols in the air, opened a gate within the ward and passed through, sealing it behind him.

Even at this late hour, Tyrlindon was busy. On almost every level of the city, soldiers were deploying to defensive positions and on the walls of the lower levels trebuchets and mangonels were being readied. As he sped to the top tier Rovann saw that the air fizzed as students and mages practiced battle sorcery.

Rovann entered the College of Mages and moved undetected until he approached a sparsely furnished set of rooms. To his relief he found Falwin seated at his desk, poring over a thick tome with a candle burning by his side.

Other books were piled in haphazard towers all over the desk.

Rovann sent a mental summons winging toward the Second.

Falwin!

The Second of the Council of Mages lifted his head like a bloodhound on a scent. "Rovann? Is that you?"

I need to talk to you.

A scowl crossed the shaven-headed man's face. He slumped back in his seat, closed his eyes and a few moments later his astral form rose up from his body.

"It is you, you irresponsible young pup!" Falwin growled. "What are you doing here? If an enemy mage should spot you—"

"I know," Rovann replied, cutting off his friend's tirade. "But I had to take the risk. You know what happened at Carrow Crossing?"

Falwin nodded. "Syrie sent word. And ever since, the king has been closeted with his advisors, deciding strategy. The king will prepare for a siege and let the Songmaker's army batter itself against the walls of Tyrlindon."

"All very well," Rovann replied, "if we faced battle on the physical plane only. But we don't, do we? Hounsey has mages with him and Fates alone know what role the Songmaker will play in all this. You can be sure there will be an attack on the astral plane as well. And yet Tyrlindon's ward is failing. It must be reinforced!"

Falwin gestured angrily at the books strewn all over his desk. "What do you think I've been doing? Growing carbuncles on my arse for the fun of it? Since I returned to Tyrlindon I've had my nose stuck in these cursed books looking for a way to do just that! Have you seen the ward? Have you noticed how unstable it's becoming?"

Rovann frowned, rattled by Falwin's words. "Yes, but surely it can be reinforced—"

"Ordinarily, yes. But something's leeching the energy away and try as we might, we can't replenish it. Our ever-helpful resident dark mage, Tallen, reckons it's Chaos. But can he tell me how it's happening or how to stop it? Of course he bloody can't! What's the use of being an adept of Chaos if you can't do anything bloody useful with it?"

Rovann winced, imagining the tirade the dark mage would have endured from Falwin. But he could well understand the Second's frustration. If they didn't find a way to stabilize the ward they would be left wide open to an attack from Hounsey and his mages.

A sudden thought struck him.

"Falwin, when I was observing Hounsey's army on the march he was hidden behind a veil of sorcery. They weren't bothering to post scouts on the astral or to set wards over the army itself. I thought it a bit odd at the time, but now I wonder if they are conducting a ritual behind that veil. Using Chaotic power somehow to weaken the ward over Tyrlindon in preparation for their attack."

Falwin's hand came up to rub his chin thoughtfully. "I don't think so. You heard what Tallen said at the meeting before we left for the Highhold. He would have to be an adept of Chaos the like of which we've never seen before. Tallen reckons nothing living could use Chaos that way: the forces would rip them to shreds."

A sudden spasm of cold dread passed through Rovann. His astral form flickered as harsh emotions roiled through him. Of course. He should have realized.

"But Hounsey isn't living," he said quietly.

"What are you talking about?" Falwin said. "Of course

he is! But he bloody well won't be once I get my hands round the traitorous bastard's neck!"

Rovann shook his head. "You don't understand. At Carrow Crossing Maegwin and I made it to Hounsey's tent. Maegwin stabbed him, put a sword right through his heart. Only he didn't die because he was already dead. Hounsey is a revenant."

Falwin stared at Rovann as though he'd gone mad. Then, perhaps reading the truth in Rovann's gaze, his eyes slowly widened. "A revenant? Fates above, what sort of power does the Songmaker wield?"

"I don't know," Rovann replied. "But I suspect his plans reach far beyond this rebellion."

Falwin scowled, hands clenching and unclenching at his sides. "Curse the man! Curse them all! What I wouldn't give to meet the Songmaker face to face, no sorcery, just him and me and a couple of battle maces. Then we'd decide this whole bloody farce once and for all!"

Rovann closed his eyes. Opened them again and took a deep breath. "So. The ward. Anything in your books that might help?"

Falwin moved over to the long desk and looked down on the tomes with undisguised contempt. "Nothing. You could write the sum of our entire knowledge of Chaos on the back of a napkin. And we call ourselves mages!"

"Then I'll try to use the Aethyr to stabilize it."

Falwin looked at him sharply. "No chance. If you channel too much, you'll die. I forbid it."

Rovann raised an eyebrow at that. The Second of the Council giving the First orders? He didn't think so. "There's no choice, Falwin. Come on."

Shifting his focus, he moved his astral body up through the college and into the sky, coming to rest just inside the shimmering ward. After a moment, Falwin joined him. Gazing around at the ward, Rovann saw that the incandescence of the bubble had faded. It looked dull and lifeless. It flickered out of existence and then back again and he knew it wouldn't last much longer.

Rovann drew sigils in the air to create a shimmering gate. He passed through so he was on the outside of the ward, leaving Falwin glaring at him from the other side.

"Be careful, you young upstart!"

"Always," Rovann grinned at him.

He looked down at his astral form and was shocked to see how frail it had become, like a translucent wraith among the glowing tides of the astral. With a jolt, he realized he'd been away from his body too long already. Any longer and he might not get back at all.

Gathering his strength about him, he drew sigils in the air and opened a gate into the Realm of Aethyr. Its vitality rushed through him, bringing strength and stabilizing his astral body. But this power wasn't for him. Instead of holding it within himself, Rovann channeled the energy out into the ward. Yet the barrier remained unstable. It continued to flicker, threatening to fail at any moment.

Doggedly, Rovann focused his strength on the weaker points, hoping to reinforce the overall framework. A silver fretwork snaked its way across the surface of the ward, focusing the Aethyr on the parts that needed it most.

But then something kicked back. A ripple ran through the barrier as the Aethyr collided with the tendrils of black Chaos that twisted across the ward's exterior. The Aethyr skipped over it as though it was oil, unable to bond with the Eorthic power beneath.

Gritting his teeth, Rovann drew more Aetheric power until it raged through his body like a tornado. Little bits of his essence began to tear away, tiny fragments of his astral form that spiraled into the ward.

"Stop!" Falwin bellowed. "That's enough! The ward can't be saved. Stop before you kill yourself!"

But Rovann didn't stop. A tiny sliver of fear ran through him as he realized that he couldn't. He'd lost control of the torrent of Aetheric power tearing through him. Strength leaked away as bits of his essence tore free until he felt like a burnt out husk.

And still the ward wasn't stable.

But then, miraculously, a thrill of vigor flowed through his astral body. Strength returned, filling him like water into a parched cup. He looked around, searching for the source of this unexpected help and saw a tiny figure floating on the astral above him. His breath caught as he recognized it.

Maegwin.

A rope of silver light ran from her fragile astral body to Rovann's. Somehow, she had formed an astral link between them and was feeding him strength.

He didn't have time to be amazed. He pulled Maegwin's vigor into himself, used it to focus the channel of Aethyr and poured it out into the ward. With a snap that shook the astral like thunder, the black flecks within the ward evaporated into smoke that drifted away on the shifting astral tides. Gradually, the ward grew stronger until it shone with incandescent silver light.

"Look!" Falwin called raggedly. "She's breaking up!"

Rovann turned and saw to his horror that Maegwin's astral form was beginning to disintegrate. Calling to Falwin, "The ward will hold! Give Hounsey a beating for me!" he sped toward Maegwin.

Desperately, he threw bands of light around her tattered form and dragged her across the empty miles of the astral, feeling her strength ebbing away despite his attempts to stabilize her. At last they reached the clearing. Unceremoniously, he pushed her down into her body and then dropped into his own.

He opened his eyes to hot agony cramping his muscles, threatening to make him black out. Clasping his hands to his forehead, he waited as pain rampaged through the front of his skull and then crawled through the leaf-litter to Maegwin's side.

She lay as still as a granite effigy. He pressed his fingers against her throat, searching for a pulse and sighed with relief when he felt a strong beat. Carefully he laid her on her side and then covered her with his cloak. A strand of hair fell across her face which he brushed away gently.

She looked so peaceful. Could this really be that vicious, angry woman she'd become at the inn? Would she have killed that man if he hadn't stopped her? A memory of the creature's words echoed through his head and he shivered.

She will serve us in the end.

He stroked his thumb across Maegwin's cheek, feeling the soft warmth of her skin. She would recall little of what she'd experienced on the astral. It would seem as a dream, fragmented images that made no sense. But he would remember what she'd done.

Pulling himself to his feet, he tested the state of his body. Every muscle ached as though he had been in a brawl. Yet he also felt oddly refreshed, full of life.

Nearby the leaves on a holly bush rattled gently in the wind. An owl glided silently overhead then alighted on a branch, watching him with unblinking eyes.

Leaving Maegwin to sleep, Rovann ran from the clearing and back to the village. As he approached the inn, he cast a glamor over himself so the patrons would see a face they recognized, an acquaintance they could ignore. He pushed through the door to find the common room in an uproar. People stood in clusters around the bar, all shouting at each other. The innkeeper was waving his arms, vainly calling for quiet.

"What more proof do you need?" shrieked a thin woman with a nasally voice. "The strange goings on tonight coincided with them turning up! They must be behind it. Who else can it be? You saw the way she attacked poor Jarnos! She was deranged, I tell you!"

She turned to Jarnos and patted his arm sympathetically. He sat at the bar looking slightly dazed but otherwise unharmed.

"So what do you suggest, Marla?" demanded the innkeeper, crossing his arms over his chest.

"Hunt them down! Bring them back to face justice. They shouldn't be allowed to get away with it!"

"And just how do you propose we do that?" asked another man sourly. "They must be witches. They've probably turned into birds and flown away."

The innkeeper snorted. "I reckon you've had too much ale, Ramond. Witches? What next? Wights and warlocks?"

Ramond scowled at the innkeeper. "You got any better ideas?"

The innkeeper leaned on the bar, glaring around at his patrons until he had everyone's attention. "We can't let them go unpunished, that's clear. But nor can we go around meting out punishment ourselves. They must face the king's justice."

"The king's justice?" cried the nasally woman, Marla. "Out here?"

"Vilna is not twenty miles away and has a sheriff."

"Sheriff?" Marla snorted in disgust. "He ain't one of us is he? Why should we trust him?"

Several others nodded in agreement. Then Jarnos, the man Maegwin had attacked, said, "She was a witch, I'm sure of it. Did you see the look on her face? I was sure she was going to kill me and drink my blood!"

An image flashed into Rovann's mind: Maegwin's face contorted with fury, a mad light filling her eyes. He couldn't equate that image with the woman who had risked her life to aid him on the astral. He knew that since the destruction of her temple she battled with inner demons. But she'd saved his life in Angard, and done the same for Tyrlindon.

And she'd tried to kill an unarmed man.

"There!" Marla glared triumphantly at the innkeeper. "Jarnos says she's a witch and he's the one most likely to know." Everyone was watching her now, listening avidly to her words. "It's up to us to make sure justice is done."

Rumbles of agreement traveled round the room and many banged their tankards on their table.

Rovann didn't like the mood of the crowd. Soon their fear would turn to violence. Time to act. Drawing a little Eorthic power, he wove a sequence of gestures in the air, spoke an incantation under his breath then breathed it out into the room, covering the patrons. For a second everyone froze before resuming their conversations, blinking as if waking from sleep.

"What was I saying?' said Marla. "Oh yes. My brother's ewe had triplets. Can you believe it? We've not had such a good omen round here in many a year."

"Aye," agreed the innkeeper. "Let's just hope it bodes well for the harvest."

Quietly, Rovann slipped out the door and closed it behind him. His use of mind-magic made him uneasy: it was too similar to the Songmaker's dark magic. Yet he could not afford a mob of angry villagers on his tail. He hurried to the stables, retrieved the horses and led them back to the glade.

Maegwin was still sleeping. For a moment, Rovann remained in the shadows, watching her.

I was sure she was going to kill me and drink my blood!

Rovann hobbled the animals then spread his bedding on the ground beside Maegwin. The clearing had become peaceful, a serene pocket of the night. Nobody would have guessed that the Unforgiven Dead had been here or that a battle had been fought. Lying back on his blankets, Rovann stared up at the cold stars far above.

Something hot blowing in his ear woke him. Opening his eyes, he saw Brye peering down at him, muzzle scant inches from Rovann's face. Rovann pushed the horse's nose away but the animal merely responded by slurping his tongue along Rovann's cheek. Satisfied, he wandered away and began cropping grass.

With a wry laugh, Rovann got up and walked into the trees to collect firewood. The sun hadn't yet risen and the air was gray and still. It smelled of dew and freshness. No taint of evil remained on the soft morning breeze. The villagers would have no memory of last night's events. Their lives would go back to normal. Rovann used this thought to justify his use of mind-magic, even though his reasons sounded hypocritical to himself.

He tried to calm his thoughts, push everything but the present from his mind. In this way, he'd learned to find peace within himself, a stillness where he found strength. He concentrated on collecting the firewood, piling sticks of all sizes in his arms and drinking in the smell of the wood, feeling its grainy texture as it brushed against his skin, listening to the sharp snap of twigs breaking beneath his feet.

When he had enough he returned to the clearing and dumped the firewood in the center of the glade. He waved his hands over the pile and flame flared to life among the branches. Rovann took some bacon and sausages from one of the saddlebags and began to fry them over the fire.

The smell roused Maegwin. She turned over, mumbled something incoherent and then sat up, looking around wildly.

"Easy," said Rovann. "The creature has gone, you're safe."

It took a moment for Maegwin's eyes to focus and recognize him. Then she relaxed. "You saved Tyrlindon?"

"Yes."

Maegwin slumped back. "I'm glad. For a second I thought we'd failed."

Rovann pushed the bacon around in the pan. "I didn't know you could walk the astral."

She shrugged. "Neither did I. I was as surprised as you when it worked."

"Why did you do it? You could have been killed."

With a frown, she scrambled into a sitting position and fixed him with a look he couldn't decipher. She was either angry or amused. "What choice did I have? I couldn't let you fight alone."

"I'm glad." He dished the bacon and sausages onto plates and passed one over.

Silence descended as they ate, punctuated by the sound of the horses tearing up chunks of grass.

After a moment, Maegwin said quietly, "I'm sorry about the inn."

Rovann kept his eyes on his food. He'd been hoping she

wouldn't bring it up. "Are you? Do you even realize what you did? What if I hadn't stopped you in time? If I'd been a second slower? Did the king save you from the noose in Mallyn just to have to hang you for a different murder?"

She ducked her head as though his words were physical blows. She placed her plate on the ground and looked off into the distance. "Perhaps I'm destined for the hangman."

Her words stung him into anger. "Really? Then why did you agree to help me? Am I a fool to trust you?"

Her head whipped round, eyes going wide. Emotions flickered across her face: irritation, shame. "You're not a fool, Rovann. Your trust is…important to me. I'm sorry."

Rovann scrubbed his hand through his hair. "I need to know if I can rely on you, Maegwin."

"I gave you my word didn't I? I will find Leo and the prince, or die in the attempt."

Rovann let out a long breath. "Without your aid I wouldn't have been able to strengthen the ward over Tyrlindon. On behalf of the king and the Council of Mages, I thank you."

She looked away, seeming uncomfortable with his gratitude. Her eyes strayed toward the road. "The villagers?"

"We have nothing to fear from them. I took care of it."

Questions crowded her face but she merely nodded, accepting his explanation. She climbed to her feet and began to saddle her horse. Rovann doused the campfire, repacked the breakfast things and then saddled his own mount. As dawn was breaking, they rode into the west.

Chapter Six

Maegwin stared at the tangled web of branches passing overhead. Bands of morning sunlight fell through them, making it seem as though the trees were covered with thousands of sparkling emeralds. From the forest floor delicious fragrances wafted up: earthy loam, pine needles, wildflowers. Birds flitted from tree to tree, singing and whistling.

It seemed to Maegwin that the world had come alive. Since her return from the astral plane, things had subtly altered. Although those events were becoming hazy in her mind like the fragments of a fading dream, their effects appeared to grow stronger with each passing minute.

She glanced at Rovann.

Is this what he sees all the time? she wondered. *Is this what it's like to be a mage? To see the world in such detail?*

A fly landed on her horse's neck and she stared, fascinated by the delicate patterns on its wings.

"Maegwin?"

She looked up to find Rovann frowning at her. "Are you all right?"

"Fine," she muttered. "Why wouldn't I be?"

"You seem a little...distracted."

Maegwin forced herself to concentrate on the King's Mage. He wore a stony expression and the way he sat his horse spoke of tension. "No, I'm well. Sorry, tell me again —where are we heading today?"

"If all goes to plan, we'll reach Roamsford Edge."

"Oh."

Roamsford Edge. A name whispered with dread. Maegwin knew she ought to be afraid but she couldn't bring herself to care. A leaf fluttered across her vision, snagging on her horse's mane briefly before blowing away again. She watched it dance and swirl through the air.

My eyes have been opened, she thought. *A gift from my mistress.*

But which mistress? Sho-La or Her darker aspect?

Maegwin shifted in her saddle, suddenly uneasy. Her thoughts traveled back to the previous evening and the black rage that had come upon her so unexpectedly. Would she have killed that man at the inn if Rovann hadn't stopped her? Surely not? But Maegwin couldn't say for certain. At the time, she'd been filled with exultant fury.

Not my fault, she told herself. *Anger brought on by the demon. Its evil bleeding into me.*

And yet...

She shook her head. No. She was not that angry, vengeful person. She was Maegwin of Sho-La. But wasn't she now Maegwin of the Dark Goddess as well? Didn't vengeance drive her as much as compassion?

She lifted her chin, unwilling to follow those thoughts. "What's my horse's name?"

Rovann looked at her. "Sorry?"

"My horse. What's she called?"

He shrugged. "No idea."

Maegwin pursed her lips in thought. The beast had been a faithful companion throughout the journey. She deserved a name.

"Tilya," she said after a moment. "After the yellow flower that used to grow in the meadows around the temple. Do you know it?"

"I do. Its leaves are useful as a poultice for bruises. Tilya it is then."

Tilya looked up at Rovann with big, watery eyes then swung her head down and continued her plodding walk.

"She likes it!" Maegwin said, laughing.

Rovann smiled briefly before returning his gaze to the road.

They stopped to check the map and Maegwin took the opportunity to slide from the saddle and wander a little way into the woodland. Not far from the path, she strayed upon an old beech tree, a brooding giant that spread its limbs out in all directions.

Stooping, Maegwin picked up a fallen branch and examined it with her newly heightened senses. She saw the fibers that made up its innards, smelt the rot beginning to creep through the bark. Near the top of the fallen bough was a tiny nodule, like a bud. A resonance came from that shoot as though it struggled for life.

Maegwin stretched her awareness toward it…

With a pop the nodule burst and a small green leaf uncurled into the daylight.

She yelped, dropping the branch with a thud.

"Don't worry. It won't bite."

Rovann was leaning on a tree, watching her with an expression of amusement.

"What happened?"

Rovann pushed away from the tree and squatted by the

branch Maegwin had dropped. "You Walked the Realms. It changes you."

"Are you saying *I* did that?" she asked incredulously.

Rovann looked up at her, raising an eyebrow. "Is that such a strange notion? I've watched you all morning looking around like a new-born, amazed at everything. I was exactly the same the first time I Walked the Realms."

She opened her mouth to speak and then shut it again. She glanced at the branch. The leaf was small and delicate, bright green with burgeoning life.

She'd done that? Really?

"But... but..."

Rovann straightened and placed his hands on her shoulders, forcing her to look at him. "It's nothing to be frightened of. I'll help you."

Maegwin watched him. His eyes were as blue as the sky, intense in their scrutiny. His palms felt warm against her skin. Her stomach fluttered, heat flooding into her cheeks.

"All right," she whispered.

He nodded and strode off, leaving Maegwin suddenly cold in his absence.

Later that morning, as Maegwin watched a flock of geese go honking overhead, she noticed a sudden change in the atmosphere. Goose bumps rode up her skin. The hairs on the back of her neck rose.

Rovann pulled Brye up and sat staring off into the west. A break in the trees revealed a long, featureless plain stretching off in that direction. "Roamsford Edge is close," he said, squinting into the distance. "Just the other side of the plain."

Maegwin made out a dark smudge on the horizon. "I don't like it. It feels wrong somehow."

"Yes," Rovann agreed quietly, "It does. The Edge is resentful and angry. I don't know what we'll find there."

Nudging their mounts forward, they left the road and headed onto the plain. The ground became rocky under a thin covering of turf and the horses found it hard going. Loose chips of stone rolled from beneath their hooves, making each step treacherous.

Maegwin focused her gaze on a clump of scrubby grass off to the right, concentrating her senses. At last, she found the energy that drove it, hidden deep within every particle. She reached out her will and snuffed out the plant's life force. The tuft of grass crumbled to dust that blew away on the breeze.

She smiled.

They traveled steadily for the rest of the day. The only sign of life they saw was an eagle that hovered on the thermals above them before winging its way south.

Rovann watched the bird with a frown on his face.

"What is it?" Maegwin asked.

"I'm not sure. Nothing I hope."

It was approaching night when Rovann finally called a halt. They made camp in the lee of a large boulder.

Rovann slumped against the rock, took out his knife and the carving he'd been working on and began whittling it. Maegwin saw that the lump of wood was starting to take shape. Although still crude, she could tell it was a woman's face. Istra. Of course.

Abruptly she got to her feet. "I'm going to look around."

Rovann seemed about to say something but then changed his mind. "Be careful."

"I will."

As she headed out onto the plain, the last warmth of the

sun faded from the landscape and a chilly breeze picked up. She stooped to the ground, looking for tracks. The prints of a small hunting cat marked the dust, but nothing she need worry about. Slowly she made a wide sweep of the land around their campsite, treading soundlessly, melting from shadow to shadow. She could have been the only person in the world, alone in the vast, dark wilderness.

The moon came out; a thin silver crescent that lit the sky like a lamp. The wind rose suddenly, whipping dust into her eyes.

And a voice carried on the breeze. *Maegwin.*

She spun around, searching. "Mistress?"

She walked into the night until a tree loomed from the darkness. It was an evergreen of some kind, with silver bark and dark green needles. A presence flickered around the tree. The shadows around its base were thick and viscous.

"Mistress?"

It was not the dark of the moon. The thin yellow crescent rode the sky above as if to deny the Dark Goddess's power. But Maegwin sensed Her close.

Closing her eyes, she focused her concentration on the tree, building a mental picture in her mind. When the image was complete she dug deep inside herself and let forth her new-found power.

The tree exploded into flames.

Maegwin was thrown sprawling in the dirt. White-hot fire enveloped the tree from roots to crown. Its leaves withered away, its bark blackened and then blistered. The blaze roared like a beast. The conflagration consumed her senses. It was primal, instinctive and utterly bent on destruction.

What have I done? she thought in horror.

Maegwin heard hoof beats and Rovann came pounding

up astride Brye, pulling Tilya along behind. He threw himself from Brye's back and approached the burning tree. His eyes were narrowed in concentration as his hands scribbled gestures in the air, his lips moving in a silent incantation.

A sudden pressure change made Maegwin's ears pop and a second later a torrent of water appeared in the sky and dumped itself on the blazing tree. The fire fizzled out, leaving the tree a black, smoking ruin.

Rovann slid to his knees, placing his palms flat against the ground as Maegwin had once seen Syrie do. Words bubbled between his lips and Maegwin recognized the language of the Eorthe, the power of the Realm of Earth. Rovann was channeling it into the tree.

Slowly it began to recover. The bark faded from black to gray. Young green leaves sprouted from the ends of the branches and the smell of pine needles filled the night air.

Maegwin stared, aware her mouth was hanging open but unable to help herself. He had such power. He could mend anything she destroyed.

"What did you do?" he rasped, breath coming in heavy gasps.

Maegwin moved her tongue, working up enough saliva to speak. "I was practicing. I didn't mean to do this."

Rovann stared at her for what seemed an age, assessing. Finally he looked away and muttered. "It's my fault. I should have guessed this might happen. I burned down my father's barn when I first came into my power."

Maegwin nodded, unable to speak. Suddenly ashamed, she stared at her feet.

"The blaze will have been seen for miles," Rovann said. "We have to get out of here."

Dumbly, Maegwin clambered onto Tilya and followed

Rovann at a canter into the night. The silent ride seemed to last forever.

As dawn was breaking, they crested a hill and Rovann signaled for her to stop. Pulling Tilya to a halt, Maegwin gazed out on a sea of gnarled and hoary trees that marched off to the horizon in all directions. She licked her lips. Roamsford Edge. A place of deadly wights and unforgiving spirits. It looked like a vast wall of impenetrable darkness.

Yet somehow they had to find a way through.

Chapter Seven

Rovann turned in his sleep. Black branches reached toward him, digging cold fingers into his body. Rending. Tearing.

He jerked awake.

Maegwin sat cross-legged, watching him. The sun skimmed the horizon. Brye and Tilya were tethered nearby, idly cropping the sparse grass. A pot bubbled over a low fire. He shook his head, clearing the clinging threads of his dream.

Maegwin handed him a bowl of stew that smelt thickly of herbs and rabbit. As he ate, he stared at the brooding mass of Roamsford Edge. The darkness between the trees was absolute, as though thick blankets hung from the boughs.

Rovann slurped the meal as quickly as its heat would allow and then sprang to his feet and began breaking camp. With a sigh, Maegwin got up and helped.

"How long will it take to get through Roamsford Edge?" she asked as she threw the saddle over Tilya's back.

"If the tales can be trusted, four or five days, providing

we meet with no trouble. We should take some simple precautions. If we encounter a wight, do not show any fear of it. We can only hope our presence will go unnoticed."

Maegwin nodded and they swung onto their mounts.

Uneasiness squirmed in Rovann's gut as they began picking their way down the slope toward the forest. The will of the great forest hung in the air, heavy like a storm. It seemed to be… waiting. For them? Rovann wasn't sure. But the forest was old and angry, eager for revenge.

And last night, Maegwin had burned a tree.

Gritting his teeth, Rovann pushed the notion aside. Breathing deeply, he calmed his thoughts and drowned his apprehension as they ducked under the branches of the first trees and entered the dark forest.

The branches overhead were such a tangled net that they blocked out the sunlight. The heat turned humid and a squashy layer of leaves covered the ground, swallowing the sound of the horses' hooves.

"There are no paths through Roamsford Edge," Rovann told Maegwin. "At least, none have been recorded. Stay close and bolt if I do."

They moved in silence, weaving their way through the maze of trunks, wary and alert. Several hours passed with no incidents and Rovann was just beginning to relax when Maegwin suddenly pulled Tilya to a halt.

She held her finger to her lips and mouthed a single word. "Listen."

Rovann stood in his stirrups, straining his ears. A snatch of melody floated on the wind, an eerie, otherworldly tune. Glancing up, Rovann spotted something in the topmost branches of a nearby tree. It was a girl, singing softly. She looked to be around twelve years old and would have passed for human except for five vicious talons extending from each foot and curling expertly around the branch to keep her from falling. Her long yellow hair billowed around her head like writhing snakes.

Maegwin gasped and the girl's gaze snapped to them. Her eyes were utterly black, like holes picked in her face. Rovann held his breath but after a moment the girl looked away, continuing her singing.

They moved quietly on, and Rovann's heartbeat didn't begin to slow until they had put more than a mile between themselves and the creature. Maegwin pulled abreast of him, face pale.

"Was that a wight?"

Rovann nodded. "From the Realm of Air at a guess."

"Was she dangerous?"

"Undoubtedly, but not in the way you might think. Not all wights are aggressive but their powers are alien to this Realm. They can do things we can't."

"Such as?"

Rovann frowned, thinking. How much should he tell her? How much was she ready for?

"Take the creatures of the Outer Darkness, who are also called The Unforgiven Dead or the Sluargh. Most consider them to be evil. But they aren't. At least, not all of them. Yet they come from a world of chaos. We come from a world of order. They are the antithesis of each other. So, they are deadly in that their very existence threatens to unravel the order of the other Realms."

Maegwin nodded slowly. "So if she wanted, that girl could have used the power of Air, which we can't combat here on Earth?"

"Yes. Although we aren't totally powerless. The Eorthe is a powerful weapon and we can channel the power of other Realms if we need to."

Like last night, he thought to himself. *When you forced me to channel Water by destroying that tree. Why did you do that, Maegwin?*

"It's not safe to camp," he said, glancing around at the rapidly darkening forest. "We'll keep moving."

They rode without speaking, the only sound the crunch of twigs and leaf litter under the horses hooves. Night fell. The moon rose and then set leaving the night as dark as a void. Reluctantly, Rovann formed a light globe to illuminate their way. The small white ball bobbed along in front of Brye, lighting the ground before the horse's hooves.

Maegwin suddenly tensed, sat upright in her saddle. "What was that?"

"Hssst! Ssstrangers!"

A whispered conversation came from a clump of bushes to their left: two voices, speaking in sibilant tones. A thrill of fear wriggled through Rovann's abdomen and his heart began to thud against his ribs. He pulled Brye around to face the bush and the voices stopped instantly. But a moment later it came again on the other side. This time it was a single voice, quietly cursing to itself.

"Rip them. Kill them. Nothing left for me. Why is there never anything left for me? Rip out their lungs and use them to make music."

Harsh voices answered from all around, "Yes, rip them! Kill them!"

"Run!" Rovann shouted.

They kicked the horses into an urgent gallop but they had not gone more than a hundred paces when the voices bellowed on either side, laced with anger. Rovann spotted something flitting through the shadows. He jabbed his arm and the ball of light flared briefly. In the sudden illumination Rovann saw dark, faintly man-like creatures skittering out of sight like cockroaches.

They kicked the horses to greater speed but the whispering voices kept pace, easily matching the pace of the galloping horses. They jumped a fallen tree, thundered up a short rise, veered to the left to avoid a holly thicket. The trees closed in, forcing Rovann and Maegwin to duck to evade low branches. Still they thundered on through the dark forest.

Rovann spotted a wall of smoky darkness rising before them. He sawed on Brye's reins and the beast screamed, digging in his hooves to stop himself colliding with the dark barrier. But too late. Brye smashed into its murky surface which gave like some kind of sponge before dissipating into a mass of writhing hands that grabbed at the horse and pulled him down.

Rovann was thrown from the saddle where he landed with a thud in the dirt, all breath knocked from him. The blackness closed over his head and he was plunged into a strange half-world of shifting shadows and cloying smoke. It dribbled down his throat, threatening to choke him. Rovann pushed himself flat, trying to pull in breaths of the cleaner air closer to the ground. Boiling hands tore at him, their smoky claws as sharp as blades as they ripped his clothes, scratched his skin.

Voices cried and gasped all around him. *Get off! Mine! Kill them! Rip them! Mine! Give it me!*

The horses screamed in terror, a sound that made Rovann's hair stand on end. Summoning the Eorthe, Rovann struggled into a sitting position and then uttered a word that sent a pulse of light blazing out from his hands. The smoky darkness evaporated with wails of pain and anger.

The two horses were down, scratches covering their hides. They struggled up and tried to bolt, but beyond the reach of Rovann's light the darkness still boiled so the horses milled in fear and confusion, desperately looking for a way through.

A few meters away, Maegwin scrabbled to her feet. Her clothes were torn and she bled from a hundred different cuts. Rovann took two steps toward her and then stopped, tottering on suddenly shaky legs.

"Rovann!" she staggered over to him, supported his weight on her shoulder. "Are you all right?"

A terrible, burning pain pierced his side. Carefully, he lifted his tunic and cursed. The stab wound he had received from one of Hounsey's soldiers near the Highhold had re-opened, torn by tiny teeth marks. The skin was red and angry and his strength seemed to seep out with his blood.

Maegwin ripped a piece of cloth from her already torn tunic, wadded it and pressed it against the laceration.

"Curse them," she growled. "They must have sensed your injury. That stab wound never properly healed and now it's worse than ever. We have to get out of here."

Rovann's light was beginning to fade. When it did, the creatures would be back. Rovann thought desperately. They were miles from the border of the Edge and would not make it through alive. No, if they were to get through this they must find help from somewhere within Roamsford Edge itself. But who or what would help them in this hostile, unforgiving place? Then he had it. A tiny sliver of hope uncoiled in his chest.

"Hold on," he said to Maegwin, tightening his grip on her shoulder to steady himself.

Closing his eyes, he sent his senses out into the dark wood, desperately searching. Finally, a soft presence, like the touch of a feather brushed across his mind.

"Come on."

He limped over to Brye and climbed into the saddle, doing his best to calm the terrified horse. When Maegwin had brought Tilya under control he nodded once to her.

"Ready?"

"Ready."

Together, they kicked the horses into a gallop. They pounded down a shallow ditch and up the other side, sending mud and leaf litter flying from the horses' hooves. The boiling figures followed them. Smoky hands reached from the darkness.

Maegwin yanked her dagger from its scabbard and swung it. On impact, a yellow flame burst from the sword's tip and the hands withdrew with a shriek of pain. Yowling, the creatures pulled back, beyond the range of Rovann's light.

Rovann took the lead, guiding Brye toward the presence he sensed. They galloped up a slope and found themselves looking down into a deep dell and Rovann cried out with relief.

A Sentinel stood in the center of the dell.

Maegwin yelled in triumph and together they thundered down the incline and into the protection of the Sentinel's Earthlight. As they passed under the great tree's shining branches, a ripple of warmth passed over Rovann.

He pulled Brye to a halt in a shower of leaves and mud, jumped from the saddle and turned to face their pursuers, words of power ready on his lips. But he saw no sign of the creatures. Perhaps they were afraid of the Sentinel. Perhaps.

He collapsed in exhaustion, lying on his back as his chest heaved and pain coursed through his veins.

Maegwin tethered the horses and then tapped him on the shoulder.

"Come sit by the trunk," she instructed.

Rovann allowed her to pull him to his feet and help him over to the tree and bade him lean against the trunk. She knelt in front of him and gingerly lifted his tunic, frowning as she looked at the wound beneath.

Rovann closed his eyes, gritting his teeth against the stinging pain. "How bad is it?"

"Let me look. Hold still."

She took out her water bottle and gently began cleaning the injury. Rovann squirmed, curling his hands into fists.

Maegwin scowled at him. "Do you know you are a terrible patient? Will you hold still?"

"It hurts!" he said, petulantly.

"And it will hurt a whole lot more if infection sets in!"

Pressing his lips together, Rovann held himself still as she worked, probing the gash gently and then hissing through her teeth.

"I don't like the look of this. See these marks? They look like teeth marks to me. Lady! Those things have torn open your old stab wound and were trying to drink your blood!"

To his unease, Rovann saw that a chunk of his side was torn and bleeding. He couldn't see how deep the wound went. He reached down but Maegwin slapped his hands away.

"Don't touch it! If we had some half decent medical supplies I might be able to treat it." She leaned back on her heels, thinking.

"Just bind it up. That will have to do."

But Maegwin wasn't listening. She craned her head back, looking up at the great tree and her eyes slid slowly closed. Her lips moved as though in silent conversation and then her gaze suddenly snapped back to Rovann. There was a strange light in her eyes.

She crawled forward, placing her palms reverently

against the smooth silver bark of the Sentinel. She appeared to be listening.

"What are you doing?"

"Hush. Can't you hear its song?"

Rovann leaned back but all he could hear was the pounding of his heart. He was starting to feel sick.

"Can I have a drink of water?"

She didn't respond. Head cocked to one side, she swayed slightly as though to an unheard melody.

"Yes!" she said suddenly. "It hears me! Quickly!"

She grabbed Rovann's hand and placed his palm flat against the trunk, covering it with her own. Her eyes slid closed and her lips moved once more. A second later, something brushed his side and he looked down to see that tiny roots, as fine as filament, had grown out of the ground and were weaving themselves into a net over the wound in his side.

Maegwin clapped her hands. "I knew it! It speaks to me, Rovann! I can hear its song! I asked it to restore you!"

Rovann leaned his head back as a soothing heat seeped into his body, chasing away the pain. Weeks ago, in what seemed another life, he'd asked a Sentinel to heal Maegwin. And now she was doing the same for him. So much had changed.

Reaching out, he found her hand and clasped it. "Thank you."

She curled her fingers around his. Her green eyes found his gaze and held it, seeming suddenly deep and full of promise. Rovann swallowed. Maegwin's lips parted and Rovann heard the soft hiss of her escaping breath. She leaned closer, so close Rovann was sure he could detect the heat radiating off her skin. Despite himself, Rovann felt himself leaning into her, eyes fixed on her face.

She blinked. Rovann cleared his throat and moved back.

"I'll get us some supper," Maegwin murmured, climbing to her feet and hurrying off.

She returned a moment later with some bread and cheese. She handed a chunk to Rovann and then slumped down beside him.

Maegwin looked up at the Sentinel's massive branches spreading out above them. "You know, just a few months ago I didn't know these trees existed. Now I've encountered two of them, and each time they've saved my life."

Rovann smiled. "Life would be dull if there was no mystery."

Maegwin snorted a laugh. "Do you think? Sometimes my old life feels like it happened to someone else. Sometimes I can barely remember it. But I can't let go of who I was. You do understand that, don't you?"

Rovann turned to face her. Her green eyes were clear and piercing. He got the impression she was trying to tell him something, making some obscure kind of apology. "What do you mean, Maegwin?"

She fiddled idly with the lump of bread. "I have sworn to help you, and I will, but beyond that I am still a priestess of Sho-La."

"I know that, Maegwin," he said softly.

She raised her eyes to meet his and Rovann saw a tangle of emotions riding behind her gaze. "Do you think we'll find the Songmaker? Rescue Leo? The prince?"

The question startled him. "I have to believe we can, otherwise what would be the point in trying?"

"If the Songmaker is as powerful as everyone seems to think, what chance do we really have?"

Rovann winced at the harshness of her words. They came too close to truths he did not want to face. He shook his head. Questions and doubts. They plagued his waking moments.

Warrior of the Realms, the angels had called him. But he didn't feel like a warrior.

You should have gone back to tending your father's sheep, he thought suddenly. *On that night twenty years ago, when you felt the tingling of the Eorthe in your palms and the pull of the Realms in your head, you should have ignored it.*

But he hadn't. And the path he'd taken had led him, twenty years later, to the foot of a Sentinel in the dark heart of Roamsford Edge. If he'd chosen differently perhaps he would have settled down with a village girl and known nothing of kings and mages, of power and command, of the One Light and the Outer Darkness. Of duty.

And he would never have met Istra.

"Tell me about her."

Rovann jumped at Maegwin's voice. He looked down and realized he was holding his half-finished carving in one hand.

Maegwin nodded at it. "You never talk about her. But I heard what her brother said to you in Stoneshowe. And Hounsey conjured her image at Carrow Crossing for a reason. Why did he try to use her against you?"

Rovann pressed his lips into a hard, flat line, the muscles of his face pulling tight. He didn't want to discuss this.

"Her name was Istra Tamarand," he said at last. "A daughter of the Clan Tamarand from Tharly in the north."

"Tharly? Wasn't that an independent state until King William conquered it?"

He nodded. "The sons of Clan Tamarand are mighty warriors and powerful mages. The Clan Tamarand now swears allegiance to the king and are some of his most loyal soldiers."

Maegwin watched him steadily. "And Istra?"

Rovann looked away. He traced the rough lines of the carving with one thumb. "The daughters of the Clan Tamarand are bards who sing of the clan's exploits. Istra was the greatest singer Tharly had seen in a generation. She was invited south, to Tyrlindon, to sing at Prince Owen's investiture. That was when I first saw her."

He paused, lost in the memory. His finger delicately stroked the wooden hair of the carving. "I wasn't King's Mage then. I was still young enough and stupid enough to believe I could accomplish anything I wanted. I determined that Istra would be mine. But the first time I spoke to her, she dumped a pitcher of water over my head. They do things differently in the north. It took me a year, countless trips to Tharly, countless gifts to her clan, and the near exhaustion of Falwin, who acted as my second, to persuade her to marry me. But eventually she did."

Dead leaves crunched as Maegwin shifted her weight and the branches overhead rustled in a sudden breeze. She stared into space and Rovann wondered what thoughts were going through her head. Closing his eyes, he laid his head against the bark of the Sentinel, sighing as the pain from his wound lessened.

"I knew she was your wife."

He snapped awake. "What?

Maegwin's expression was guarded as she watched him. She picked up a dead leaf and began shredding it. "Istra. Sometimes you mumble her name in your sleep."

Rovann raised his eyebrows. "I do? I didn't realize. I'm sorry."

"For what? Loving her?"

"No. I'm sorry for…"

What? he asked himself. *For not being able to forget? For letting your guilt cloud every moment of your life?* His throat suddenly closed and he looked away.

Maegwin laid a hand on his arm. "What happened?"

Rovann didn't answer. Why did Maegwin want to know? Why did she insist on tormenting him like this? But when he looked at her he saw only kindness in her bright green gaze. For perhaps the first time since he'd met her, Rovann saw a priestess of Sho-La, goddess of wisdom and compassion.

He opened his mouth, intending to deflect her question as he always did when asked these things, but under her scrutiny he suddenly found words flowing out. Perhaps it was their unfamiliar surroundings or the absurdity of their situation. Or perhaps it was because there was no guarantee of them surviving this mission. Or maybe it was because he found Maegwin easy to talk to. Whatever the reason, he felt as though a dam inside suddenly broke and the words came rushing through.

"She came to live with me in Tyrlindon and for a while we were happy. But a year later, the renegade attacks tripled, Leonardo Sottra, my mentor, was killed and I was made First of the Council of Mages. I was away from Tyrlindon much of the time. We were fighting the Song-maker's mages all over Amaury.

Istra began to fail. She was born to the mountains you see, used to the open air and being surrounded by clan. She did not do well in a city, surrounded by strangers who neither knew nor cared for the customs of her people. She began to fall into bouts of black despair. I would have sent her home to Tharly, to keep her safe until the war was over, but the Songmaker had captured Silverport and so the northern roads were too dangerous."

He swallowed thickly, his insides tightening with remembered pain. Why was he telling Maegwin this? Inside, a voice was crying, *shut up! Don't talk about it!* But now he'd started, he didn't seem able to stop.

"The doctors told me it would pass. They gave her medicines and told her to rest. Then we received word that the Songmaker was massing an army at Sandford Moor. I am King's Mage, First of the Council of Mages. It was my duty to lead the king's forces. So I went. I left her." His voice cracked and he had to swallow several times before he could continue. "The housekeeper found her on the bedroom floor. She'd slashed her wrists. Perhaps she had tried to change her mind before the end because it looked as though she had been trying to crawl to the door. By the time the housekeeper discovered her, she was gone."

He was amazed at how calmly the story came from his mouth. Memories of that time filled his head. His calm words to Maegwin spoke nothing of the chaos that had followed Istra's death. It didn't tell of how he'd cursed the Council and raged at King William. Of how Tyria and Syrie had moved into Rovann's house to take care of him when he wouldn't take care of himself. It spoke nothing of the six black weeks when Rovann lived in a dark pit, refusing to see Istra's grave, refusing to do anything other than lie in bed and drink cheap ale.

Nor did it mention that during those six weeks the Songmaker, sensing a weakness, had overrun towns on the eastern borders, how Mallynshire had been persuaded to declare for the rebels, how close Talshire and Tyrlinshire had come to falling to the Songmaker's forces.

In the end, his oaths had saved him. He had lost his wife, but he still had his duty. So, one morning he'd risen from his bed and taken up the mantle of his life. Once more, he became King's Mage, First of the Council of Mages. And so he'd been ever since.

"I'm sorry," Maegwin whispered.

Tears streaked her cheeks. She took his face in her hands and kissed him on the forehead. It was a long time since anyone had touched him like that and Rovann was reminded of the night beneath Carrow Crossing and her warm lips on his in the darkness. On impulse, he put an arm around her and pulled her close. Maegwin leaned into his embrace and rested her head against his shoulder.

With Maegwin's warm weight against his side and the soothing power of the Sentinel weaving inside him, Rovann fell asleep.

He awoke to hazy dawn light filtering through the branches. The horses were awake and impatient, pulling on their tethers. Looking down, he saw that the Sentinel's roots had disappeared, leaving behind a tender, pink patch of skin but no wound or festering bite marks. Maegwin's scratches too seemed to have disappeared.

He shook his head in wonder and looked up into the branches of the great tree. "My thanks, Old Heart."

Slowly, he disentangled himself from Maegwin and climbed to his feet, stretching like a cat. Careful to remain under the umbrella of the Sentinel's branches, he paced around the edge of the glade. A waking landscape met his gaze. Bird chorus filled the air and a fox slunk through the undergrowth, eager to return to its den with the onset of day.

There was no sign of the smoky creatures.

He untied the horses and said, "Right, I give up. Go and eat!"

Brye snorted, tossed his mane and then led Tilya to the edge of the dell where there was plenty of thick grass.

By the Sentinel, Maegwin suddenly sat bolt upright, clutching at her dagger in fear. "Rovann?"

"I'm here," he said, turning.

Relief flooded her face. "Where are the horses?"

"Having breakfast."

"And the wights?"

"Gone. I'm guessing they're nocturnal. We should be safe in the daylight."

"And when it gets dark again?"

Rovann sighed, looking around with his hands on his hips. "We have to assume that they'll come at us again. We must be ready."

Maegwin nodded. She held his gaze for a moment and Rovann knew she would never speak of what he'd told her last night. He was grateful for that.

She stood and stretched her arms above her head. "Maybe we should follow the horses' example. How does bread and cheese for breakfast sound?"

Rovann grinned crookedly. Bread and cheese was all they had left. "That sounds lovely."

Once they had eaten, they saddled the horses and rode out in to the waking forest. Rovann remained alert, eyes flicking from side to side as they rode, senses thrown wide to detect danger. But the forest seemed quiet.

In the late morning the sky clouded over and a squally rain battered the forest. The trees swayed menacingly in sudden winds, ripping up flurries of leaves that twirled to the ground. He and Maegwin were soon drenched through to their skin. The horses plowed on, heads down and ears drooping, looking thoroughly miserable. The only consolation was that wights from the Realm of Air were unlikely to be abroad in such weather.

But, he reminded himself morosely, *Water wights will love it so we are probably no safer than before.*

The downpour eventually stopped around midday. By that time, they had covered only a fraction of the distance that Rovann had hoped and he ground his teeth in frustration. Maegwin was silent and miserable, staring at the tangled wilderness ahead as though willing a path to present itself.

Finally the clouds cleared and the summer heat once again asserted itself. Water began to evaporate, sending swirls of steam and vapor wafting through the air. The horses steamed and a wet horse smell imprinted itself on Rovann's clothes.

Despite his best efforts, he began to drowse in the saddle. From the corner of his eye he noticed that Maegwin was nodding too. The horses walked with their heads drooping, noses almost touching the ground.

Wake up! he shouted at himself in sudden alarm. *Something is wrong!*

"Maegwin!" he croaked. "Maegwin!"

But his voice was little more than a dry whisper and she didn't hear. Everything had become such an effort. Even turning his head seemed to take more strength than he could muster.

It took a while for him to notice that the horses had stopped walking. He lifted his head to see they were standing in an open glade. In the center of the glade was a round pool, untouched by water plants or hanging branches. It appeared as smooth and flawless as glass.

Rovann's eyes widened and he gasped. A huge goat-like creature sat by the pond. It was twice the height of a man, with white, shaggy hair. Wicked looking horns swept back from its head and a beard dangled halfway down the broad chest.

Its eyes were as red as hot coals.

Rovann gasped. It couldn't be. A capaill? Here, in the Realm of Earth?

He'd heard of such creatures but never thought to see one outside the Realm of Water. The capaill was the most malevolent wight of Water, a predator of the highest order. The creature suddenly jerked its head and the horses reared, throwing Rovann and Maegwin into the dirt. Rovann landed with a thump and rolled to his feet, turning to the horses. It was too late. The terrified beasts had fled into the wood.

Deep in his subconscious Rovann heard the wight's voice and realized he had been listening to it for hours as it slowly drew him and Maegwin here.

Let me drown you. I will give you oblivion.

To Rovann's horror, Maegwin began to obey the capaill's command. She climbed to her feet and took a hesitant step in its direction. The wight watched her impassively, its red eyes burning.

The creature's compulsion tugged at his mind, trying to find a way in. It was agony to disobey, but he battled stubbornly, shutting out the creature's will. But Maegwin continued to take slow, tentative steps toward the pool.

Water will consume you, fill your lungs, still your heart. It will take away your pain.

Images flickered in Rovann's mind: still pools, gently trickling streams, the soft sway of the sea against a beach. He floated in a still lake, held perfectly balanced by the water, having to make no effort at all. Nothing hurt anymore. Peace enveloped him. He just needed to surrender to the capaill.

Rovann clamped his jaws shut, bit down on his tongue to send a sudden stab of pain through his head. The shock shattered the capaill's images. Rovann strained, trying to reach Maegwin but his arms and legs would barely move. They felt filled with lead.

All he could do was cry out wordlessly. The capaill's gaze flicked to him. He began walking toward the creature. He could not refuse. Maegwin had already covered half the distance. The lurid light in its eyes spoke of rending and devouring.

Rovann dug deep, trying to reach his power but found it shut off from him. Anger flared.

Curse you! he raged at himself. *You are the First of the Council! Think! How can you break this creature's hold?*

Then he had it. Gathering all his will, all his strength, he pushed it into his right arm which reached out, scooped up a rock and hurled it with all his strength into the middle of the pond. It landed with a loud splash, sending water cascading into the air in diamond droplets.

The effect was instant. As the rock ruptured the surface of the water, the capaill let out a bellow of rage that shook the trees. Its power broke with a snap that made him stagger.

Maegwin whirled, grabbed Rovann's arm and together they staggered from the glade. Fear powered Rovann's legs and they hurtled through the tangled forest, jumped over fallen logs, slipped in the mud, and stumbled on once more.

As they ran Rovann listened for sounds of pursuit, expecting to feel the capaill's teeth at his neck any moment. But he didn't. Finally, he and Maegwin skidded to a halt and doubled over, panting.

Maegwin gasped, "Where is it? Have we lost it?"

Rovann wiped his face then straightened, looking

around. "I don't know," he gasped, "Perhaps it can't leave its pool. Maybe that's why it tried to lure us in."

"I hope you're right because I don't think I can run anymore."

Rovann slumped to the ground. "That makes two of us. We can't go on without the horses anyway."

Maegwin leaned wearily against him. "What do we do? The horses could be anywhere by now."

Arooooo.

A mournful cry echoed through the forest. Maegwin spun.

"Wolves!"

"They're probably after the horses," Rovann replied.

Arooooo.

The call was closer now and, to Rovann's dismay, it was answered somewhere off to the south.

"After the horses?" Maegwin asked. "Or after us?"

Rovann shook his head. He had no answer for her.

To think they could have passed through Roamsford Edge unharmed now seemed like the gravest folly. What had he been thinking? He knew the risks, didn't he? So, why had he brought them here, miles from any help?

Fool! He cursed himself.

They couldn't do this without aid. The Sentinel had saved them once but the great tree couldn't help them get through the forest.

"We're getting nowhere," he grated to Maegwin. "We need help."

"Help?" she snorted, raising her hands to indicate the surrounding forest. "From where? It seems there is a creature behind every leaf who wants us dead!"

Rovann rubbed his hands together, thinking. "I have to try. Keep watch. Wake me if we're attacked."

Maegwin nodded tightly.

He folded into a cross-legged position on the muddy ground, closed his eyes and opened his senses. With all his strength, he sent a mental summons winging out into the fabric of the Realms.

Angels of the Aethyr, I need your help!

A strange vibration hummed on his senses like a lute played out of key. Faint voices echoed in his mind. He stilled himself, emptied his thoughts so that he might hear.

We cannot help you, Rovann of the Realms. The threads that bind the Realms begin to fray. If we reach across our borders, we will begin the Unraveling. But the time is close. We are ready and when the time comes, we will ride with you to war.

Then the voices faded away, soft music that drifted slowly out of range.

Angels! What do you mean? he shouted.

There was only silence.

But suddenly another voice intruded on his senses, this one was human, male and commanding.

"Why do you resist? Do you enjoy pain? Do you think I will take pity and let you go? You are no fool. Surely you realize the only way to save your life is to give me what I want?"

Rovann's vision shifted and suddenly he was seated in a chair, looking out at an opulent chamber. He saw expensive, velvet covered furniture and paintings on the walls. But there was something wrong with his sight. It swam and misted, turning everything in the room blurred.

In a hoarse voice that scraped from a parched throat, Rovann answered, "Curse you, traitor! I will not betray my father. I will not be your puppet. Let me out of these restraints and I will carve your heart out!"

Pain exploded as something slammed into the side of

his head. He tasted blood. His eyes stung. The chamber swung further out of focus. Through tear-filled eyes he saw a figure looking down at him but could make out no features.

Rovann tried to lash out but his arms were weak and wasted, his muscles atrophied from the paralysis the Song-maker had placed on him.

The Songmaker?

A jolt like electricity went through Rovann's body in sudden understanding. *I am looking through the prince's eyes.*

Whilst searching for the angels he'd found the mind of Prince Owen instead. The prince's eyes were burning. He tried to blink but although the muscles around his eyes bunched and contracted his eyelids wouldn't close.

What is going on here? Rovann thought. *What is that bastard doing to Prince Owen?*

The prince was in terrible pain but he wasn't broken. In a defiant voice he demanded, "Show me your face, traitor. Why won't you reveal yourself? What are you hiding?"

The figure moved out of Rovann's sight and he heard the creak of a nearby chair. "Perhaps I like the mystery."

"Or perhaps you're frightened. Is that why you keep yourself concealed? So that when I get free I won't be able to come after you? That won't save you. I'll find you. And when I do, I'll kill you."

There was soft laughter. "Indeed. Now, I ask again. Where is the King's Mage?"

It was Prince Owen's turn to laugh. "Ah, that's it, isn't it? You're frightened of Rovann! You're frightened he's coming for you. And you should be, traitor, you should be. There's no place you can hide. He'll find you and tear you to pieces!"

There was a snarl and something impacted with the

prince's face, snapping it to the side in a shower of blood. Red-hot pain lanced through the prince's skull and for a second he teetered on the edge of unconsciousness.

Rovann could feel the prince's strength ebbing so he began to channel energy from his astral form into the prince, trying to give him enough strength to hang on for a few more days.

Perhaps the Songmaker detected the faint surge of power because there was a creak as he rose from his seat and then he was suddenly crouching in front of the prince, gripping his chin with hard fingers. All Rovann could see were the indistinct features of a man.

"Who's there?" the Songmaker asked. "I can see you. Who are you?"

Rovann didn't answer. *Who are* you? he thought.

The Songmaker laughed. "That is First Mage Rovann unless I am much mistaken. I won't ask how you have managed to inhabit the prince's mind."

The Songmaker brought his face close to the prince's, staring deep into his eyes. "Your prince is proving most obstinate, King's Mage. He refuses to tell me where you are. I know you're not in Tyrlindon. Nor Silverport or Mandrake. Where are you, King's Mage? What are you up to?"

The urge to lash out almost broke Rovann's restraint. Here was his faceless enemy, closer than he'd ever been. If he could somehow seize control of the prince's body he could get his hands around the man's neck and squeeze. And then all this would be over.

With an intensity that shocked him, Rovann longed to do it. He longed to look down and watch the life leave the man's eyes.

But he'd lingered too long already. He couldn't risk the

Songmaker detecting his intent. The Songmaker thought Rovann was abroad in the kingdom somewhere and hadn't yet begun to suspect he knew of his hideout. Rovann intended to keep it that way.

He withdrew his awareness from the prince's mind, felt a sensation of traveling at speed and then he landed in his body with a jolt. As soon as he opened his eyes, he jumped to his feet.

"Maegwin!" he called, "Come on! We have to leave!"

Maegwin remained seated, looking up at him quizzically. "Why? What's happened?"

He didn't answer, pacing to the edge of the clearing and back again, mind racing. Maegwin rose and grabbed his wrist, forcing him to look at her.

"What is going on?"

Rovann could hardly force himself to speak. "The prince is dying."

"How can you know that?"

"I've seen him." He turned in a slow circle, scrubbing one hand through his hair.

"Rovann, stop. You aren't making any sense."

He pulled in a deep breath then raised his chin. "I linked to the prince, almost like a Sharing. I saw what's being done to him. He won't last unless we reach him." He did not mention that he had asked the angels for help and that they had refused.

Maegwin's eyes were troubled "You saw the Songmaker?"

"No. I couldn't make out his face. But I heard him."

"And Leo? Was he with the prince?"

Rovann hesitated. He felt suddenly ashamed that he'd not even thought about the minstrel. Leo had risked his life to try to save the prince and was captured at the same time. Was he being tortured too?

"I'm sorry, Maegwin," he said. "Leo isn't important to the Songmaker. He's unlikely to have kept him alive."

She stared at him, digesting his words. Then she shook her head. "No. Leo is alive. I know he is. And we'll find him."

Rovann didn't reply. Maegwin had been close to Leo. The young minstrel had become her friend after the destruction of her temple and she'd do anything to save him. It was why she'd agreed to accompany him, after all. He watched her for a moment.

A large, ungainly bird landed noisily in the branches above. Bees droned in and out of the bars of sunlight filling the glade.

At last, he looked away. "Come on, we have to keep moving."

With no horses, no allies and very few weapons, they set off once more.

Chapter Eight

Urgency churned in Rovann's gut. He had to find a way through Roamsford Edge. Had to. If he didn't then Prince Owen would become the Songmaker's puppet and give the renegade mage control over all of Amaury. Unacceptable.

As they walked through the tangled mass of the forest, moving as quickly as the terrain and their tired bodies would allow, his thoughts whirled. There must be a solution. Must be. But he couldn't find it.

"What's that?"

Maegwin's sharp cry made him halt. They were passing through a grove of huge, silver-skinned beech trees. The ground was open, free of clutter. Rovann saw nothing amiss.

"What's wrong?"

Her head was tipped back, staring into the branches of the great tree above them. Rovann squinted upward but all he saw was the softly swaying branches and heard only the whisper of leaves. But then something dark detached itself from the trunk high up. It watched them for a moment before taking off and winging away to the south.

"Curse it all!" Rovann growled. "We're being tracked!"

"By what?" Maegwin asked, turning concerned eyes on him.

"I don't know. Let's get moving."

Time crawled by in the forest. Every sound, every movement in the undergrowth had them jumping and scrabbling for their weapons. But no attack came. Twice more they saw the strange winged creature flying above, but each time Rovann readied his power to bring it down, it fled south.

Even so, Rovann had the feeling that something was drawing closer. A dark shadow was growing in his mind, bringing a burning fear. He could not fight these creatures. He needed the help of the angels of Aethyr, but they had refused him. Without their aid, there seemed no way out of this. Unless...

He halted as a sudden thought gripped him. The path to the Aethyr was closed but did that mean the other Realms were closed also? Might he still reach them? The words of a friend came floating back to him.

If you need me, I will answer. Do you not have fire in your Realm as well?

Tanyaka the dragon. The Realm of Fire. Was it possible?

"Maegwin, wait."

"We can't delay here," she replied, looking around uneasily. "I don't like this place."

"Nor do I." The wind picked up, shaking the branches and sending leaves skirling through the air. On the wind came a sickening stench: smoke and death. "They're coming. We have to discover a way to fight them."

Maegwin's face had gone pale. She hugged her arms around her chest. "What did you have in mind?"

"Some mages can channel the power of other Realms. I am one such. I am an adept of the Aethyr but that Realm has been closed to me. But I'm hoping the others haven't. I'll use Fire to fight these things."

Maegwin stared at him. "Like you did when you torched the bridge at Carrow Crossing?"

"No, not like that," he said, shaking his head. "That was nothing compared to what Fire wights can wield. I'll need far more."

"Then how?"

"There's a dragon of Fire, Tanyaka, who I hope will aid me. Wake me if they get here before I'm back."

Rovann glanced around and then sank onto his knees on the soft moss covering the forest floor. He closed his eyes and slipped easily into that other dimension of awareness, somewhere between waking and dreaming. Gathering all his strength, he created a gate and sent a mental summons into the Realm of Fire.

A presence drew close on the far side of the gateway, a towering life-force, as strong as a mountain. Her voice exploded in his head. "Rovann?"

Relief flooded him. "Tanyaka. I wasn't sure you'd hear me."

Her spirit resonated with sadness. "Much is changing within the Realms but at least for the moment the way between Fire and Earth remains open."

Rovann drifted closer to the gate. "Tanyaka, my friend, I need your help."

"If it falls within my power, you'll have it."

Rovann hesitated. He felt as though he was about to jump into a pit without knowing what lay at the bottom.

"We're being hunted by wights that move like smoke. I believe they may be from your Realm."

"Reyari. Ash wraiths," Tanyaka replied. "Many have been leaving the Realm of Fire, eager for the power they can exert in Earth and in Air. They're savage hunters and won't give up."

"I know. I don't have the power to match them. I'm not an adept of Fire so can't wield enough to fight them. But with your help, perhaps I can change that."

Tanyaka was silent for a long time. Finally, she said, "You understand the risks?"

"I do."

"Very well. I will lend you the full power of Fire. But beware, Rovann. Fire is seductive. It will devour you if it can, make you its tool."

"I know, Tanyaka. I promise to be careful."

Almost at once an alien force flowed into him, a raw elemental power that burned with unimaginable heat. It filled him as though he were an empty vessel, fusing with every fiber of his spirit.

Tanyaka's voice echoed in his mind. "Use only what you must. If you're in trouble, remember that earth and water will smother fire, but air will only feed it." Then her voice faded, leaving Rovann feeling vulnerable and alone. What did he know of this alien power? How was he to wield it?

Pushing away such doubts, he opened his eyes and stood. Maegwin was already standing, gazing steadily out into the darkness of the trees. She turned to look at him and then took a step back.

"What's wrong?" he asked.

She moved toward him cautiously. "You look different." She took another stride and then gasped. "There are flames dancing in your eyes."

Rovann nodded as Fire coiled through his veins.

"Share it with me," Maegwin said abruptly.

"What?"

She licked her lips. "Will you leave me unprotected? How am I to defend myself when they come at us?"

Rovann frowned. "I'll protect you."

"Not good enough," she said, shaking her head. "There'll be many. Too many for you to handle alone. Share the Fire with me. Let me fight at your side."

Rovann hesitated. "No, Maegwin. You are not a mage."

"Not a mage?" she snorted, anger flashing in her eyes. "I have Walked the Realms, I have given my life force to save Tyrlindon, I have used the power of a Sentinel to heal you! Don't tell me I am not a mage just because I haven't studied at your precious college! I ask only for the means to defend myself! Don't you trust me?"

And that was the question. Did he trust her? Dare he? He sighed. She was right. The simple truth was that even with the power of Fire he may not be able to fight the creatures alone. And he could not leave her unprotected.

He raised his eyes to hers. "Come here. Give me your hand."

As they moved through the darkening tangle of Roamsford Edge, Maegwin probed this new power. The Fire coursing through her body obliterated the need for sleep, the need for food: all the weaknesses that made her human. She was sure she could run forever. It was a strange and slightly frightening sensation. But it was wonderful as well.

When the Fire had first entered her body, she'd wanted

to scream in horror. It had felt like an alien presence taking her over, like breathing water or drinking molten iron.

She understood Rovann's warning. Fire was seductive. It promised power and untold strength. What might she do with such power? A voice in the back of her mind whispered in warning. *Fire is a destroyer. It will try to devour you.*

Night fell but the day's heat lingered. Rovann didn't speak and Maegwin had no wish to disturb the silence of the night. Instead, she contented herself with exploring her new power, trying to figure out its uses.

Arooooo.

The mournful cry of wolves echoed through the darkness and Maegwin saw shadowy shapes flitting through the trees. She tensed, ready to unleash Fire if the wolves attacked. But the pack came no closer, content to remain as elusive shadows that flitted through the night-darkened spaces between the trees.

"What are they doing?" Maegwin asked as they ran.

Rovann looked off into the trees and frowned. "I don't know, I've never known wolves to behave in such a way. I don't think they're hunting us. They seem to be keeping watch."

"Or shepherding us."

Rovann didn't answer but his silence declared his unease.

Then, far to the west, in the trackless depths of the forest a lone wolf raised its voice in a howl.

Arooooo.

Maegwin went cold. That howl spoke of danger: a warning. The wolves fled, melting into the forest like ghosts. It seemed that the normal vibrations of the Edge had become muted and the darkness had taken on a creeping quality, as though something stole through it toward them.

And the wolves had fled…

"Rovann!" she whispered urgently.

"I feel it," he said quietly, "They're coming."

His face had set in an unreadable mask, his mouth a tight line. Maegwin glanced at the shadowy undergrowth. A narrow face was peering at her from behind a boulder, glaring with undisguised malice. A second later, it was gone.

Maegwin recognized the smoky creatures. As before, they were surrounding her and Rovann. Suddenly the sound of whispering broke out, many voices holding hushed conversation. It made Maegwin's skin crawl. She spun in a circle. The creatures were everywhere. Sharp, evil faces and elongated bodies that boiled along the ground like smoke.

Rovann's voice was calm. "We have to find a suitable place to stand and face them."

Maegwin nodded. At last, she'd fight. The Fire within her flared hotly at the thought.

Ahead, the terrain rose steeply. Rovann pointed. "There."

The trees receded and suddenly they were pounding over open ground. A large shadow loomed across their path, blocking out the night. Maegwin squinted. It was a cliff. This would be a perfect place to meet the creatures. The face would guard their backs, meaning the creatures could only come at them from the front. A worthy battleground.

Drawing her dagger, Maegwin placed her back to the bluff. Rovann stood by her side. The forest was dark and impenetrable but to Maegwin's heightened senses, it was a tangled mass of life, a great shadowy tapestry that throbbed with endless possibilities. And through that tangled darkness, creatures of smoke swarmed toward them.

Rovann raised his hand and muttered foreign words. Light flared, cocooning them in a golden bubble. Maegwin gasped at what the light revealed. They were surrounded. The smoky wights had found them.

Their hissing voices filled the night air. She made out vague words although the language was incomprehensible. The sounds spoke of tearing winds and fierce infernos and smoke that slowly crept through the world, drenching everything in its cloying grasp.

One of the creatures roiled toward them. It tipped its head to one side, regarding them. "Yes, tender meat, juicy meat. It will make good slurpings. Bones to crack and guts to swallow. Rip them. Tear them. Plenty for all of us."

As if this was a signal, the creatures rushed toward Maegwin and Rovann like a horde of rats. A wave of terror broke through Maegwin's composure. Sweat slid down her forehead.

Rovann raised his hands and Fire blazed from his fingers. His movement shattered the spell of Maegwin's fear. Following his example, she focused the burning energies inside and her dagger blossomed with a raging crimson fire.

A shudder went through the creatures. Perhaps they recognized Fire, instinctively understood its destructive appetite. For a miniscule instant, less than a heartbeat, they faltered. But only for a heartbeat. A second later, they came on once more, a terrible wave of undulating darkness.

As churning black hands reached toward her, Maegwin ceased to think. She locked all emotion and thought deep inside. Instead she moved automatically, allowing the Fire within to guide her movements. She spun away from the grasping hands, leapt and as she landed, sent a wave of Fire cascading into the creatures.

They blew apart like brittle leaves.

The wights made no sound but the vibrations of their death screams reverberated in her chest. She threw herself backward into a roll as one of the creatures tried to jump at her and jabbed her dagger at the creature as she came back to her feet. It died in a conflagration of Fire.

A great gale of burning ash suddenly ripped through the forest, a rain of cloying powder that clawed at Maegwin's eyes, nose, mouth. She doubled over, coughing, wiping hot dust from her face. The air tasted scorched, like the poisonous fumes of a volcano. It tore at Maegwin's lungs. She couldn't breathe. She was suffocating.

"Use Fire!" Rovann screamed.

She didn't know what he meant but she obeyed his command. Dazedly she channeled Fire, not really knowing what she was doing, letting it pound through her veins and arteries. After a moment in which her sight turned dark and she was sure she would pass out, the tightness in her chest relaxed, and blessed air filled her lungs.

But she had delayed too long. Burning talons punched into her thigh, sending agony through her body. Maegwin screamed and collapsed onto one knee. Before her, a dark creature rose up, snapping jaws flying for her throat…then it blasted apart in an explosion of burning particles.

Rovann pulled her to her feet. Her left leg was weak, barely able to hold her weight. Blood leaked through her leggings. Yet she felt no pain. The Fire obliterated it.

Rovann's warning came back to her. *It is tempting to draw too much Fire, and in doing so, be destroyed.* She recognized the warning but she no longer cared. Deliberately, she removed all resistance within herself, like opening a sluice. Behind that sluice lay the raging torrent of Fire, unrestrained and wild.

Maegwin opened herself, let Fire pour unchecked through her body. Then she turned it on the wights, hurling an inferno of pure crimson power. As the creatures were blasted apart the Fire clamored for more death, more lives to feed its appetite.

And something within Maegwin responded.

Is this enough destruction? she asked her mistress. *Take this life. And this one.*

Somewhere, deep in the shadowy recesses of her soul, she heard the Dark Goddess answer. *Yes, my child. I am pleased.*

Maegwin could no longer see Rovann, the trees of Roamsford Edge, or the star-filled sky above. All she saw were the smoky wights and the power she wielded to destroy them in droves.

But still the wights attacked. A dark wave filled the endless spaces of the forest. Dimly Maegwin wondered at their lust for blood. Why did they hate humans so? In a way, she understood them. They were like her, driven by desire and hunger. Somewhere nearby she heard a high-pitched, gleeful laughter. It took a moment before she realized the sound came from her own throat.

Then, through the tumult of the battle a voice spoke clearly.

"No. I will not allow this. Stop."

Everything froze.

Maegwin's Fire fluttered like a candle flame and guttered out. A wight leaping toward her throat hung suspended in mid-air. Her feet were rooted to the spot. She managed to turn her head just enough to look at Rovann and she realized that he too was frozen. He was staring at something beyond the ring of wights.

Swiveling her eyes in that direction, Maegwin saw an enormous wolf watching them from the edge of the clearing. Its pelt was bright silver and a thick growth of fur grew around its shoulders almost like the mane of a lion. The wolf's golden eyes glowed like lamps.

Awe stirred in her chest. The wolf's presence dominated her senses. Even the trees, the very forest itself, seemed to draw back as if to show reverence.

The wolf moved its head from side to side slowly, taking in the scene. The huge eyes blinked. Then the wolf's form began to shimmer. A moment later a man stood in its place. He was a giant, at least eight feet tall with long silver hair and a broad, muscled chest.

"This is a breaking of law," the man said. "I will not allow it. *Reyari* of Fire, I tolerate your presence here only because you do no harm to the forest. Do not test my patience. You have been warned. Be gone."

With a terrible hissing, the wights dissipated like smoke blown on the wind. In the next instant, the stasis which held Maegwin evaporated and she staggered. Her left leg buckled and she collapsed to her knees.

The man stared at her. She wanted to look away, hide behind something. She felt as exposed as if she were naked, as if this man could look inside her and expose everything she sought to keep hidden.

His lips curled back in a snarl, revealing teeth as sharp as any wolf's. "You will find that your powers of Fire are gone. I have banished them back to the Realm from which they came. I cannot allow you to threaten my forest."

My forest?

To Maegwin's astonishment, Rovann spread his hands wide to the man and bowed. "My thanks, Old Heart. We wish only to travel to the far side of the Edge. The wights, it seemed, had other ideas."

"The Reyari will not bother you again."

"Who are you?" Maegwin demanded.

The great golden eyes swung to regard her. She fought the urge to cringe. "My name is Fenris."

With a gasp, Rovann suddenly dropped to one knee. His blond hair fell forward as he bowed his head in supplication. "Lord, forgive my ignorance."

Fenris looked down at Rovann and an expression of amusement flickered across his face. "You are courteous, First Mage Rovann, as Tanyaka said."

Rovann looked up. "Tanyaka? You know her?"

Fenris growled softly. "She is a guardian of the Realm of Fire, just as I am a guardian of the Realm of Earth. She told me you had asked for her aid. Why? Fire is not natural to this Realm, you might have destroyed the whole forest. Why did you not ask Earth for help?"

Rovann rose to his feet, looked Fenris in the eye. "They were creatures of Fire. What could the powers of Earth do against such ferocity?"

Fenris frowned. "Plenty. Earth is stronger than Fire. It is constant, enduring. Fire is volatile and transitory. First Mage of the Council of Mages, there is still much you have to learn."

His golden eyes scanned the dark depths of Roamsford Edge. "The creatures of the Edge are restless. Your presence has caused quite a stir, as you have seen. Come, walk with me."

Fenris turned and began walking slowly through the trees. Rovann scrabbled to his feet and hurried to the giant's side. After a moment's hesitation, Maegwin did the same, keeping a wary distance from the tall man. This close his scent was almost overpowering. He smelled *charged*, like air after a lightning storm.

"You're an elemental," she said suddenly.

Fenris looked at her in surprise. "Of course."

As they walked, Roamsford Edge opened up, as though it moved back for Fenris to pass. His feet left no indentation in the ground and his passage made no sound. But for the evidence of her own eyes, Maegwin could almost have thought he was a ghost. She felt small in his presence, insignificant.

"Why did you help us?" Rovann asked.

Fenris walked silently for a moment before answering. "Tanyaka asked me to. And I could not permit such a battle of alien forces to continue. A clash of Fire would be cataclysmic for the forest. But that is not the whole truth either." His massive head swung toward Rovann and his voice dropped lower. "I cannot allow your quest to fail. This mage you call the Songmaker uses powers that threaten the Realms themselves."

Rovann did not meet Fenris's eyes. Instead he stared off into the forest, digesting the elemental's words.

Fenris turned to regard Maegwin instead. "And as for you, tell me why the demons of the Outer Darkness are so interested in you."

Maegwin gasped. "Me?"

The man regarded her with eyes that could bore holes through rock. "One of the Sluargh has already escaped from the Outer Darkness, who knows how many more will follow? Those trapped behind the veil whisper your name. Why?"

Fenris's gaze was unflinching. Maegwin looked to Rovann for help, but he said nothing. He too wanted an answer.

The elemental said, "The forest is uneasy in your presence, even though you carry the song of a Sentinel inside you. Why would this be? Why is the forest afraid of you?"

An image flashed through Maegwin's mind of her standing before a mighty tree and it bursting into flames.

Because of what I might do, she wanted to say but she could not bring herself to speak the words. Instead she shook her head mutely, unable to frame a better answer.

But Fenris was unforgiving. His amber eyes caught and held her, waiting for an explanation. If she did not win his trust, she knew he would kill her. She tried to find a reply, something that would satisfy him. She opened her mouth and closed it again. Finally she shrugged.

He growled deep in his throat, a rumble that seemed to come from the very earth itself. "I do not know you, Maegwin of Sho-La. You must give an account of yourself."

If you don't, you will die.

The unspoken threat hung in the air.

Silence stretched. Even the forest was quiet, waiting for her to doom herself. Fenris's shining eyes became the center of the world.

Maegwin stepped forward. Her voice shook only slightly as she said, "I can't. Perhaps you need to discover the answer yourself."

She held her hand out to the elemental.

No! A voice inside her cried. *He will see the mark of your mistress! And then he will kill you!*

But she had no choice.

Fenris watched her for a moment and then folded her palm in his huge, meaty hand. The Eorthe slammed into her. She had experienced the Eorthe twice before, once when mage Syrie had used it to take them to Carrow Crossing and again when Rovann had tapped it to help them escape Lord Cedric Hounsey. This was different. It probed every inch of her, laying bare all her secrets. But where the Fire had seemed alien and deadly, the power of Earth felt *right*.

Finally, the power withdrew and Fenris dropped her hand. An unreadable look shone in his eyes.

There is turmoil within you. His voice suddenly blossomed in her mind. *But there is also light. Which will you choose?*

I don't know, Maegwin answered him, unable to be anything but honest under that sharp gaze.

That choice is yet to be made. I hope, when the time comes, you will take the right path.

Maegwin bowed her head, understanding that he was giving her a chance. Hot tears pricked the back of her eyes. *I will try.*

And that is all I can ask.

Fenris blinked and spoke aloud. "Come."

Rovann bowed his head in quiet acceptance and Maegwin said nothing, not trusting herself to speak. They walked in silence through the dark wood. The place held no fear any longer.

They traveled steadily, at an easy pace. Yet the forest seemed to fly by on each side. As dawn was turning the eastern sky pink, they found themselves stepping out from under the last trees of Roamsford Edge. Ahead stretched a vast, undulating plain, covered in tall, waving grasses.

Maegwin spun around, looking back toward the forest. Fenris was gone but she caught the barest glimpse of a huge wolf disappearing into the trees. She shared a look with Rovann and then turned to stare out over the prairie.

Far in the distance, where the details became hazy on the horizon, Maegwin thought she saw a line of jagged hills. On the top of one of those peaks she spotted a gray speck.

"Tyrvanan," Rovann breathed. "That's where we'll find the Songmaker."

Chapter Nine

Rovann took a few faltering steps onto the prairie and stopped. A fierce wind whipped his hair out behind him and squeezed tears from the corners of his eyes. The grassland seemed to go on forever, rolling away to the horizon like a shimmering green blanket. Above, the sky was a vast blue bowl dotted with wispy clouds. The world seemed empty and eerily quiet: the only sound was the ceaseless moan of the breeze and the occasional *pee-wit, pee-wit* of birds.

Squinting into the distance, he could just make out the fortress of Tyrvanan. Apprehension twisted his stomach. Why here? Why this place? The ancient city was an older version of Tyrlindon and the model the capital had been based on. But Tyrvanan had been a ruin for many centuries. So why had the Songmaker made his base here?

Rovann frowned, raking a hand through his tangled hair. It could not be coincidence.

Maegwin spoke suddenly. "What are you waiting for? Let's get moving."

She seemed full of restless energy: pacing around, twirling her dagger absently.

What happened between you and Fenris, Maegwin? he wondered silently. *Why did he feel the need to test you?*

"Come on."

It was hard going. The tall grass tugged at their legs and threatened to turn an ankle. After an hour they seemed to have made little progress. Behind them Roamsford Edge stood silent, watchful.

"Rovann!"

Maegwin cannoned into his chest, sending him sprawling onto his back with a grunt that knocked the breath from his lungs. A red-fletched arrow whizzed through the air where he'd stood and thudded into the dirt.

He scrambled to his feet. Maegwin rose into a crouch, drawing her dagger.

A group of men emerged suddenly from the grass, sharp spears raised and arrows nocked to bows. Rovann spread his hands slowly to either side, showing he was no threat. The men had sun-darkened skin and black hair tied into braids. Their hard expressions boded ill.

"Who are you?" he demanded. "Why did you shoot at us?"

Their attackers scuttled back in alarm.

"They can speak!" a man exclaimed.

"Of course we can speak!" Maegwin snapped. "And we can fight as you'll discover if you don't stand down!"

The men shifted warily, eyeing each other. One of them, possibly the leader, stepped forward and regarded Rovann silently, brown eyes looking him up and down.

"What are you doing, Dranvey?" another man cried. "They're wights! Kill them!"

Dranvey, a tall willowy man with copper skin, frowned. "Who are you?"

"Travelers," Rovann replied. "We mean no harm."

"Lies!" shouted the other man. "So they can talk? So what? It's just a wight trick. Kill them!"

Dranvey glanced at his companion. "We must be sure, Preyen. You heard what the Lord Shaman said." He turned back to Rovann. "If you are human then why do you bring the magic of the wildwood onto the plains? We watched you leave the Great Whispering."

His companions nodded their agreement.

"Yes, we came from the Wildwood," Rovann agreed. "Is that a problem?"

It was the wrong thing to say. With cries of anger, the men raised their weapons. Arrows were aimed at Rovann's heart.

"You see?" yelled the younger man, Preyen. "Wights! Kill them now!"

"Wait!" Rovann shouted, holding up his hands. "We're just travelers!"

"Nobody passes through the Great Whispering," Preyen cried. "Slit their throats and be done with it, Dranvey."

There were murmurs of assent amongst the rest of the men but the leader didn't react. He gazed steadily at Rovann, a penetrating look in his eyes. "Preyen speaks the truth. He's our most skilled tracker and has spent many years patrolling the border of the wildwood. None but wights come from the Great Whispering and whenever they do it means ill for us. They kill our herds and cause havoc."

"Do we look like wights?" Maegwin snapped, stepping forward. "Are you blind as well as stupid?"

Rovann cursed inwardly. But to his surprise the leader turned to look at her, eyes narrowing in thought. "The Lord

Shaman instructed us to keep watch on the Great Whispering, saying two people may be passing this way. Two people of great interest to him. I thought it a fool's errand but perhaps I was mistaken. If you're not wights, maybe you're the ones the Lord Shaman is looking for."

The younger man, Preyen, stepped up to his leader, shoulders hunched with suppressed fury. "What are you doing? You can't allow them to live! You have seen what wights can do. They will kill us all!"

Dranvey's voice hardened. "I am hunt leader, Preyen. I will do as I see fit."

Preyen's jaw worked, a vein in his temple throbbing. He glanced at Rovann, raw pain shining in his eyes.

"You can't," he whispered. "Not after…"

Suddenly Preyen's face twisted into a mask of hatred. Before anyone could stop him, he launched himself at Rovann, crashing into his chest and sending them both sprawling into the dirt. As they went down, Preyen punched him in the stomach, knocking all the wind from him. Rovann grappled, trying to push the young man off but the warrior was wiry and strong, aiming kicks and punches that Rovann struggled to repel. Then suddenly a knife flashed in Preyen's hand, speeding toward Rovann's heart. He grasped Preyen's wrists, deflecting the blow, but the knife scored a gash across his shoulder and blood suddenly flowered through his shirt.

Arms grabbed Preyen, yanked him away, and Maegwin helped Rovann to his feet.

"Are you all right?"

He nodded.

Two of the band held Preyen, who was still struggling.

"How dare you?" the hunt leader hissed at the younger man, his voice cold and low. "Have you forgotten you are

Shinnar?" He back-handed the young man across the face, whipping his head to one side.

"They are wights!" Preyen bellowed, unrepentant. "How can you be so blind?"

"Blind is it? Look at this!" he pointed to the blood staining Rovann's left shoulder. "Do wights bleed?"

Preyen's eyes widened slightly, the crazed look receded and he hung his head. "I...I don't know."

Dranvey stared at him for a moment longer. Seeming to reach a decision, he turned to Rovann and Maegwin then dropped into a small bow with his arms crossed over his chest. "We are the Shinnar. My name is Dranvey, hunt leader of the Eagle Clan. We will take you to our chief and shaman. They can decide what is to be done with you. If you are wights after all, you'll be killed. If you are not, you'll likely be taken to the Lord Shaman in Tyrvanan. And Preyen will make reparation for the injury he has done you." Turning to his men he barked, "Bind their hands and bring them."

Rovann cooperated meekly as the Shinnar dressed the gash on his shoulder and then bound his hands behind his back. His thoughts raced. The Lord Shaman? In Tyrvanan? Was Dranvey talking about the Songmaker?

Dranvey led them out into the prairie and the rest of his men took up positions around them, weapons trained on the two captives.

The men moved effortlessly through the grassland. Where Rovann and Maegwin stumbled and tripped, the Shinnar seemed to glide over the terrain, completely at home in the undulating prairie.

They moved in uneasy silence. Rovann scanned the faces of his captors and saw eyes full of mistrust. Preyen walked at the back but Rovann felt the young man's eyes on him, making the space between his shoulder blades itch. He just hoped he wouldn't feel a knife hit that spot when Dranvey wasn't looking.

Slowly the landscape began to change. The thick clumps of grass were replaced by harsher stony ground. Clusters of pebbles lay in the dusty soil and Rovann left footprints behind. The bushes clinging to the dirt here were small and stunted as if they struggled to find enough sustenance to grow any bigger.

But there was life everywhere. Far in the distance Rovann saw black specks that might have been buffalo and nearer at hand, a rampant herd of wild horses thundered past, snorting and frolicking. A coyote and her young quickly padded away and a large red and black bird sat in a bush squawking angrily.

Rovann thought back to when he had mind-linked to Prince Owen. Had he let slip his intentions to the Songmaker? Had he inadvertently warned the Songmaker he was coming? Was that why he'd asked these people to keep an eye on Roamsford Edge? A coil of uneasy fear squirmed in his stomach. It seemed that his enemy was always one step ahead of him. The attack on Carrow Crossing. Lord Cedric Hounsey laying a trap. Was this another?

Rovann shook his head and pushed such thoughts away. His ideas were going round in circles and getting him nowhere.

After several hours of marching signs of civilization began to dot the grassland. A herd of horses grazed on the sparse grass, guarded by two men and a large black dog. The beast ran toward them barking but then dissolved into a chorus of excited yipping and wagging of its tail. Dranvey patted the dog and waved to the men, calling out a greeting. The men called something back that Rovann couldn't make out and the group turned west, sending the hound running back to its masters.

In the late afternoon they reached an ancient lake-bed, long since dried out. Large, conical tents filled the space inside. Made from pale hide, each was painted with patterns in bright colors. To one side of this impromptu village sat an enclosure filled with goats. The place had a transitory look, as though its occupants could leave at any moment.

Rovann dared a question. "You're nomads?"

Dranvey shrugged. "Of course. We follow the herd's migrations from summer to winter. The land gives us all we need."

Rovann thought of Tyrlindon and the amount of energy and resources that went into feeding and running the massive city. He had the distinct impression the Shinnar would be appalled by it.

"Come," Dranvey commanded and the men prodded the prisoners with spears to get them moving.

A gaggle of children spotted the incoming war band and gathered in an excited group around the men, pointing and crying greetings. But when they saw the strangers they scattered and Rovann heard the words, "wight" and "wild-wood" whisper through the encampment.

Dranvey marched them through the village to a tent in the center. Much larger than the others, a garish pattern of red and white stripes covered its sides. An emblem of a stylized eagle with an elongated beak had been painted above the door.

Dranvey ordered his men to wait outside whilst he ducked through the tent flap. From inside came the dull hum of conversation and then Dranvey emerged again.

"Follow. You too, Preyen."

Rovann ducked under the opening and found himself in

a dimly lit space filled with the aroma of burning herbs. Two men stood by a brazier, talking quietly. The hunt leader went to his knees before them.

"Great chief, wise shaman, I bring these strangers for your judgment. We were patrolling the Great Whispering as the Lord Shaman ordered. We watched them emerge from the trees, accompanied by a man who changed into a great wolf. They claim they are not wights. Preyen dishonored himself by attacking them. I leave their judgment to you."

One of the men laid a hand on Dranvey's head, bidding him to rise. The man's face was flat and expressionless as he regarded Rovann without fear. Yet there was something else in his gaze, a sorrow that reminded him of King William.

"I am Brennan, chief of the Eagle Clan. Why do you trespass on Shinnar lands?"

"We meant no offense," Rovann said quickly. "We are traveling through only. If you allow us on our way we will be gone by nightfall."

This did not placate the chief. He crossed his arms over his chest, showing massive biceps that rippled in the torch light.

"This isn't the first time we've heard such promises. We took in a girl who claimed she was a traveler lost in our lands. In truth she was a Water wight. She drowned four of my people before we managed to slay her. We won't make that mistake again. "

He jerked his head and the second man emerged from the shadows. Eyes as black as stones stared from a wrinkled face as tough as old leather. The man's white hair was elaborately decorated and hung with tiny bones. Rovann tensed, sensing the power emanating from the shaman.

The old man peered first at Rovann and then Maegwin. His pupils were so large they seemed like two pools of ink.

"By the World Mother's tits!" he cursed. "They conceal themselves from me! Slit their throats, Brennan. And hurry up about it. I can smell dinner cooking." He began to shuffle away as though this audience was over but Brennan halted him with a hand to his shoulder.

"And if they are the ones the Lord Shaman wants?"

The old man glared at his chief. "Fine!" he exploded, spittle flying from his lips. "I'll test them. Must I do everything myself around here?"

"Test us?" Rovann asked.

The shaman approached and grinned evilly. "Do you refuse? We can always slit your throats instead. What do you say?"

Rovann kept his tone neutral. "What does this test involve?"

Brennan answered. "Kandar, you will give them the test of salt and iron. Nothing more." There was a warning in the chief's tone.

Kandar glanced at his chief and back to Rovann. Finally, he grunted and moved to the back of the tent, muttering under his breath. He returned carrying a long iron rod and a small earthenware pot which he placed with reverence on the floor by Rovann's feet.

"Wights can't abide the touch of iron or salt," the old man said. "So if you're not wights, you'll be able to pick up the rod and taste the salt. Easy, eh?"

Brennan folded his arms across his chest, watching impassively. Kandar grinned at Rovann, showing a row of yellow teeth.

"Well? What are you waiting for?"

Rovann stooped and lifted the iron rod. Taking the lid from the earthenware pot, he scooped a pinch of salt into his palm. Then he straightened, holding the rod out in front of him and rubbed the salt onto his tongue.

Brennan remained expressionless. Dranvey let out a sigh of relief and at the back of the tent, Preyen shifted uncomfortably.

Kandar frowned. "The woman too."

Maegwin shot the shaman a venomous glance. "I'm no wight." She grabbed the rod from Rovann, took a pinch of salt from the pot and swallowed it. "See? Now do you believe us?"

Brennan slowly uncrossed his arms and let out a long, slow breath, seeming to visibly sag. "I'm relieved. It is not the way of the Shinnar to dishonor guests in this way. You will be accorded Shinnar hospitality until you can be escorted to the Lord Shaman."

Kandar cackled suddenly, a sound that set Rovann's hair on end and caused Maegwin to step back in alarm. "The Lord Shaman! Ha! Perhaps you'll wish we'd slit your throats after all!"

Rovann frowned. "I told you we were travelers. We have passed your test. Why then do you make us your prisoner? Is this Shinnar hospitality?"

Brennan's jaw clenched. He appeared about to say something but changed his mind. Instead, his eyes flicked to Preyen. "Come here, tracker."

The young man shuffled forward, head hanging. Brennan regarded him steadily. "You attacked these people?"

Preyen raised his head and nodded dumbly. "I thought they were wights. I couldn't allow them to trick us. Not after…what happened.

A shadow of pain flashed in Brennan's dark eyes. "It is not the Shinnar way. You have brought shame to our people. You will make reparation. I release our guests into your charge. You will find them a tent to sleep in. You will see to their needs and you will guard them. Ensure they do not try to flee."

The young man nodded dumbly.

"Wait!" Rovann grated, taking a step toward the chief. "Why are you making us prisoners? I have not survived Roamsford Edge to be captured now. I will not allow it!"

In a flash, a wave of cold enveloped his body, freezing him in place. Kandar stepped forward and Rovann saw that his eyes had turned ice-white.

"You will do as you're told," the shaman whispered in a voice heavy with threat. "Or you will die."

Rovann struggled. The sorcery holding him felt strangely familiar as though it was a distorted form of the Eorthe. It held him like an iron band. Slowly, the band began to squeeze.

"What do you say, little birds?" Kandar asked. "Will you be good? Or must I pluck and roast you?"

"Kandar!" Brennan rebuked. "Stop it!"

The sorcery eased up slightly, just enough for Rovann to breathe. The chief stepped close, his brown gaze searching Rovann's face. "I will have your word. You will not try to escape. What say you?"

Rovann worked his mouth, trying to grab enough air to speak. "I give my word."

Brennan turned to Maegwin. "And you?"

Kandar turned his scrutiny on her, ice-white eyes roving over her face. He seemed to be searching for something.

"I promise," Maegwin gasped.

Kandar straightened suddenly. "They stink of mage craft! Can't you smell it, Brennan? They have power and try to hide it. We should kill them and have done with it."

Brennan glanced at the shaman. "The last time I looked, Kandar, it was I, not you who was chief of the Eagle Clan."

Kandar shook his head. "Bison's balls, Brennan! Are you blind?" He pointed a bony finger at Rovann. "I don't trust him. He seems to me like a feral dog: harmless one minute, but savage when the mood takes him. And her," he shifted his finger to Maegwin, "I trust even less. Inside she's mangled and twisted. If he is a dog then she is a rabid one."

Maegwin's eyes widened. "How dare you? Is this how you treat strangers who've done you no harm? With disrespect and insults?"

The chief said, "Kandar will apologize for his remark, it was ill-judged and beneath a Shinnar."

Although Kandar nodded in acquiescence, the expression of smug satisfaction on his face was unmistakable. He had wanted this reaction from Maegwin. Rovann narrowed his eyes at the old man. What was he up to?

Kandar bowed elaborately, a movement that made him look like a hunched up spider. "My apologies. You are, of course, our honored guests." His voice was heavy with sarcasm.

Brennan sighed. "Release them, Kandar."

The sorcery around Rovann evaporated and he staggered, catching himself on the tent pole.

From outside came the steady beating of a drum. *Boom-doom, boom-doom.* Brennan's eyes flicked toward the entrance. "You've given your word and I accept. It's time for the evening meal. Will you join us?"

Rovann inclined his head. "We would be honored."

A hint of a smile turned the corners of Brennan's mouth. "Then come."

He strode from the tent. Kandar scowled at Rovann but didn't question his chief's decision.

Outside, the sun was dropping toward the grasslands and beams of red light painted the tents crimson. Rovann and Maegwin followed Brennan and Kandar through the village to an open space on the north side. The villagers were seated in a circle around a bonfire. Several large iron pots stood in a row, giving off a series of delicious scents.

Brennan indicated for the newcomers to sit next to him. Hesitantly, they made their way around the circle and sat on his left side. Rovann sensed dozens of pairs of eyes on him, tracking his every move, but nobody raised a word in protest. The chief had accepted them. That was enough.

Kandar shuffled into the center of the circle to stand before the bonfire. He looked slowly round the gathering, meeting the gazes of those present. Then he threw his arms and spoke in a voice meant to carry far across the prairie.

"Great Goddess of the Sun and Moon, hear me! We gather at dusk, the time twixt your two domains to remember our place within your Realms and to hope that one day we will join you in the glory of the One Light."

He bowed to the bonfire. After that women began dishing out food from the iron pots. A plate of sliced meat was pushed at Rovann. He took it and began to chew mechanically but he barely registered the taste.

His thoughts were spinning with everything he'd learned. Kandar's power earlier had been shocking. And his invocation… *Remember our place in your Realms, and one day join you in the glory of the One Light.*

What knowledge did the Shinnar have of the Realms? Of course, there was danger in assumptions. He should have remembered that. Who was he to assume the Shinnar were ignorant? Why could they not understand the powers of the universe, just as the mages of Amaury did? And what of Kandar? What power did he control? Some form of the Eorthe, Rovann was sure. Only rougher. Wilder.

Rovann glanced at Kandar. The shaman was busy shoveling chunks of stewed meat into his mouth as if it might be his last meal. The bones in his hair clacked and shook as he chewed.

Noticing Rovann's gaze he barked, "What's wrong, little bird? Not tasted bison before? Or is there something about my handsome face that fascinates you?"

"My apologies," Rovann replied. "I was just thinking about your prayer before the meal. You mentioned a goddess."

Kandar nodded, not looking up from his platter. "So I did."

His tone did not invite conversation but Rovann persisted. "Which goddess do you worship? There are many —or so I'm told."

Kandar shook his head and licked grease from his fingers. "No. There's only one. But you already know this, I think." The shaman looked up, eyes narrowed, regarding Rovann shrewdly. He felt suddenly as though he was engaged in a mental sparring match.

"You don't like answering questions do you?

"Not as much as you seem to like asking them."

"What do you know of the Seven Realms?"

"Why do you ask?"

"In Amaury we study the Seven Realms. I didn't know the Shinnar do too."

Kandar pointed a bony finger. "By the swinging teats of the World Mother! Do you think mages are alone in their knowledge of the Realms? Wrong, little bird! The Shinnar were the first. Your ignorance will be your doom."

Rovann stared at him, unblinking. "Then enlighten me."

Kandar leaned forward. "No."

Rovann pulled in a deep breath to keep from swearing. "Fine. Keep your secrets."

The shaman threw back his head and cackled wildly.

Rovann turned to his food. He chewed the tough meat methodically, trying to bury his annoyance.

"What was that all about?" Maegwin murmured.

"Nothing."

"Nothing? We are prisoners, Rovann! When are we going to escape?"

Rovann stared at his plate and spoke quietly from the corner of his mouth. "We aren't. Bide your time and do as I do."

Maegwin scowled but didn't pursue the matter. She pointed to a spot beyond the circle where a tent sat by itself in the gathering gloom. It melded almost perfectly with the shadows of the prairie and had been painted entirely black. The door flap was pulled shut.

"A moment ago a woman went in with a plate of food and another came out with an armload of blood-covered bed linen. What's that all about? Watch Brennan."

The chief was deep in conversation with an elderly lady. From her hand gestures Rovann guessed she was telling a story but her accent was so strong he struggled to make out the words. Brennan listened and nodded at intervals but his eyes strayed to the black tent. A spasm of pain washed over his face. The old woman, noticing his gaze, said something softly and laid a hand on his arm. Brennan smiled sadly and patted her hand. After a pause the crone resumed her tale.

Preyen stepped in front of them, startling Rovann from

his observations. "You've finished your meal? Good. I'll take you to your tent."

It was not a request. Preyen led them to the far side of the village. There, a much-patched tent stood next to the goat corral.

"You'll sleep here," Preyen announced. "I will stand guard. Call if you need anything. In the morning you'll be taken to the Lord Shaman."

Maegwin sank gratefully onto a cushion and closed her eyes, glad to be away from the busy camp. The noise, aromas and scrutiny of the men, women and children at dinner had wearied her. And yet, she didn't feel as irritated as she should. The easy acceptance shown by the Shinnar had reminded her of...what? The temple? But no, that couldn't be right. The ordered life in the temple had been vastly different to this.

But they worship a goddess, she reminded herself. *Just like you.*

She clasped her hands in the prayer position and bowed her head.

Sho-La, mistress. You are my light, my guide. Is this the path you chose for me? What would you have me do?

There was no answer.

Rovann coughed softly. Maegwin opened her eyes to see him standing close to the brazier which warmed the tent's interior. An apologetic smile flickered across his face.

"It seems the Shinnar have made a few assumptions."

"What? Oh. I see."

There was only one bed: a hide stretched over a pole frame and piled with furs.

Rovann cleared his throat. "I'll sleep by the door."

Despite herself, a grin pulled the corners of her mouth. "That would be foolish. I suspect the nights are cold out here."

Rovann brushed hair from his forehead. He'd lost the leather thong he used to tie it back, so now it lay in pale locks on his shoulders. With a shake of his head Rovann seemed to accept the absurdity of the situation and smiled, the corners of his eyes crinkling in amusement.

He bowed flourishingly, "As always, you are right, most esteemed lady!"

"Don't mock me, mage!" Maegwin cried. She swept up a cushion and threw it at him. He ducked with practiced ease. "You've done that before!" she laughed.

He nodded, grinning. "Avoiding all sorts of thrown objects has become a specialty of mine. I had plenty of practice with Istra—"

His easy mood evaporated like smoke blown on a breeze. Silently he removed his boots and cloak and then climbed into the bed fully clothed. Rolling into one of the furs, he turned away from her.

Maegwin watched him for a moment, wondering if she should say something. Then she sighed, pulled off her boots and slid into bed beside him. But despite screwing her eyes tight shut and trying to relax, sleep eluded her.

Irritably she flipped onto her back and stared at the ceiling. In the top of the tent's cone, a large black spider sat in the middle of a shimmering web. It didn't move, waiting patiently for prey to enter its lair. From beyond the walls of the tent came the muffled conversation of the men guarding them. She was reminded that despite the Shinnar's hospitality, she and Rovann were still prisoners.

"These people are not what they seem," she whispered.

She hadn't expected an answer so she was surprised when Rovann said, "What do you mean?"

She rolled to face him. "I'm not sure. They seem like savages but I don't believe it." She cast about, trying to find the words. "It's almost like they're the remnant of something, bigger, older. More powerful. Like they were once much more than they are now. Does that make sense?"

Rovann turned onto his back and looked at her. "I think maybe it does. The Shinnar are old. Like Tyrvanan. It was once the capital of a mighty civilization. Is it coincidence that the Shinnar dwell in sight of the ancient city? Or that the Songmaker has made it his base?"

Maegwin frowned. Above her, the spider moved. A fly had hit the web and was struggling to escape. The spider crawled across the web slowly. It had no need to rush. Its prey couldn't escape.

Are we like the fly? she wondered. *Walking into a trap?*

"Are the Shinnar the Songmaker's servants? Allies?" she asked.

"I'm not sure," Rovann said, frowning. "Kandar knows far more than he's willing to tell me. There's history here, something important, but at the moment I have no idea what it is. "

Maegwin sighed, suddenly weary. "Well, it can wait until tomorrow. All I want right now is a good night's sleep. Will you try not to snore?"

Rovann snorted indignantly. "I'll try if you will!"

"I don't snore!"

"Oh really? Then it must have been someone else who's kept me awake most nights, making enough racket to wake the dead!"

Maegwin opened her mouth to retort but then closed it

again, refusing to be baited. Instead, she pulled the fur up to her chin. "Good night."

"Good night, Maegwin."

Silence descended and Maegwin found herself wishing she'd kept the conversation going. She liked the sound of his voice, especially on the rare occasions when he relaxed. At those times the King's Mage vanished and Rovann the farmer's son came out, playful and easy-going. Soon the steady hiss of his breathing told her he was asleep. A few strands of his golden hair had strayed onto Maegwin's pillow. They smelled faintly of wood smoke. He lay only a few scant inches from her. It would be so easy to reach out and touch him but she didn't. Rolling over, she sank into sleep.

The noise of the camp woke Rovann the next morning: barking dogs, neighing horses and the clank of pots and pans. Gray light seeped under the door, showing that the sun had not yet risen. Groggily, he sat up and stretched his arms overhead, working a kink out of his back. By his side Maegwin lay curled into a ball like a child. During the night she had kicked off the fur covering her and it lay in a crumpled heap by her feet. Rovann reached down and pulled it over her. The morning was chilly.

Her eyes popped open. "Is it morning already?" she asked in a voice heavy with sleep.

"Barely," he replied.

Maegwin groaned and sat up, rubbing at bleary eyes. "Did I snore?"

Rovann climbed out of bed and waggled his hands over the brazier. After a few minutes the coals began to glow molten red, helping to chase the early morning chill from the tent. "No, you didn't snore, luckily for me. I'm just going to see what's happening."

He ducked under the door flap and out into the freshness of the morning. The sharp air filled his lungs like icy water. It was alive with the chirps and chirrups of birds singing their chorus to the sun, which was just poking its orange head above the horizon.

Preyen approached Rovann. The young hunter stood with his feet shoulder-width apart and gripped a tall spear in one hand. He bowed slightly in greeting. "Peace and honor, stranger. You slept well?"

Rovann bowed, mirroring the Shinnar formality. "Peace and honor, Preyen. Yes, the hospitality of the Shinnar humbles me."

Preyen gave a tight-lipped smile at the compliment. "That pleases me. Chief Brennan and Shaman Kandar have been meditating on the meaning of your presence. When you're ready, they request you join them for breakfast."

There was a stiffness to Preyen's words that suggested he knew more than he was saying. Rovann nodded and ducked back into the tent.

Maegwin sat cross-legged on a cushion, tugging a bone comb through her hair.

"What is it?" she asked as Rovann grabbed his cloak and swung it over his shoulders.

He sat on the edge of the bed and pulled on his boots. "Brennan and Kandar want to see us."

Maegwin paused, the comb poised in mid-air. Her eyes went distant as though she was watching scenarios run through her head. She set the comb down. "Then we'd better not keep them waiting."

The doors to the chief's tent had been pinned back to let the air in and the brazier was unlit. As a result, when Rovann stepped within he felt goose bumps ride up his skin from the early morning chill. Four people sat in a circle inside: Brennan and Kandar with two elderly women who were talking urgently to the clan chief. As Preyen led his charges into the tent the women fell silent, turning searching gazes on the strangers. The elder woman said to Brennan, "We'll keep the Sorrow Fires burning but it won't be long now."

Brennan nodded wearily, a look of bleak despair flickering over his features. The women climbed slowly to their feet and left the tent. Brennan gestured irritably to the cushions. "Sit."

Rovann glanced at Kandar. The shaman was watching him with eyes as bright and dangerous as a hawk's. Rovann lowered himself onto a cushion in front of the two men. Maegwin followed his example. Like the two Shinnar, she sat with legs crossed and hands resting lightly on her knees. But for her pale skin, she could have been one of them.

Rovann waited in silence. After a moment Kandar pushed his sleeves up, revealing thin, sun-browned arms.

"Eat!" he commanded, indicating a basket of fried corn cakes. Following his own advice, he scooped up one of the round cakes and began munching.

Rovann made no move to take any of the food. He watched the shaman warily.

Kandar grinned as if somehow he had scored a point. Bits of chewed cake dropped out of his mouth and landed in his lap.

The top of Maegwin's lip curled in disgust, probably an unconscious gesture, but it made Kandar grin even wider. He took his time eating, chewing each mouthful deliberately. Only when he had demolished the whole basket did he deign to speak. He leaned forward with his bony hands clasped together.

His eyes were sharp and dangerous as he said, "As we speak, a messenger is getting ready to leave for Tyrvanan. Word of your presence will reach the Lord Shaman by midday. We expect his response by nightfall."

Kandar's gaze flicked to Maegwin and then back to Rovann. He watched them, a calculating look on his face as he gaged their reaction.

"I'd rather you didn't do that," Rovann said quietly.

The shaman cocked his head. "I'm sure. I suspect your reason for being here runs contrary to the Lord Shaman's wishes. Why else would he ask us to keep watch for you?"

Rovann pressed his mouth into a flat line.

Kandar shook his head, making the bones in his hair rattle. "Ah, there's the crux of it. You won't tell us who you really are, nor why you're here. Your silence invites mistrust. The Lord Shaman will be informed and you will be given into his care." He grinned evilly. "Although I'm not sure 'care' is the word I'd choose."

Rovann blinked. Pulled a deep breath through his nose. They'd reached a crossroads and he had to make a choice. Should he tell the Shinnar the truth and hope they would aid him? That seemed unlikely. Or should he call sorcery and use it to escape the Shinnar? But if he did that the Songmaker would be alerted instantly to his presence and ruin any chance of surprise. But what real chance of surprise did they have anyway? Rovann was beginning to suspect that this had all been planned from the start.

No, there really was no choice. He would have to fight Kandar.

The old shaman's eyes narrowed as though he'd guessed

the track of Rovann's thoughts. Sudden power flared around him, his eyes going ice-white.

"Chief! Chief! Come quickly!"

The sudden cry froze them all.

An old woman burst into the tent, chest heaving. "Forgive the intrusion, my chief, but you must come now. Sallis's death is here!"

Brennan surged to his feet and followed the woman from the tent without a word. Kandar spat a curse and Preyen slowly closed his eyes, teeth gritted as a low moan of pain escaped his lips.

"Hunter!" Kandar snapped. "Recover yourself." The old man climbed to his feet. "Guard the strangers. If they try to leave, kill them."

He hurried out, robe flapping around his spindly legs. Rovann looked at Maegwin and found the same thought mirrored in her eyes. This might be the opportunity they needed. With Kandar distracted, they might be able to escape.

Rovann hesitated. "Who is Sallis?" he asked.

Preyen stared at him with wide eyes. He opened his mouth and then shut it again. At last he murmured, "Sallis is Brennan's daughter." Then more quietly, he added, "And my betrothed."

"Your betrothed?" Maegwin said softly. "Then shouldn't you be by her side?"

Preyen's gaze flicked to Maegwin and away again. "It is not my place. When the World Mother calls, only the shaman and her blood kin may be in attendance."

"The World Mother? What do you mean?"

In a choking whisper Preyen said. "Sallis was attacked by a wight five days ago. Even Kandar's magic cannot save her."

In a flash, everything suddenly made sense: Preyen's attack on him, his insistence that they were wights and should be killed. Would he, Rovann, have reacted any differently if it was his betrothed who lay dying?

"Rovann can save her," Maegwin announced suddenly.

He glanced at her sharply. What—?

Preyen froze, seeming suddenly like a hunted animal. He stared at Maegwin without blinking. "Don't torment me."

She took a step toward the young tracker.

"Maegwin," Rovann warned, voice low.

She paid no heed. "If you want your betrothed to live I suggest you listen to me. Rovann has the power to heal her, if you'll trust us."

"Maegwin, enough!" he strode over and grabbed her arm, forcing her to spin around and look at him. "Don't make promises we cannot keep! I do not have that kind of power."

"Perhaps not," she answered quietly. "But I do."

"What do you mean?"

"The Sentinel. It's here still, inside." She tapped her chest.

"No," Rovann said, shaking his head. "Even if that was the case, you couldn't tap into it."

She looked up, met his gaze. "No. But you could."

It took a second for the meaning of her words to sink in. "What are you saying?"

She visibly steeled herself. "You could use the Sentinel's power to heal Sallis. You could wield it for me. Like you did at Carrow Crossing?

When I seized your power for my own? Dear gods, why would you ask me to do so again?

"No," he said. "No."

She laid a hand on his arm, her grip hard. "What choice is there? We need the Shinnar's help. If we don't win them over we'll end up being delivered to the Songmaker like pigs to market. Forgive me, Rovann, but that's not how I envisioned this quest ending. Did you?"

Rovann stared at her, appalled by her suggestion. Why was she willing to do this? He didn't want that kind of responsibility. But he couldn't deny her logic.

"Ah, Realms! You're sure about this?"

"I'm sure."

He turned away from her and approached Preyen. The young Shinnar watched him warily. "My name is Rovann de Lacey, First Mage of the Council of Mages and King's Mage to King William of Amaury. Maegwin spoke the truth. It's possible I might be able to heal the chief's daughter."

Preyen's eyes widened, showing he recognized Rovann's title. He swallowed a few times, running his tongue around his lips. His eyes darted from Maegwin to Rovann. At last he blurted, "Follow me."

As they stepped out into the camp Rovann guessed where they were heading. The black tent stood alone, stark against the morning light like a warning. Doubt crept through him. Had he promised more than he could deliver? Was Sallis already beyond his aid?

Signaling for them to follow, Preyen held up the tent flap and ducked inside. Rovann's nostrils flared at the stench. Despite strong herbs burning in braziers, the rotten stink of infection hit him like a wall. Realms, what had Maegwin gotten him into?

At the back of the tent a group of figures stood around a bed. Preyen moved forward and bowed awkwardly.

"My chief, forgive me."

Kandar sprang at him, fists clenched. "How dare you break the ancient laws? It is forbidden for any but blood to look on the faces of the dying! And you bring strangers here! Get out before you cause irreparable damage!"

Preyen stood his ground. "I'm sorry. But these people say they may be able to save her." He looked imploringly at Brennan. "My chief?"

Brenan's face was a mask of grief. His eyes were dull and lifeless, as though something within him had broken.

"Can you save her?" he croaked.

"I can try."

"What?" bellowed Kandar, turning on his chief. "Have you lost your mind? Mother's swinging tits! He might kill her, Brennan! I won't allow it!"

"Won't allow it?" Brennan rasped in a voice full of menace. "You forget yourself, shaman. Perhaps Sallis will die but at least I will go to my grave knowing I did everything I could."

Irritably he waved Rovann and Maegwin forward. "How can you save her when my shaman cannot?"

"I am a mage," he said quietly.

Kandar snorted as though the statement confirmed his suspicions but Brennan silenced him with a glare. The chief stared long and hard at Rovann. "If you heal my daughter you will have my gratitude unending. If you betray me I will kill you myself."

Rovann bowed his head, accepting the chief's words.

Brennan ushered everyone out. Kandar shot him a venomous glance as he passed; a glance full of promised vengeance should this go ill.

He and Maegwin were left alone in the tent. She looked frightened: pale and drawn. Silence descended but for the rasping breathing of the figure in the bed.

"Maegwin," he said softly.

She glanced at him, eyes round, chest heaving. "I'm all right. I am. Let's get on with it."

Nodding, Rovann stepped up to the bed. A tall, black-haired girl lay there. Her nut-brown skin sagged against the bones of her skull and her closed eyes were sunk deep into their dark sockets. The blanket draped over her rose and fell erratically. He knelt on one side of the bed and gently peeled back the blanket. Covering the girl's lower abdomen was a bandage and compress which he carefully unwound.

At the sight, Maegwin gasped. A massive puncture had torn Sallis apart from ribs to belly. Although the wound had been closed with small, careful stitches, Rovann knew the internal damage must be terrible. How was this girl still breathing?

Then he realized. Kandar.

Once again Rovann was reminded of the danger of assumptions. Kandar had a command of the Eorthe that surpassed Rovann. Perhaps surpassed even Syrie.

He swallowed. "Maegwin, come here."

She looked to Rovann like one of the wary colts on his father's farm: wanting to trust but not quite managing it, ready to bolt any second.

"Do you remember the Sharing we did back in Tyrlindon?" he said softly. "This will be similar. Ready?"

She gulped. Nodded.

Rovann gently placed his palm against the soft skin of her cheek and closed his eyes. Feeling the link snap into place, he sent his senses questing toward her. Her memories assailed him, flitting like butterflies, but he ignored them. They were not what he needed. Instead, he searched for the tiny spark of light that was the Sentinel's residual touch within her. As he probed he touched something dark and painful that scuttled away from him like a spider but he didn't follow. Leave Maegwin her secrets.

Then, like a flower opening to the light, the Sentinel's power enveloped him and Rovann was momentarily stunned by the imprint it had left on her soul. It blazed like the One Light itself.

Taking hold of that power, he channeled it into Sallis's broken body. In his mind's eye he saw the Shinnar girl fill with a light, a light that fused torn muscle, repaired damaged organs, burned infection from her blood. Rovann watched in wonder as the Sentinel—as Maegwin—achieved what he and Kandar with their vaunted titles and revered powers could not.

Finally Sallis's breathing settled into an even, natural rhythm. Color returned to her pallid cheeks. But she did not stir. Her consciousness had fled far, far from her body and was already walking death's road. Rovann wasn't sure he could bring her back.

He sent his awareness soaring out into the Realms and onto the path that led to the One Light. He found her waiting for him: a tall girl with long black hair and almond eyes.

"You've come for me?" she asked.

He nodded. "Your body lives still. Will you return?"

She hesitated and Rovann could understand her reluctance. The pull of the One Light was strong, seductive. At last she nodded and held out her hands. Rovann curled his fingers around hers and pulled but suddenly the white light grew around him and then he was falling down, down, into oblivion.

He awoke to darkness. Fatigue flooded his limbs. But he was alive. His heart beat steadily and breath moved in and out of his lungs. He whispered a word of the Eorthe and a globe of light fared into existence. It revealed that he was lying in bed back in the Shinnar tent with Maegwin asleep beside him.

And Kandar hunched at the end of the bed.

Rovann yelped in surprise as the shaman shifted like some enormous vulture stretching its wings.

"It would have been better if you'd told me who you are at the beginning," the old man rasped.

"Better for whom? You? Or the Lord Shaman?" He pushed himself into a sitting position to be best placed to defend himself from the shaman.

But Kandar only grinned. "You have nothing to fear from me, King's Mage. Brennan has spoken."

"What happened, Kandar? Why are you here?"

The Shaman waved his hand dismissively. "You fell into the in-between. I brought you back."

Rovann frowned, unsure of Kandar's motives. "And Sallis?"

"Sleeping. Healing, thanks to you." He stood abruptly. "Which is what you should be doing. Rest. There is much to discuss in the morning." He watched Rovann for a moment with lidded eyes before turning and stalking from the tent.

Rovann stared after him for a long moment. Relief warred with disbelief inside him. They'd done it. Sallis was healed. He could scarcely believe it. He turned to watch Maegwin. Red-gold hair had spilled across her pillow and she looked peaceful in sleep. Gently, he reached out and flicked a stray strand from her face. Her eyes fluttered open.

"What time is it?"

"I've no idea. Late I think."

"Sallis?"

Rovann grinned. "Alive and well."

Her eyes widened. "You mean it worked?" She scrabbled into a sitting position. "It really worked?" A look of wonder spread across her features. "We did it!"

Suddenly she threw her arms around him, slamming into his chest with enough force to elicit a grunt.

"Ouch! Careful!" he laughed, returning the embrace.

"Sorry." She straightened, hands resting on his shoulders and her green eyes found his. He couldn't read her look but her eyes suddenly seemed depthless, like he could fall into them.

She leaned forward, enveloping him in her clean scent and pressed her lips to his. For a second, Rovann froze. Then something jolted through his body and suddenly he was kissing her back, arms circling around to pull her close.

After a moment Maegwin pulled him down onto the bed, hands tearing at his clothes. Rovann's thoughts scattered. His world shrank to the moment, here, with Maegwin. Her touch, her smell overwhelmed him.

And he allowed it to sweep him away.

Chapter Ten

Much later Rovann lay in drowsy half-sleep, limbs relaxed, thoughts fuzzy. Maegwin had drifted off with her head resting on his chest and her warm weight against him felt… *What?* he asked himself. *Pleasant? Reassuring? What exactly is happening here?*

Rovann wasn't sure. He couldn't quite place the emotions running through his body. The constant tension that rode his limbs and his thoughts seemed to have drained away. At least for the moment. He'd not felt this way since Istra died. He struggled to find a word. Content?

A rap on the door pole caught his attention. He turned toward the sound. "Yes?"

A young Shinnar boy poked his head through the flap, eyes averted. "The shaman wishes to speak to you, sir."

"Now? In the middle of the night?"

The lad nodded. "Yes, sir. He said it was important."

Rovann sighed. "Very well. I'll be out in a minute."

As the boy ducked out, Rovann peeled back the covers, extricated himself from Maegwin's embrace and quickly dressed. Outside, he found the shaman waiting for him, hunched into his smock like a vulture.

"What do you want, Kandar?" he asked.

"Are you rested?" The old shaman's voice sounded different somehow, less mocking.

Rovann nodded slowly. What was this about? Another of the old man's schemes?

"Good. There is much I would show you."

The shaman clamped his bony hand around Rovann's forearm and guided him from the tent. The camp was quiet and a fat moon hung in the sky, dusting the prairie with silver. Kandar led Rovann to the northwest corner where a large outcrop of rock rose from the ancient lake-bed. Atop this, looking down on the encampment like a sleepless sentinel, stood a narrow tent. The moonlight illuminated the tent's garish decoration: hundreds of painted eyes. Some stared at Rovann, others watched through heavy lids.

He shivered, rubbing his arms.

Inside, the interior was so dark Rovann could see nothing. Yet the darkness stank of power: a cold, metallic scent like the air after a thunder storm. He was reminded suddenly of Lord Cedric Hounsey's tent back at Carrow Crossing. The hairs rose on his neck and he took a step back, raising his arms to defend himself.

"What is this, shaman?" he demanded.

In the next instant Kandar's voice rang out and a lamp flared to life in the center of the tent, casting the old man's hawk-like face into an eerie mix of light and shadow.

"No need to be so defensive," the shaman snapped. "What do you think I'm going to do? Eat you?"

Rovann squinted in the sudden illumination. The tent was not what he expected. It was meticulously tidy with a circle of cushions sitting around a small bowl of smoking herbs. Various implements of Kandar's trade hung from the ceiling: bunches of dried leaves, bones of dead animals tied together with twine, the shriveled head of something that may once have been a lynx. Two chests made of stretched hide lay at the back of the tent painted with strange symbols that might have been part of the Shinnar alphabet.

Kandar waved his skinny arms irritably. "Sit down, sit down! What are you waiting for? Do you expect an old man to stand all day? By Shalia's sagging teats!"

Hesitantly, Rovann lowered himself cross-legged onto the cushions. Kandar sat opposite. The shaman rested his hands on his knees and regarded Rovann levelly. He returned the stare. The shaman had brought him here, let him speak first. He'd be damned if he'd play the old man's games.

At last Kandar spoke. "It would have saved much time if you had trusted me."

"Would it?" Rovann replied, raising an eyebrow. "Or if I revealed my identity would you have just packed me off to your Lord Shaman even more quickly?"

"*My* Lord Shaman?" Kandar snapped, eyes bulging. "He is not *my* Lord Shaman, you ignorant idiot!" Spittle flew from his lips. "Do you think we welcome him here? Mother's swinging tits! I am surrounded by fools!"

Rovann leaned back, surprised by this sudden outburst. Didn't the Shinnar serve the Songmaker? "Then what is he to you? Why did you take Maegwin and I prisoner?"

Kandar threw his head back, waving his arms in the air. "Questions! So many questions! Take a breath, little bird, or you might choke yourself." He descended into a fit of cackling, bones clicking as his braids swung.

"This is pointless," Rovann growled. "I'll not play your

cursed games, shaman." He made to rise but the old man's hand shot out, fingers wrapping around his wrist like a vise.

"Wait, King's Mage." All mirth was gone from his manner and his eyes had turned cold and hard. "You have healed one of our own and that changes things. To risk your life for another is the greatest of gifts. Curse my hairy arse, but you've earned the right to your questions. Ask."

Something inside Rovann shifted, a lessening of the tightness around his chest. His thoughts began to churn, throwing up question after question. There was so much that he needed to understand. So much.

"What is Tyrvanan? Who is the Lord Shaman?"

Kandar leaned back, waggling his fingers dramatically. "Such simple questions you would think! Ah, but the answers are as long as the history of the Shinnar." He tapped his finger on his chin, thinking. Then he climbed to his feet and took a cloth-wrapped object from a chest.

He shuffled back to his seat, placing the object reverently on the ground between them. Rovann's eyes flicked to it and then up to the shaman's wrinkled face. He seemed to be gathering his thoughts.

"What do you know of Tyrvanan, King's Mage?"

"Not much" Rovann answered. "Only that it was once part of an ancient civilization. Queen Sophia studied Tyrvanan's ancient design and used it when she built Tyrlindon."

"Did she?" The shaman's eyebrows shot up and his eyes looked troubled. "I didn't know that. I wonder if it worked out well for her?"

"What do you mean?"

Kandar waved his hand. "No matter. The Shinnar are an old people and we weren't always nomads. Once we had an empire that stretched all the way to the Wildwood in the east and the coast in the west. And the capital of our empire was Tyrvanan."

Rovann glanced around the tent, trying to equate this simple, nomadic existence with the powerful people Kandar described.

The old man snorted. "Yes, difficult to believe, eh? But there you have it. Time has not been kind to the Shinnar people." His black eyes came to rest on the wrapped object on the floor. "But some might say we have brought this doom on ourselves." His eyes snapped up. "Back then the creatures of the Wildwood were our allies and we didn't fear them as we do now. We were scholars, artists, craftsmen and builders. We worshipped Shalia, the World Mother, and studied her Realms. We knew our place." He paused, spindly hands hovering above the wrapped bundle as if unsure of whether to proceed. But then, seeming to reach a decision, he quickly peeled back the layers of cloth.

It revealed a small book, brown with age.

"The last surviving copy of the writings of Barbul, High Priest of Tyrvanan. It tells the truth of the betrayal at Tyrvanan and the blasphemy of the Lady."

Kandar's voice had turned low and hesitant. He stared at the book as though watching the events written within. "Religious war came to the Shinnar. As our empire grew, so did our greed for power." He fixed Rovann with shrewd eyes. "I think you appreciate as well as I, that power is a terrible thing. The priesthood became intolerant of deviation from the true path of Our Lady. They instigated a pogrom, exterminating all opposition to their will. "

Rovann sat transfixed. He wanted to do nothing that might break the flow of Kandar's words.

"The priests said that our Lady commanded us to burn the Wildwood. So we did. Thousands of the Shinnar, whipped into a fervor of hatred, descended on the Great Whispering with burning torches. The wood burned for three days before rain came to save it. And Roamsford Edge does not forget."

Kandar ran his hands over the cover of the book and then gently opened it. Its pages were yellow and brittle, covered in a spiky black script that Rovann did not recognize.

"That wasn't the worst of it. Barbul writes that the priests performed a ritual, something even he was not a party to. Through gathering every ancient source I could I've come to believe that the ritual was concerned with opening the Realms. Well, it didn't work. The power they tried to unleash recoiled. It destroyed them. It destroyed Tyrvanan." The old shaman crumpled up his lips as though he was sucking on something sour. "Barbul's hairy arse crack! It destroyed the Shinnar! Everything wiped away. Our city. Our way of life. Our faith. The survivors became nomads, a shadow of a once mighty people. And the wights of the Wildwood swore vengeance against us. We have been fighting for our lives ever since."

Outside, a coyote barked. Rovann shivered. Kandar's words hung in the air like smoke.

The shaman closed the book with a thump. "You asked who the Lord Shaman is. The truth is, I'm not sure. But I fear. I fear history is turning full circle. Old powers stir within Tyrvanan, within the Shinnar."

Rovann frowned, leaning forward to ease an ache in his ankle. "Kandar, you say the Lord Shaman is your overlord. How then can you not know who he is?"

Kandar closed his eyes and nodded slowly. "Many summers ago, when I was just a boy, five people entered our lands. They were very old or at least they seemed so to me.

They claimed to be descendants of the priests of Tyrvanan and begged leave to return to their ancestral home. My father was shaman of the Eagle Clan and spoke vehemently against letting them return. But they promised us great things – to free us of the scourge of the wights of Roamsford Edge. At that time wights of Fire were constantly harrying the prairie burning huge swathes. We were forced into the far north where the grazing is sparse. The newcomers said they could rid us of this threat.

The chiefs agreed to let them try. So the old ones were allowed to take up residence in the ruins of Tyrvanan. And they did as they promised. The attacks by the Fire wights stopped. These newcomers held powers previously unknown to the Shinnar."

Rovann said nothing but his chest tightened. A suspicion he barely dared to recognize was beginning to grow in him.

"Nobody is sure when the Lord Shaman came from beyond the Great Whispering. He is the strongest of them all and under his leadership much of Tyrvanan was rebuilt. It has become busy once more although Shinnar are rarely allowed inside."

"And now a priesthood rules the Shinnar once more?" Rovann asked.

Kandar looked up sharply and the venomous look that crossed his face told Rovann what he needed to know.

"Curse my hairy pits! I'm shaman of the Eagle Clan, as my father was before me. I have dedicated my life to studying the Seven Realms of the World Mother and guiding my people as best I can. But I could not keep my people safe from the wights nor heal Sallis. I'm not a mage. I don't have that power. Yet now I bow my neck to those that wield the same magic as those that betrayed the Shinnar back then. So how do you think I feel? As the seasons turn I see the power of Tyrvanan growing. I don't like it."

Something flashed in Kandar's eyes. Fear?

Quietly Rovann said, "I think you've guessed I am here to confront the Lord Shaman, although I know him by a different name."

Kandar didn't move but the air in the tent suddenly felt very close. "The Songmaker?"

Rovann nodded. "The Songmaker."

Kandar was not his enemy, Rovann understood that now, but neither was he yet his ally.

"In Amaury, around fifty years ago, a schism began in the Council of Mages. The schism was led by five mages who preached supremacy. They preached that those with power should bow to no authority, not even the king's. They were exiled. That would have been about forty years ago around the same time Tyrvanan was occupied once more. Quite a coincidence don't you think?"

Kandar nodded slowly, eyes narrowed. "Quite a coincidence."

"When they left Amaury, the unrest didn't leave with them," Rovann continued. "Mages began leaving the council and it soon flowered into a rebellion which has lasted for forty years. For a long time it remained low key; sacking trade caravans, sowing dissent among the people, stirring up anger against the king. But several years ago the rebels found themselves a new leader and everything changed." Rovann scrubbed his hand through his hair. The incense was making him light-headed or was that just his own fear? "My country is being torn apart by civil war. And it all seems to center on here. On Tyrvanan."

The night had become very still. The lamp was burning low and flickering shadows danced on the tent walls. He could see little of Kandar's face, only his eyes gleaming in the gloom.

"War. Dissent. Such events pass. But I fear this may not. There is disturbance in the Realms and beyond the borders of the world. I hear dark things whispering my name."

There was real fear in Kandar's voice and the sound of it frightened Rovann all the more because the shaman made no effort to hide it. What had Kandar seen lurking beyond the edges of the world? What waited for him there if he dared to look? Rovann felt suddenly as though a gulf lay just beneath his feet with only a slender bridge across it. One misstep and he would fall.

The shaman leaned forward, his hawk's gaze intent. "Don't go to Tyrvanan, King's Mage. It's a trap."

"How do you know that?"

Kandar tapped his chest with a spindly finger. "I feel it. In here. He is waiting for you. And for her."

Rovann sucked a deep breath through his nose. "What do you mean?"

Kandar looked down at his hands clasped in his lap. His lips moved as if he was muttering to himself. "Why me? By the icy balls of hell! Why me?"

Rovann leaned forward, grabbed the shaman's wrist and forced him to look up. "Kandar, what did you mean? Who is he waiting for?"

A frown drew the old man's bushy eyebrows down. He shook his head and Rovann feared he wasn't going to answer. His gaze slid to the tent flap and back to Rovann's face. In a low, urgent voice, he said, "Do not take her to Tyrvanan. It is what he wants, what he's wanted all along."

"Who do you mean? Maegwin? You're mistaken, Kandar. It's me the Songmaker is after."

The shaman's eyes were as hard as lead as he stared at

Rovann. "No it isn't. It's her. Heed my warning, King's Mage. Run. Take her and leave. Get far away from here. Return to Amaury and mount your defense elsewhere."

Kandar's words raised the hairs on the back of Rovann's neck. He fought the urge to flee. "I can't do that, Kandar. I've come a long way to find the Songmaker and to rescue Prince Owen. I have to find him."

"Stubborn! Why must you be so stubborn!" The old man waved his hands in the air in frustration. "Listen to me you arrogant young idiot! If you take her to Tyrvanan you will lose her."

Cold dread punched Rovann in the stomach. For a moment he couldn't breathe. Couldn't think. He gasped, struggling to find words. "Is this a prophecy, Kandar? Are you a seer? Do you mean that if I take Maegwin to Tyrvanan she will die?"

Realms, no! Please, not another one!

But Kandar was shaking his head. "No. I mean if you take her to Tyrvanan she will betray you."

Silence. Empty silence that stretched away into the vast distances of the prairie. And Kandar's eyes, deep and unreadable, full of knowledge.

Betrayal? Maegwin?

"You're lying!" Rovann said. "How do I know you aren't the one laying a trap for me?"

The old shaman didn't reply.

Rovann looked away, anger swirling in his stomach. He clenched his hands into fists then forced them to relax. No. He wouldn't do this. He wouldn't allow this devious old snake to manipulate him.

"This conversation is at an end," he snapped, fixing the old man with a glare. He allowed a trickle of power through his defenses, just enough for the shaman to sense it. He was rewarded when Kandar's eyes widened slightly.

"I healed the chief's daughter. The Shinnar are in my debt."

Kandar watched him for a moment as though considering continuing their discussion. But then he bowed his head. "We are. Brennan has decreed that you shall have whatever aid you desire.

"Good. Then find a way to get Maegwin and I into Tyrvanan."

Chapter Eleven

Maegwin sank to her knees outside the tent and dashed her face with cold water, gasping as the shock chased away the remnants of sleep. She'd woken and found Rovann gone but that didn't worry her. She wondered about that. Where had this trust in the King's Mage come from? It had snuck upon her drop by drop, building gradually through the shared struggles of their journey until the realization dawned, opening before her like some bright, beautiful flower.

Rovann was hers. Hers. She struggled to believe it. Just the thought of what they'd done made her giddy. She'd never felt so…alive.

She glanced up. A clear, crisp dawn was stirring. Stars were still visible in the lightening sky, hanging overhead like fireflies. Somewhere up there, among those distant stars, Sho-La walked. But right now Maegwin's mistress seemed far away, remote. How could the Dark Goddess hold any power over her now?

Sho-La, mistress, she prayed, bowing her head. *Lady of*

Light. I've come back to you. Joy has replaced the hatred in my heart. Thank you for sending Rovann to me. Thank you for my second chance.

Tears stung her eyes and she blinked rapidly then looked around. Of course, there were no guards on her tent anymore. Rovann had made sure of that. He'd earned the trust and respect of the Shinnar when he healed Sallis.

When we *healed Sallis*, she corrected herself. *See what we can achieve together.*

She picked up the bowl of water, carried it inside the tent and put it down on the small wooden table. A platter of bread and cold meat had been laid out for her and someone had been in and lit the brazier. Maegwin climbed onto the bed and lay with her hands behind her head. It was cold without Rovann by her side.

The swish of moving fabric startled her. She jumped up but it was only Rovann ducking under the tent flap. In the light from the brazier his eyes sparkled with excitement. He came to sit on the bed and took hold of Maegwin's hands.

"Ah, good you're awake."

Maegwin said nothing. His hands were warm and reassuringly strong where they curled around hers.

"They're going to help. Kandar is going to get us into Tyrvanan."

A shiver slid down Maegwin's spine. She went suddenly cold, dread swirling inside. She pulled her hands from Rovann's and scrambled to her feet, trying to gather her thoughts.

"When?"

He stood and moved to stand behind her. "Now. Today. As soon as it can be arranged."

She didn't answer. Her heart pounded against her ribs. Her stomach churned. Tyrvanan. The Songmaker. At last.

At last the chance to rescue Leo or take vengeance if he was dead. At last the chance to avenge her sisters. At last the chance to fulfill her promise to her mistress. This is what she'd wanted all along. Wasn't it? So what was wrong with her? Why was she suddenly terrified?

Because I don't want to be her anymore, she thought. *I don't want to be that woman bent on revenge. When I made my vow to the Dark Goddess I thought it was the only path for me. But I was mistaken. Rovann has given me a choice.*

He laid a heavy hand on her shoulder and she flinched. "What's wrong, Maegwin?"

She leaned forward and kissed him on the lips, savoring the warm feel of his touch. "I'm fine."

There was a knock on the tent pole then Dranvey and Preyen ducked through the flap. The hunt leader bowed.

"Forgive the interruption. Chief Brennan wants to see you."

Rovann shot her a questioning glance. *Are you ready?*

She nodded minutely and they followed the two Shinnar warriors out into the camp. First light was touching the plains, a purple and gold wash that made everything seem fuzzy and indistinct.

Brennan's tent was a hive of activity: people ducking in and out of the door flap running errands and carrying messages. Inside, Brennan sat calmly in the middle of the bustle, directing it all. Kandar was nowhere in sight. As she and Rovann entered the tent the chief stood. Following Rovann's example, Maegwin bowed to Brennan with her arms folded across her chest. The ghost of a smile played across the chief's lips: amusement at a stranger's approximation of the Shinnar greeting. Then he bowed in turn.

"I'm glad to see you're both recovered. Will you be seated?"

They arranged themselves on the pile of cushions and Brennan lit a large pipe. The smell of burning herbs was so strong it made her eyes water. Brennan pulled in a great lungful then blew out a spume of blue smoke that spiraled toward the hole in the ceiling. Brennan offered the pipe to Rovann who gingerly took it, not wanting to offend. He pulled in a breath and then let it out again before passing the pipe to Maegwin. She shook her head and quickly passed it back.

If Brennan took any umbrage at her refusal he didn't show it. Instead he set the pipe in a wooden stand where it smoked away to itself and said, "I've talked with Kandar and he's told me of your intentions. I owe you my daughter's life, First Mage Rovann and Lady Maegwin, but I ask myself: should I repay this debt with the lives of the Eagle Clan? For the Lord Shaman will surely seek reprisals when he learns of our involvement with you."

Rovann narrowed his eyes at the chief who stared blandly back. "What choice do you have? Would you sell your daughter's saviors to the Lord Shaman? You're not a dishonorable man, Brennan."

"It's a dangerous game to appeal to my honor," the chief said, "when the lives of my clan are at stake." He sighed. "But you're right. You've earned whatever help you need from us. Besides, Kandar believes that if we don't aid you we risk another catastrophe like the betrayal at Tyrvanan. I trust the judgment of my shaman." He leaned back, one hand reaching up to rub his chin. He regarded them with his deep eyes for so long that Maegwin began to feel uncomfortable. At last he said, "We may have found a way to get you into Tyrvanan."

Maegwin watched Rovann, gaging his reaction. The King's Mage's shoulders slumped forward as he let out a sigh. His voice was soft as he muttered, "My thanks to the Shinnar, Brennan. I will do all I can to keep your people safe. You have my word on that."

"Defeat the Lord Shaman. Give us back our independence. Then we'll be happy. The Eagle Clan will travel west, to the coast. Grazing is poor there, but we might, just might, be beyond the Lord Shaman's reach. "

Maegwin wafted away a cloud of smoke that was starting to make her cough. Although she dreaded the answer, she forced herself to ask. "So how do we get into Tyrvanan?"

Brennan turned to her. "In Tyrvanan there are many people who do not hunt or raise animals. The burden of feeding and clothing them falls to the Shinnar. A portion of our hunt, our herds, and our cloth is given to Tyrvanan in tithes. Ours isn't due for a full cycle of the moon but we've taken it early before and if we do so again perhaps it won't arouse suspicion. We'll disguise you as Shinnar and you'll deliver it." He shrugged. "It may or may not get you into Tyrvanan."

The tent flap opened and Kandar came hurrying in carrying a sack, closely followed by Preyen. Kandar dropped onto a cushion while Preyen stood by the tent wall. The shaman nodded a greeting.

"Even with a disguise there's still a chance you'll be discovered," he announced as though he'd been part of the conversation all along. "The Lord Shaman is as cunning as a coyote, curse his hairy arse to all the hells. You're sure you want to do this?"

Rovann glanced at the open tent flap as if he could see Tyrvanan waiting for them across the vast plain. "We know the risk. It's acceptable. But we ask none of your people to accompany us."

Kandar snorted. "Don't be an idiot! How would you find your way? Oh, it might appear easy but the distance is further than it seems and the plains can be treacherous." He tapped his chin for a moment and then pulled at one of the bones in his hair. "Yes, I think I'll come with you. It's about time I took a proper look at Tyrvanan." His hawk's gaze was bright with determination.

Preyen suddenly cleared his throat and strode to the center of the tent. Pulling in a deep breath he blurted, "I'll go with you."

"No," Rovann said quietly, shaking his head. "I can't vouch for your safety."

Preyen stood up straighter as though insulted. "I don't ask you to. You saved the life of my beloved; I have a debt to repay." The young tracker stared at Rovann, daring him to argue.

Brennan and Kandar said nothing, merely watching the youth.

At last, Rovann nodded.

Kandar cackled. "That's settled then. Now we have to make you look as much like Shinnar as possible." He grabbed the sack and tipped its contents onto the floor. A tumble of old clothes fell into a messy heap.

"These were the best I could find," Kandar said, picking up a tunic and sniffing it loudly. "Mothers tits, these stink! Did somebody die in them, Brennan? No matter, it will only add to your disguise, eh?" He stared at Maegwin and then at Rovann with a finger resting on his chin and the tip of his pink tongue sticking out of his mouth. "Curse my hairy crack! Our biggest problem is your skin. Too light. How do you avoid sunburn? You're both pale as maggots!"

"There's a root that can be ground to make a dye for

their skin," Brennan said, frowning at the shaman. "Would that work?"

Kandar nodded. "Maybe. Or maybe they'll just look like two white people who've been rolling in shit! Don't know till we try." He grinned, a terrifying sight to Maegwin's thinking. "We'll make Shinnar of you yet!"

Rovann smiled but Maegwin stifled a frown. So this was how it would be. Creeping up on the Songmaker in disguise, like a scavenger on a carcass. It didn't feel right. None of this did.

Brennan rose. "We'll leave you in Rhiann's hands."

The men left and three women entered carrying large baskets. The first woman bowed with her arms crossed over her chest.

"I am Rhiann, wife to Brennan. For healing my daughter you have my unbound thanks. I am here to serve you. Will you let us attend you?"

Awkwardly, Maegwin bowed to Rhiann. "We are honored."

Rhiann signaled the other women forward. In their baskets were small bottles, bundles of roots, a pestle and mortar, bowls, brushes and sharp little knives that appeared to be made of some sort of bone.

"We'll start with your hair." She began uncorking some of the glass bottles.

Another woman entered carrying two buckets of steaming water which she carefully poured into dishes Rhiann had set out on the floor. Maegwin watched, fascinated, as the women began grinding the roots with the pestle and mortar. They moved with practiced ease as if they did this task often.

I am watching a cultural ritual, Maegwin thought. *I wonder how many outsiders have witnessed this. Any?*

She'd heard of such things before. The people of Mallynshire wove brightly colored nets to hold back their hair and it was said Silverport natives were recognizable from the silver rings through their noses.

In only a short time the roots had been ground into a fine black powder that reminded Maegwin of the soot that used to gather in the fireplaces of the temple. Rhiann carefully poured the ash into waiting bowls of water and stirred the mixture together with twigs. What resulted was a thick dark sludge like mud dredged from a dirty pond. It stank.

Maegwin wrinkled her nose in distaste. Then, catching Rovann's warning glance, she wiped the frown from her face and tried not to flinch as Rhiann began brushing out her hair with a bone comb.

Rovann grinned at her discomfort as, when Rhiann had combed out her hair, she started slapping the dye onto Maegwin's smooth tresses. Damn the man. He was enjoying this!

When this was finished, the Shinnar woman wrapped Maegwin's hair in a towel and left it to dry while she turned her attention to Rovann. Now it was Maegwin's turn to smile. The cocky grin slid from his face to be replaced by a frown as Rhiann pulled his hair around.

Maegwin snorted a laugh and then shoved her hand over her mouth to stifle her giggles. Rovann crossed his arms over his chest and scowled at her which only made it worse. What had happened to the all-powerful King's Mage? Rovann looked like a naughty child suffering the attentions of his mother.

But as the dye began to take hold, Maegwin was shocked by the difference. As Rovann's blond locks turned to the dusky blue-black of raven's wings he was transformed into another person, a warrior of the Shinnar. She started to understand why the making of the dye seemed so sacred to these people.

A rite of passage, she thought. *Becoming a Shinnar. They're accepting us into their culture.*

It was a humbling thought.

One of Rhiann's helpers took the towel from Maegwin's head and started brushing her hair. The tresses that fell down her chest were black as coal. She watched, bemused, as Rhiann took a bowl of the dye and added a yellow paste from a small earthenware pot. The result was a cream the color of wet sand.

Rhiann and the other women seated themselves cross-legged on the floor around Maegwin and bade her close her eyes. Although she knew what was coming, the cold of the ointment still came as a shock as they began to rub it onto her exposed areas: face, neck, hands, wrists.

After a moment she was told to open her eyes and saw that the unguent left her skin stained the color of weak tea. Rovann had been dealt with in a similar fashion and they were left staring at each other in amusement.

The clothes that Kandar had brought were quickly sorted into the correct sizes and given to Maegwin and Rovann to put on. Kandar was right. They smelled like somebody had died in them. Maegwin gritted her teeth as she pulled the garments over her head.

Lastly, a number of Shinnar ornaments were attached to their hair: red and amber beads for Maegwin, grouse feathers for Rovann. Then the women stepped back to view their handiwork.

Rhiann cocked her head to one side, lips pursed in thought. "It will do. The dye will last several days provided you're not caught in a rainstorm. But you must be careful: the disguise won't fool any Shinnar who look too closely.

You don't have the facial structure or build of a true Shinnar."

"Thank you, Rhiann," Rovann said, bowing formally.

The women returned the gesture gravely, then picked up the supplies and led them from the tent.

Outside, a group had gathered. A gaggle of children broke into peals of laughter, pointing at these new Shinnar. Rovann gave a sheepish grin in return but Maegwin scowled, uncomfortable with the attention.

The camp had been transformed. The tents had been taken down and packed onto wooden travois attached to the harnesses of small, bad-tempered looking ponies. Belongings and food had been packed away. What wouldn't fit on the travois had been stuffed into rucksacks and each member of the clan carried something. Even the children had a small pack dangling from their shoulders.

The crowd parted, allowing Brennan and Kandar to approach.

Kandar grinned, "Didn't I say we'd make Shinnar of you yet?"

"How is your daughter?" Maegwin asked Brennan, uncomfortable under the shaman's scrutiny.

The chief smiled. "Better. Greatly improved. She's been chiding me for spending so much time by her side when I should be leading the clan, a sure sign she's recovering."

Rovann gestured at the camp. "You're leaving already?"

The smile faded from Brennan's face and he shared a long look with Kandar. "The moment you confront the Lord Shaman he'll know of our involvement in your plans. Whilst I and my warriors would gladly fight, we have the women and children to take care of. For that reason we'll run and hope the Lord Shaman doesn't catch us."

Rovann nodded and Maegwin could see him considering the price the Shinnar were willing to pay for him. If Rovann failed, the Songmaker's retribution against the Shinnar would be swift and brutal. Had he signed the Shinnar's death warrant?

No, she thought fiercely. *Rovann will succeed. We will succeed.*

She glanced at the King's Mage. He caught her look and winked. She smiled weakly in return, a sudden cold hard dread squeezing her heart.

What if he fails? a traitorous thought whispered in her head. *What if the Songmaker kills him?*

And then suddenly she was leaning over, hands on knees as her heart pounded and the breath left her.

No. No. I will not allow it.

"Maegwin?" Rovann was there, warm palms resting on her back. "What is it?"

Fear, she thought. *After all this, it turns out I'm a cursed coward. I'm terrified of losing you.*

"Nothing," she said, straightening. "I'm fine."

Trying to calm herself, she turned to stare out over the plains. Sho-La's presence was everywhere: in the whisper of the wind, the swish of the grasses. Her touch was in the sunlight that kissed the prairie, the clouds that scudded across the blue sky.

But she could also hear the murmur of the Dark Goddess. Her voice echoed in the scream of a hawk as it ripped its talons into a rabbit's body. Her speech rumbled in an angry river as it uprooted a bush and carried it away. Her touch was in the ivy that choked the life from an acacia and her song was in the last breaths of an old mare that lay down in the grass to die.

The Lady of Light and the Dark Goddess. One and the same. How was Maegwin to choose?

A crow landed heavily in a tree at the edge of camp and cocked its head, watching Maegwin with its sharp black eyes.

Kandar took a bone rattle from his belt and shook it at the crow, advancing on the creature. "Be gone doom-bringer! There is no death here for you!"

The bird squawked and flapped heavily into the air. As it flew off across the prairie, its raucous cries sounded to Maegwin like gleeful laughter.

"That was an ill omen," Kandar said quietly, "I don't know why the doom-bringer was here but it bodes ill for your quest."

Rovann watched the crow disappear with a frown on his face. Then roused himself. "Is everything ready?"

Brennan nodded. "Come."

He led the way to a high-wheeled cart with two shaggy ponies standing in the traces. Several large packages tied with deer hide filled the cart's bed.

Kandar reached up and untied one of his hair bones. It was as thin as a needle and had yellowed with age. He offered it to Rovann. "Your magic accomplished what mine could not. I acknowledge you as a fellow shaman. Will you take this token of the Shinnar?"

Perhaps Rovann saw some significance in the bone that Maegwin could not, as he took it with solemn reverence.

"Would you?" he held the bone out to Maegwin.

There was a sharp intake of breath from Kandar as Maegwin accepted the bone. To her surprise, it was warm and seemed to vibrate slightly in her fingers. Kandar's eyes were hard and cold as he watched her tie the bone into Rovann's hair. After that things happened quickly. Maegwin and Rovann climbed into the back of the cart whilst Kandar and Preyen took up seats on the board. As Preyen

195

flicked the reins and the cart lurched into motion, Maegwin resisted the urge to look behind.

They moved steadily through the early morning and ate a breakfast of boiled eggs and flatbread as they traveled. Preyen found a track that had been worn down by the passing of many carts and once on it they made better time.

Rovann stared ahead at the looming hills, silent and brooding. Perhaps he was contemplating what was to come, or planning his rescue of the prince. Maegwin had little energy to spare for his worries. She was so frightened she thought she might vomit. She wished she could tell Rovann how she felt. Hesitantly, she reached out and placed her hand on his arm. He glanced at her in surprise but then smiled and laid his hand over hers. A small thrill passed through her body.

She opened her mouth to speak but then snapped it shut again. What could she tell him? How could she explain her feelings when she didn't understand them herself?

As the day moved on the hills drew steadily closer. At midday they stopped to cook a meal of beans and bread and water the horses. Another group of Shinnar passed by in the distance and hailed them. Preyen responded with greetings but the other party did not come close and Maegwin breathed a sigh of relief when they continued.

The repast was eaten silently, each lost in their own thoughts. Tyrvanan's presence seemed to loom over all of them. By mid-afternoon the hills dominated Maegwin's sight. They were bald and rounded at their summit, inhospitable and austere. Tyrvanan squatted atop one like a big ugly toad. Now she could see it more clearly, Maegwin realized that the fortress was not alone. It sat amongst the tumble-down ruins of lesser buildings, all made of the same gray granite.

There were ruined porticos and pillars, stepped pyramids that had lost most of their upper levels, a cracked and pitted road. With a shiver Maegwin realized that in its heyday, Tyrvanan might have rivaled Tyrlindon itself. Now, only the fortress remained.

They finished the meal and set out once more. The ground began to rise gently and they were soon climbing toward the hills. Soon, the old highway appeared beneath the horses' hooves and Maegwin saw that it had been constructed from a series of interlocking stone blocks that formed a complex geometric pattern. The clip-clop, clip-clop of the horses' hooves seemed unnaturally loud after the near silence of the prairie. The road wound up through the ruined city, past once-grand houses, crumbling temples, squares with cracked fountains, wide streets choked with grass, slowly being claimed by the prairie.

Kandar suddenly raised his head and sniffed at the air like a dog. Rovann's nostrils flared and he turned from side to side as if searching. Dread swirled in Maegwin's stomach and she rose into a crouch, scanning for danger.

"What is it?"

"I don't know," the shaman replied. "There's something here, I sense it."

Rovann jumped to his feet. Maegwin's heart lurched. What had they seen? Rovann stood in the wagon bed as straight as a rod. His stance spoke of tension, fists clenched at his sides, staring up at the fortress.

"What is it?" he murmured to himself, "I've never felt anything like it."

A breeze suddenly swirled around the cart. The bones in Kandar's hair rattled. Rovann's black locks lifted from his shoulders, giving him the look of a wild prophet.

Then she tasted it. There was something on the wind, a

sickly-sweet tang of iron or ozone. The air seemed charged, as though lightning had recently struck.

"I feel it," she whispered, climbing to her feet beside Rovann. She closed her eyes, sensing the intensity of the sensation increase. Understanding exploded on her.

She sensed Tanyaka. Or rather, Fire, the burning, angry essence of the dragon's destructive Realm. But there was also peace, a cool serenity that could only come from the Aethyr. And there were other things as well; dark seas of Water and lashing winds of Air. Tall trees and growing creatures of Earth. And worst of all, there was the nothingness of the Outer Darkness. It was all of them, mixed up together.

She opened her eyes to see that clouds had moved in, encasing the sky in a leaden blanket. All was silent. Not even an insect chirruped in the grasses of Tyrvanan's deserted city. She could feel it strongly now: all the powers of the Realms were here, converging.

"Stop the cart," Rovann ordered suddenly.

Preyen yanked the ponies to a halt and frowned at the King's Mage. "It's not wise to linger here. By now the watchers at Tyrvanan will have noticed our approach and wonder at our hesitation."

Rovann paused, chewing his lip. "Get out and examine one of the horses' hooves. I need a moment to think."

A look passed between Rovann and Kandar.

"What is it?" she asked. "I can feel the power here, so don't try to fob me off!"

Rovann said nothing. Kandar said nothing. Maegwin ground her teeth in frustration. Around her the wind swirled, carrying the scent of power.

"It's a hub," Rovann murmured at last. "Tyrvanan is built on a hub."

Maegwin didn't understand but from Kandar's sharp intake of breath, it was plain the shaman did.

"You're sure?"

Rovann nodded. "Yes. All the powers of the Realms converge here. It can't be anything else."

Kandar's eyes narrowed and his gaze went distant. He began speaking under his breath, a low chant that was little more than a whisper. "I would never have believed it," he breathed at last. "The old tales speak of these *ralya*, these hubs, but I thought them just stories."

"What is a hub?" Maegwin demanded, looking from Rovann to Kandar.

The King's Mage scrubbed a hand through his hair and then turned in a slow circle, eyes flicking over the landscape. "A legend. A myth. The myths say there were once places where the Seven Realms converge. It seems those tales were true."

"So this is how the priests got their power," Kandar said, almost to himself. He grabbed one of the bones in his hair and yanked on it. "It's no wonder they gained dominion over the Shinnar. How could we shamans hope to stand against this? Curse their hairy backsides into the deepest pits of Darkness!"

"What does the Songmaker want with a hub?" Rovann asked, staring up at the towering bulk of Tyrvanan.

What was that she heard in his voice? Fear?

"So what do we do?" she demanded. "Turn back?"

"No. We continue."

Preyen finished 'inspecting' the horse's hoof and climbed aboard the cart. It lurched into motion. A cold wind drove through the hills, bringing a squall of rain that blew straight into Maegwin's face, stinging her skin and plastering her hair against her head.

Cursing, she hunkered down in her cloak, conscious of Rhiann's warning concerning the dye washing off. A moment later she sat bolt upright as a crawling sensation prickled all over her body.

"Seeking magic!" Kandar snapped. "It will discover you!" He yanked a long yellow finger bone from his hair and began waving it in a series of strange gestures. Deep, barely comprehensible words dropped from his lips. His eyes rolled back in his head.

Rovann froze, watching the Shaman. Preyen glanced about, wide-eyed, as though expecting an attack. But none came. After ten beats of her thumping heart, the crawling sensation faded from Maegwin's skin.

"I've woven a masking charm," said Kandar, swinging around and fixing them with his deep eyes. "It should make the seeking magic think you're Shinnar. Maybe the Lord Shaman knows you're coming but there's no point making it too easy for the hoary bastard, eh?"

"No point at all," Rovann said.

As they set off once more Maegwin jammed herself between the boxes of tribute in the back of the cart. Pulling up her knees, she rested her forehead on them and tried to still the screaming fear that was clawing up her throat.

Sho-La, my light, my guide. Give me strength. Please.

But no succor came.

Please, mistress. Hear me. Help me.

The cart lurched to a stop and Maegwin peered over the side. A black gate filled her vision. It was locked and looked a forbidding barrier to Maegwin's eyes. But worse than this was the huge, towering bulk of Tyrvanan. As Maegwin craned her head back she saw that it rose high into the sky and seemed to suck all light from the world.

Maegwin swallowed.

Chapter Twelve

Rovann craned his head back, staring up at the imposing edifice of Tyrvanan. With the austere granite of the fortress's exterior and the gray sky behind, the place looked inhospitable, bleak. Like a warning.

He pulled in a deep breath and then blew it out, trying to sort through the swirl of emotions that surged through his innards. Trepidation. Wariness. Uncertainty. But most of all, relief. He was finally here. Finally. After the long years of chasing the Songmaker it would end here.

One way or another.

If he concentrated he could list all the moments that had led him to this place: the battle of Sandford Moor, finding Maegwin in Mallyn, witnessing the abduction of Prince Owen, the death of Leo, facing Lord Cedric Hounsey at Carrow Crossing, fighting their way through Roamsford Edge, enlisting the aid of the Shinnar. It all led to this moment right here, right now, like a winding path beneath his feet.

And it had all begun with a teenage boy burning down his father's barn.

The ponies snorted, the sound shockingly loud in the silence, startling Rovann from his thoughts. He glanced at his companions. Kandar sat hunched on the board, gazing silently at the wooden gate of Tyrvanan as though he wanted to burn a hole through it. Preyen shifted in his seat uncomfortably, eyes wide as he stared around.

And Maegwin? Rovann frowned as he watched her. She appeared nervous, more nervous than he'd ever seen her. She licked her lips, dry-washing her hands in an unconscious gesture. In fact, she'd not seemed herself since they left Brennan's camp. Wasn't this what she'd wanted all along? To face the Songmaker? To rescue Leo if he still lived and avenge him if he didn't?

"Maegwin, are you—"

"Preyen!" barked Kandar suddenly. "Are you going to sit there all day? Go and announce us!"

There were no guards on the gate, Rovann noticed. Arrogance perhaps? But no, there was no need for guards; he could sense the strong warding magic around it. *I'm just a Shinnar,* Rovann told the fortress. *A Shinnar who is no threat to you.*

Preyen passed the reins to Kandar and hopped down from his seat. He knocked three times on the gate, a dull, heavy noise that boomed in the still air. They waited, sharing uncomfortable glances, until finally there came the scrape of bolts and the clanking of chains. A small door set within the large gate swung open and a Shinnar woman poked her head out. Preyen handed her a token and there was a rapid exchange of words which Rovann couldn't follow. Preyen gestured to the cart and Rovann's guts knotted as the woman's gaze flicked over them. Eventually, she nodded and disappeared inside.

Preyen climbed back into the seat and said to Kandar, "They're going to let us in."

The shaman took this news with a grunt then turned to Rovann. "There's a courtyard beyond the gate where Preyen and I will be required to wait with the cart. They will take you into the fortress to check the tallies and make sure we haven't shirked on what's owed. You have the tallies Brennan gave you?"

Rovann patted the set of weights in his pocket. Kandar nodded.

From behind the wall came the crunch of turning gears and the massive gate swung slowly inward. Preyen flicked the reins and drove the cart into the courtyard beyond in a clatter of hooves and creaking wheels.

The enclosure beyond the gate was large, its flagstone surface showing evidence of recent repairs. The stonework bore elaborate carvings. Stylized animals with large eyes and elongated features chased each other across walls and up pillars. Rovann chewed his lip, trying not to stare. Was this ancient Shinnar artwork? Or some affectation of the Songmaker's?

They waited on the cart, unsure. The Shinnar gatekeeper lingered, trying to see what lay in the packages. Maegwin leaned forward, letting her hair curtain her face and Rovann turned away from the Shinnar woman, pretending to be studying the door that led to Tyrvanan's innards. At length that door opened admitting a man and woman who strode purposefully toward them. The Shinnar woman scurried back to her position by the gate, keeping her head bowed and eyes averted.

The newcomers were not Shinnar, instead bearing the

lighter hair and complexion typical to the northlands of Amaury. They wore some kind of uniform that consisted of wide crimson trousers and short tunics. Each carried a tall, gnarled staff. On their left shoulder they bore a bronze pin shaped like a thistle. Sudden fury made Rovann's skin prickle and he turned away, grinding his teeth to keep from speaking out.

Those pins were given to graduates of the College of Mages in recognition of their vow of service. These people had broken that oath and yet they carried their badges as if they had a right to them.

How dare they? *How dare they?*

Rovann bowed his head as they approached, trying to look every inch the subservient Shinnar but his fingertips itched at the nearness of these two enemy mages. The woman placed her hands on the cart's edge and looked over the contents with a disinterested air.

"You are Eagle Clan?" She asked in the heavy, rolling accent of Silverport.

Rovann nodded.

The woman's brows pulled together in a frown. "Your tithe is not due for another cycle of the moon. Why have you come so prematurely?" Her voice was cold, aloof, used to being obeyed.

Maegwin answered in the meekest tone Rovann had ever heard from her. "The herds are migrating earlier than usual this year and we must follow. In a month's time we'll be far from here. We respectfully bring our tithe early to offer to the Lord Shaman."

The woman's eyes flicked to Maegwin and away, as though she was beneath notice. Instead, she addressed her comments to Rovann. "Trivlyn will inspect your tallies."

She dismissed them with a wave of her hand and

hurried back into the fortress, leaving the man standing by the cart scowling, clearly unhappy at being left to deal with this. He gestured irritably. "Come." He strode off without waiting.

Rovann shared a look with Kandar. The shaman kept his expression deliberately neutral, betraying no emotion. Finally, he nodded.

Rovann climbed down from the wagon seat. He landed softly on the flagstones but suddenly stumbled as a surge of power ripped up his legs, burning along his nerves like the stinging of tiny wasps. Just in time, he threw out an arm and caught himself on the edge of the cart. He breathed slowly, fighting the urge to cringe, until the pain finally receded.

Beneath his feat the power of the hub vibrated. It felt like the heartbeat of the world.

Maegwin moved to help him but he waved her away. Straightening, he led the way across the courtyard to the door the man had taken. Ducking under the low stone lintel, he and Maegwin entered a long featureless corridor. Ahead, the mage, Trivlyn, was disappearing into a room.

They followed carefully, walking with the hesitation and awe proper for plains-bred Shinnar, all the while quickly assessing their surroundings. Rovann pushed his senses outward into the fortress and found that it buzzed with a myriad of life-forces. He detected the earthy presences of Shinnar but mostly he felt the humming power of mages.

"Where will he be holding the prince?" Maegwin whispered. "And Leo?"

"Close to the heart of his power, I think."

"One of the towers?"

"Most likely. Somewhere near the center of his web."

"Like a spider," Maegwin said quietly.

He nodded, accepting her analogy. "Whatever happens

we can't let the mages in that room find out who we are. Somehow we have to overpower them, but, and this is very important, we must not use magecraft or we'll be detected."

Maegwin smiled grimly. "I understand."

They ducked through the door and entered a small square room, unadorned but for a large desk set against one wall. The mage, Trivlyn, was talking to a pale-faced man seated behind the desk which was piled with brass apparatus.

Rovann let the breath slowly leave his lungs as he took in the scene. Only two. There was a chance.

They shuffled forward to stand before the desk with heads bowed. Rovann brought out the bag Brennan had given him and held it out.

"We are the Eagle Clan. We come to pay our tithe to the Lord Shaman."

The man squinted at Rovann, curled his lip in contempt, and then took the pouch in his spindly fingers. He tipped the tallies—a series of wooden sticks with marks notched into them—out over the desk with a clatter.

He barely glanced at them. "What have you brought?"

Rovann hesitated. What had Kandar told them? His mind suddenly went blank. "What is owed, lord."

The man clasped his hands in front of him, fingers pressed together. "And what would that be exactly?"

Rovann opened his mouth and shut it again, unable to think of anything to say.

Maegwin leaned forward in her approximation of a Shinnar bow and murmured, "Forgive us, my lord, but we don't know. We deliver it but our chief and shaman arranged the tithe. It is not our place to ask them questions."

The man frowned, dark eyes narrowing in suspicion. "What's your name?"

"Maegwin, my Lord."

The man's gaze flicked to Rovann. "And yours?"

Rovann glanced up and the man's eyes suddenly widened in recognition. "You're not—"

"Maegwin!"

She blurred into motion, throwing herself at Trivlyn who stood by the side of the desk. In one fluid movement she snatched his staff and cracked it across the man's temple with a sound like a snapping branch. At the same time Rovann lunged, grabbed the man behind the desk and yanked him forward. The man began a strangled incantation before Rovann drove an elbow into his face, knocking him unconscious.

Maegwin stooped over Trivlyn, checking his pulse. "What should we do with them?"

"Strip his clothes," Rovann instructed.

As Maegwin bent over the mage, Rovann turned his attention to the tally man's uniform. With deft fingers he unbuttoned his tunic and then flipped him over so he could pull it from his back. In only a few minutes the two men had been stripped down to their underclothes.

Rovann stared down at them, struck by how different they looked without the trappings of their magecraft. Normal. Vulnerable, even.

Maegwin bound the two men's hands and gagged them with strips of cloth. Then she dragged them behind the desk out of sight.

Rovann fiddled with the mage's uniform, running his thumb over the expensive fabric. They were the robes of a traitor. He wasn't sure he could bring himself to wear them.

Get on with it, he told himself. *Stop being ridiculous.*

With an annoyed growl, Rovann pulled the Shinnar clothes over his head, untied the bones from his hair and shook his head to dislodge the last of the beads. The bone that Kandar had given him he placed carefully in his pocket. After a moment's hesitation he pulled on the mage's trousers and tunic. It was a little tight but would have to do. Looking at Maegwin dressed similarly, Rovann realized that the Shinnar disguise might be a problem. Whilst it had been instrumental in getting them *into* Tyrvanan, now they were inside it marked them out as different to the rest of the inhabitants. He had no doubt that to any observers they would look like plains-bred Shinnar dressed in mage robes. Not good.

He shrugged. There was nothing to be done about it.

"Ready?" he asked Maegwin.

She nodded, hefting the mage's staff.

Rovann led the way into the empty corridor. They turned left, away from the courtyard where Kandar and Preyen waited, and toward what Rovann hoped was the center of Tyrvanan. At the end of the corridor they found a dusty stone staircase.

"Up we go," Rovann muttered. "Try to look confident, as though we belong here."

He pulled his shoulders back and did his best to imitate the arrogant swagger of the mages but the skin between his shoulder blades crawled as they made their way up.

The stairs were long and winding. After each step his anxiety rose. The stairwell was too enclosed, nowhere to run. Nowhere to fight. But finally they reached the top and Rovann slowed, creeping forward, listening for movement. There was nothing.

A wide stone archway stretched across the top of the stairs and as he carefully crept under it a prickling sensation flared across his scalp, making the hairs on his neck prickle. He glanced up. Carved on the stone lintel in a flowing script were the words: *The Outer Darkness.*

He blinked. Breathed out slowly as recognition dawned. He'd seen this design before: Tyrlindon. *The twin cities,* Rovann thought. *It's true.*

Like Tyrlindon, each of Tyrvanan's levels was a reflection of one of the Seven Realms. But, Rovann suspected, unlike Tyrlindon where the mirroring was merely symbolic, here it was something far more tangible and dangerous. Tyrvanan was built on a hub, a place where the Realms converged. Rovann went cold as he realized what that meant.

Gods! Tyrvanan touches the Seven Realms themselves! Each level is a gateway!

"What are you doing?" Maegwin hissed. "We can't linger here!"

Rovann turned, eyes roving over the empty staircase, the empty corridors running off in three directions. "This isn't right. Where is everyone? Why have we encountered no one?" He sent his senses out through the fortress once more. The myriad life-forces he'd detected were gone.

Rovann stood still, hardly daring to breathe, looking up at the inscription on the lintel. He frowned as a thought struck him. "Maegwin, what does that say?"

"No idea. I don't recognize the script."

"No," he said slowly. "Of course not. It's written in a dead language that neither of us should be able to read. But I can. Why do you suppose that is?"

Maegwin stared at him blankly.

He rubbed his chin, spun round to take in the echoing, empty halls. "Do you remember the Highhold? Hounsey had laid a trap for us. Somehow he trapped us in time, replaying the same moment over and over."

Her eyes widened. "So you think…"

"I don't know. Maybe. But the Songmaker couldn't resist leaving a little clue for me. I can read that inscription. It responds to my power. As it was meant to. The bastard is giving me a message."

Taunting me, he thought.

The Sluargh had been escaping from the Outer Darkness. Could this be where they'd been coming through? Was this what the Songmaker was trying to tell him? On the edges of his perception he sensed the Realms, all of them, slowly bleeding together. Slowly disintegrating.

"This is a trap," he hissed. "We have to get out of here. Come on."

He turned, placed his foot on the top step. The air exploded in a flash of white. Rovann's forehead smashed into the wall and he crumpled to the ground, ears ringing, sight blurring. Groaning, he dragged himself to his feet and turned to face their attackers.

But the stairs were empty, not a soul in sight.

Maegwin lay slumped against the wall, rubbing her shoulder and grimacing.

"Are you all right?"

She nodded, holding out her hand for Rovann to pull her up. For a moment she leaned against him, sucking in deep breaths. "What happened?"

"I don't know."

Rovann wiped blood from his eyes and gasped as he pressed his fingers to the cut across his temple. No time to deal with it now. Warily, he approached the staircase, shuffling in tiny movements with his senses flung wide.

Then he found it.

On the top step rippled an emanation of power so faint he hadn't noticed it when they passed. Hesitantly, he reached out his hand, palm out, feeling a tingling against his hand like the warmth of a candle. Then, careful not to draw too much, he channeled a tiny amount of energy into the anomaly. The air began to shimmer like heat haze and a shape gradually revealed itself. A rotating disk of utter darkness blocked the stairwell.

Around it the walls and stairs seemed to bend, melting like wax. Rovann backed away.

"What is it?" asked Maegwin.

"Chaos," he murmured. "A ward of the Outer Darkness itself."

"Put there by the Songmaker?"

"I don't know. I've never seen anything like it before." He met her eyes. "But its presence here is already beginning to disrupt the surrounding reality." He pointed to where the walls and floor seemed to be melting. "Chaos is antithesis to order. They cannot exist together. I've no idea how the Songmaker has command of such power."

He shook his head, unable to explain, not even knowing the answer himself. "We can't go back. The ward was designed to trigger as we passed. Come on."

They moved down a wide corridor, unadorned but for a tri-colored mosaic on the floor. Maegwin took the lead and they padded along silently, two ghosts lost in this silent crypt.

"Where is everyone?" Maegwin muttered to herself.

Rovann had no answer. All around him a strange alien power pulsed, a power he couldn't quite identify. It was like hearing whispers of conversations in a foreign language. With every step he took it grew stronger.

Maegwin gripped his arm. "Someone's coming!"

Footsteps echoed down the passage and with them came a high-pitched whistle like wind through a tunnel. Maegwin dropped into a fighting crouch with the staff held in both hands. Rovann readied his power.

A group of tall, heavily armed men burst around the corner. They bore the dark skin of the Shinnar but had hair so pale as to be almost white and a blue crescent moon tattooed on each cheek. The men moved with steady purpose, eyes hard and faces grim, naked swords held in their hands. The scream of the wind grew louder and louder. Rovann braced himself, brought sorcery crackling to the end of his fingertips.

The men rushed toward them—and then passed straight through.

A sensation like an icy blade slid through his stomach. He turned, mouth hanging open in shock as the men continued down the corridor and clattered down the stairs, passing through the Chaotic ward as though it didn't exist.

The wind died. Silence fell.

Rovann leaned heavily against the wall and ran suddenly nerveless fingers through his hair. Maegwin dropped her staff with a thud on the mosaic floor and hugged her chest.

"Ghosts!" she whispered. "Holy Mother protect us!"

"What is this?" Rovann muttered. "What is he playing at?" He threw his head back suddenly and bellowed. "Face me, damn you!"

His words echoed off the walls then faded slowly into silence. Dust sifted gently down from the ceiling. It was the Highhold all over again.

Fool, he chided himself. *How could you blunder into the same trap twice?*

Fighting down a rising sense of dread, he growled, "Let's keep moving."

Beyond the corridor the space opened into a complicated network of galleries, passages and rooms. Perhaps they once formed part of the living quarters for the priests of Tyrvanan. Now the rooms were abandoned and empty. Dead.

Rovann led them quickly, boots making dull thuds on the dusty stone floor. Every sound seemed amplified in the eerie silence. At length they reached another staircase and warily climbed it. Above the lintel at the top were carved the words, *The Realm of Fire*.

Rovann paused under the lintel and tentatively reached a hand out behind. Sure enough, he felt the tell-tale tingling of power against his palm. Another ward blocked the stairs behind them, this one bearing the signature of the Realm of Fire. They were being herded upwards, unable to go back. Unable to escape. The very power of the Realms was being used against him.

Sucking in a breath, he led them on.

On this level the rooms were larger and contained the crumbling remains of furniture. But like the level below, it was empty. He and Maegwin could have been the only people in the world. Rovann halted at an intersection that had five corridors leading off. He threw up his hands in frustration and kicked at a pile of dust.

"Curse the man to the lowest levels of hell!" he growled. "I'll carve his heart out for this!"

This was not how he'd planned things. He thought he'd finally face his enemy and one of them would walk out alive. But not this. Somehow the Songmaker had eluded him again. Tyrvanan was a trap. Just as the Highhold had been a trap. The Songmaker had eliminated Rovann, the greatest threat to his power. Which meant he was free to wreak whatever havoc he wished against Amaury. Against the Realms themselves.

Black despair swirled in his stomach. From nearby he heard wailing and only realized it was coming from his own throat when Maegwin grabbed his shoulder, yelling at him to stop. He crashed to his knees and suddenly she was there, pulling him close, wrapping her arms around his shoulders. He rested against her as his thoughts spun out of control. In his mind's eye he saw Tyrlindon in flames, saw King William dead, saw Prince Owen sitting on the throne as the Songmaker's puppet. Then, even worse, he saw the Realms breached, saw the Sluargh of the Outer Darkness rampaging unchecked, saw the power of Chaos rip reality to shreds, finally reaching the One Light itself which it snuffed out like a candle flame.

All because he'd been too blind to realize the trap he was walking into.

Shivering overtook him. A racking sob burst from his throat.

"Rovann," Maegwin said, shaking him. "Rovann!"

He couldn't focus. His thoughts scattered, fragmented. Desolation ripped through his mind, obliterating his restraint.

"King's Mage!" Maegwin yelled in his ear. "Control yourself! Remember who you are!"

He couldn't. It was impossible. Around them, sorcery began to ignite the air in tiny sparks as his hold slipped. The floor rumbled, showers of dust falling from the ceiling. The air pressure increased, suddenly pressing down like a lead weight. Blood dripped from his nose.

"No!" Maegwin shouted. "You will not give up! I will not allow it!"

She pulled her arm back and slapped him so hard it snapped his head to one side and left him momentarily stunned. But the shock and pain cleared his thoughts. Brought him back to himself. He doused his power, forced his despair aside and looked at Maegwin.

She gazed at him steadily, her green eyes full of concern and determination. Deep within, Rovann thought he could see the power of the Sentinel curling in the depths of her emerald gaze. He was reminded that he was not alone. There were other powers in the world working toward the same goal as he: the Sentinels, Fenris, Tanyaka, his friends back in Tyrlindon. Maegwin.

He reached out and gently cupped her face in his hands. "Thank you. You are my strength, Maegwin."

She smiled, her eyes lighting up. "As you are mine."

He kissed her, drawing comfort from her solid presence. Then, curling his fingers through hers, he pulled her to her feet. "So, we keep going?"

She nodded. "Always."

Side by side they walked down the corridor and into a long gallery. There they paused in shock.

Six tall, white-haired women were walking slowly beside a bier being carried by two men. A girl-child lay on the bier, eyes closed. Her skin was pale and waxy, with dark circles under her eyes and a blue tint marring her rose-bud lips. Dead, Rovann realized.

He pressed himself flat against the wall and indicated for Maegwin to do the same. The somber procession moved slowly by, paying them no heed. The strange sensation came again: a blade of ice slicing through his belly. Maegwin paled and bowed her head, hiding her face from the women. Her grip on the staff was tight enough to turn her knuckles white. Finally, the odd procession turned a corner out of sight.

Rovann stared after them. "Just as I thought. Like the Highhold. We're in the past. Or perhaps, we're seeing events from the past being replayed."

"Then they *are* ghosts?" Maegwin whispered in a shaky voice.

Rovann laid a hand on her shoulder. "They can't harm us. They don't even see us. To them, we're the ghosts."

Maegwin smiled weakly but did not seem convinced. Rovann squeezed her shoulder and they moved off at a steady trot.

The strange scenes increased the closer they traveled toward the heart of Tyrvanan. In a small vestibule they discovered a young woman enduring a barbaric rite. Two older women held the girl down whilst an old man pressed a branding iron shaped like a crescent moon into her cheek. The girl's lips curled back in a scream but no sound came from her mouth.

On the next level, marked as the Realm of Air, two young boys silently chased a small dog through a gallery. Further on, a wounded man dressed as a Shinnar warrior limped down a hallway, trailing blood on the floor. Still further, a young couple sat side by side in a window seat, gazing silently at the landscape below.

None of the apparitions so much as flicked a glance in Rovann and Maegwin's direction.

Eventually they reached a level inscribed as the Realm of Earth. Here, in every room and corridor people were replaying unconnected bits of the past. To Rovann it was like walking through some bizarre carnival with silent mummers performing in every available space.

Then, in a large chamber that might once have been a

dining hall, Rovann stumbled to a halt, turning cold with horror.

An ancient battle played in the room, or more accurately, an ancient massacre. Tall men systematically strode through the room, slitting the throats of cowering men and women. The victims were dressed as priests and the armed men as guards, possibly risen up in rebellion against their former masters.

He led them quickly on, ignoring the bodies that fell to the floor at their feet. Maegwin's eyes were clouded with remembered pain. Perhaps the scene reminded her too keenly of what had happened in her temple. Rovann took her hand and she squeezed it, smiling at him briefly.

They entered a wide circular room and Maegwin halted suddenly, letting out a gasp of surprise. The chamber lay empty, with no ghosts playing scenes from the past, but the whole of the curving wall was taken up with a beautifully painted carving.

Rovann walked into the center of the chamber then turned in a slow circle, taking in the delicate hieroglyphs, the intricate swirling patterns, the strange, almost runic markings marching in regular columns through the design.

"What is it?" he asked aloud.

He hadn't expected an answer so he jumped in surprise when Maegwin said behind him.

"It's a prophecy."

Chapter Thirteen

Maegwin stared in silence. How could she find the words to explain? Shivering wracked her body and she crumpled at the knees, slumping onto the floor. Rovann watched silently, waiting for answers.

It's a prophecy.

Her gaze skipped over the carving, shying away from what it tried to tell her. But it spoke all the same, whispering harsh truths.

Why had she come here? she asked herself savagely. Why had she ever set foot in Tyrvanan? She was beginning to realize that she'd been doomed from the moment she stepped through the gates. Tyrvanan was a place of ghosts, of ancient magic and forgotten rituals, a place dead and empty of life.

Except it wasn't empty. Not for her.

Rovann thought the ghosts of Tyrvanan couldn't see them. But he was wrong. Yes, they didn't see Rovann, but she knew with a certainty that they saw *her*. It had begun with the soldiers on the lower level.

The group pelted toward them, teeth bared in a snarl, weapons held tight. They crashed into her— and passed straight through. One of the men turned at the last minute and met her startled gaze. He bowed his head in deference, eyes wide with fear or awe.

Maegwin shuddered, wiping a hand over her face. She shook her head to dislodge the memories and pulled in a deep breath. Rovann was staring at her expectantly. Deliberately, she looked away from him, focusing instead on the intricate designs on the wall.

After their first encounter with the shades the journey through Tyrvanan had become a long walk of terror for her, a slow revelation of her secrets. Every ghost they saw acknowledged her in some way.

The two lovers sitting by the window had scrambled to their feet as she passed. Even the guards in the massacre hall had nodded to her as they slit the throats of the priests and priestesses within. Rovann saw none of it.

But it had been the girl being tattooed that had given Maegwin her first clue as to the real truth of Tyrvanan. As the maiden was held down, a hot brand pressed into her skin, she'd curled her hand into a benediction, the symbol of circle and hook. It was the same blessing the Holy Mother had used when she'd welcomed Maegwin into the temple all those years ago. And the blue crescent moon being branded into the girl's cheek was the same tattoo Maegwin wore on her shoulder, hidden beneath her clothes.

The mark of Sho-La.

Now, as she stood gazing at the circular room, with its inscribed walls, Maegwin realized she'd reached the end of a journey that began all those weeks ago when her temple had been destroyed and she'd killed four men. All this time she'd thought she had a choice. She thought she'd chosen to accompany Rovann, chosen to help find Leo and Prince

Owen, chosen to seek revenge against Lord Cedric Hounsey and the Songmaker.

But what if she'd never had a choice at all?

The runes running in columns through the design were of a language she didn't recognize. But around the edge of the whole motif was a geometric pattern which symbolized the cycle of the moon: full, half, quarter, dark.

She knew the patterns intimately. They were the symbols of the Dark Goddess.

Her pulse quickened. She felt light-headed and weak. She climbed to her feet and stumbled toward the carving. As her hand brushed against the ancient design a voice spoke in her mind. Female, deep and resonant.

"We await the coming of Shel-Masa's general. She will unite the people and bring all into the light of the World Mother. She will rend the Realms, destroy all borders and free the followers of the old ways. And the Earth Mother will hold dominion over all life even unto the ending of the world."

The voice died into silence leaving Maegwin listening to the thump, thump, thump of her heart.

"What is it?" Rovann asked, gently grasping her shoulder.

The touch jolted her. She slapped his hand away, stalked off a few paces and stopped. It was suddenly hard to think, to breathe, to function. Rovann took a step but she held out a hand to stop him.

"Please, I need a minute."

Even when she closed her eyes she felt the power of the carving demanding her attention. It wanted to claim her. Written up there, in an ancient language, was her future. The symbols of the moon told her. The girl-child's tattoo told her. The way Tyrvanan's ghosts had saluted her told her everything. Finally it all made sense.

The Shinnar followed the Earth Mother which, Maegwin now realized, was just another name for Sho-La, an old name, an ancient name. But the priests of Tyrvanan had left carvings of the moon on its walls, carvings that showed where their true allegiance lay. They had turned to the dark aspect of the World Mother.

They were followers of the Dark Goddess. Like her.

"Maegwin?" Rovann's voice was soft but she detected an undercurrent of impatience. "You said it was a prophecy?"

She looked at him. His blue eyes were as intense as the very first time she'd met him.

Oh, Rovann, she thought. *Don't ask me. Please don't ask me. I have a choice still. I do. And I will make the right choice, I promise you.*

"It's just a myth. It speaks of the World Mother and her followers." She told only part of the truth and the bits she left unsaid squirmed inside like worms.

Rovann frowned. "How can you read it? I know most of the old languages yet I can't decipher this."

But to her relief, he didn't wait for an answer. He moved over to the wall and ran his hand over the carving. Almost to himself he said, "There's a mystery here. What am I missing? If only there was more time."

Frustration echoed in his tone. Every delay endangered the prince's life, yet to miss vital clues could also spell ruin. They walked a tightrope, one slip either way meaning disaster.

Rovann closed his eyes and Maegwin detected the slight thrum of his power. After a moment he opened them again and shook his head. "No. It doesn't speak to me. Whatever this carving is, it won't give up its secrets to me." He straightened. "We're on the level of the Realm of Earth. If this place is like Tyrlindon, we only have two levels to go until we reach the center of Tyrvanan."

Maegwin nodded. She closed her eyes. Around her pulsed the presence of Tyrvanan's past, as though another reality existed just beyond her senses. Vibrations ran through the ancient fortress like veins of ice through rock.

They moved quickly, almost at a run, no longer showing any caution. They reached the stairs to the next level, the Realm of Aethyr, and took the stairs two at a time, not even pausing when the ward snapped into place behind them.

After all, there was no going back.

This level, like the others before it, was populated by scenes from the past. In every corridor, hallway, room, people went about the tasks of their lives. For most part, they were priests and priestesses wearing long white robes and with the blue crescent moon of Sho-La tattooed into their cheeks.

Rovann made his way through as though they were merely a nuisance but to Maegwin they were like memories, bits of her old life reminding her of what she used to be. Except for the slightest of differences in the priesthood's garb, this could have been Maegwin's own temple, could have been her and her sisters walking these silent corridors. And, more importantly, the ghosts wanted to welcome her. Each one acknowledged her with a nod or with a blessing.

At last, she and Rovann found the steps leading to the final level of Tyrvanan. Above the lintel were carved the words, *The One Light*. Together they stared upward. Rovann's face was stone. Only his eyes betrayed the tangle of emotions within. They blazed with passion and not for the first time Maegwin was glad she wasn't his adversary. He looked at her and she looked back. He didn't speak but she knew what he was trying to say.

This is it.

A whirl of images flashed through her mind: the look of surprise on Meryk Hounsey's face as she killed him, the gallows in Mallyn, the storm over Angard, Leo's indomitable good cheer, the sadness of Hesha's death, Cedric Hounsey's cruel laughter, Fenris's probing gaze, Kandar's distrust of her.

She reached out and clasped Rovann's hand. He coiled his fingers around hers and for a second she wished she was somewhere else, anywhere else. How would her life have been if different circumstances had befallen her?

It was a pointless question. Together they walked up the stairs and stepped out into the Realm of the One Light.

She'd expected to find the Songmaker waiting for them, surrounded by his mages, parading the tortured prince. What they found was a gallery that circled an inner chamber. The doors to this chamber had rotted away and through the open archways Maegwin saw that the space was empty.

They moved to the doorway and peered through. Like the room on the level below, it was perfectly circular but bore none of the intricate carvings of its counterpart. In fact, except for several windows high in the domed ceiling, the chamber had no features at all. It was dull and empty. Lifeless.

As Rovann took a step into the room something suddenly thrummed on her senses like a warning. The hairs rose on the back of her neck. Desperately, she grabbed Rovann's arm.

"Wait! It's not—"

Her words cut off as people appeared in the archways

and charged at them. Maegwin raised her staff, sorcery crackled around Rovann, but the men and women ignored them, moving to form a circle in the center of the room. As they passed, Maegwin felt the familiar sensation—a blade of ice slicing right through the middle of her belly. More ghosts.

Rovann looked around warily, clearly rattled by the absence of the Songmaker or any of the renegades. This was not what he'd expected. His forehead creased into a frown. Anger throbbed in his voice. "He's playing with us. Damn you!" he shouted, lifting his arms wide. "I know you're here! Come out and face me!"

Maegwin grabbed his elbow. "Look!"

Something was happening within the gathered circle of people. A mural suddenly flared into existence on the floor: seven circular bands, one inside the other. Each of the rings was painted a vivid color: silver, green, blue, yellow, red. The inner most circle shone a bright gold but the outer band was dyed black, as deep and unforgiving as the night.

"The Seven Realms," Rovann breathed.

A woman stepped forward and spread her arms wide to the rest of the gathering. Maegwin jumped at the shock of being able to hear her words. After the silence of the lower levels, the woman's voice was piercingly loud, as though she was shouting right by Maegwin's ear.

"Sisters. Brothers. I don't have to tell you how important a day we've reached. Our architects have labored for months to make the dimensions of this tower correct. The tower of Tyrvanan now sits exactly on the point where the Seven Realms touch. My friends, using this power, we can open the Realms and bring the World Mother the dominion She has asked of us. We'll complete our life's work and take our place by Her side. Are you ready?"

The others nodded, joy shining in their eyes. Or was it fear?

"Let us begin."

They started to sing. There were no words that Maegwin could discern but the melody was beautiful, the male voices in perfect harmony with the female, as though they spent many hours practicing. It was a slow, almost mournful song, the notes rising and falling in perfect counterpart to each other. It swept Maegwin away, carried her up on a wave of sound.

In response, the mural on the floor began to glow, casting a dancing pattern of color on the walls and ceiling. It floated up from the floor until it formed a sphere of colored bands. It was like looking at a miniature universe, with the tiny orb of the One Light at its center and the other Realms layered around it.

As they sang, the priests and priestesses held cupped hands out before them and a shining light materialized on their palms. The light began to stretch into long shafts that reached out toward the floating sphere.

"What are they doing?" Maegwin whispered.

Rovann said nothing. His eyes were fixed, unblinking.

Inch by slow inch the threads of light extended. When they reached the sphere and touched the first of the Realms, the Outer Darkness, Rovann gasped, flinching as though struck. But the ropes carried on moving, straight through the Outer Darkness and into the red band that marked the Realm of Fire.

"Fates preserve us," whispered Rovann.

"What are they doing?" Maegwin asked again. "Tell me, Rovann!"

His mouth was a thin line and Maegwin could see the tension in his jaw. "They're attempting to open the

Realms, or more specifically, the One Light. Perhaps they believe their goddess resides there and are trying to free her."

"But surely they don't have that kind of power?"

"This is a hub, Maegwin. A gateway to the Realms themselves. Who knows what can be done here? It's no wonder the Shinnar shamans despise the priests for what they did. This is sacrilege."

The ropes of light had reached the silver brilliance of the Realm of Aethyr. With a coughing gasp, one of the priests staggered and pitched face-forward on the floor, his head making a horrible cracking noise. In response, the others sang louder, pushing the strands through the silver band of Aethyr toward the center.

With an almost audible snap the ropes reached the One Light and a silent concussion rocked Tyrvanan. Maegwin staggered and reached a hand out to steady herself. Four of the priests lay dead in the circle, rivulets of blood running from noses and ears. The rest of the group continued singing, pouring their power into the hub and out into the Seven Realms.

The high priestess looked up at the ceiling and yelled, "In the name of the World Mother, Shel-Masa, we open the Realms! Come to us, mistress!"

But the One Light refused. At each new probing touch, it only grew brighter, stronger, until with a mighty concussive burst, it threw the threads back, sending them whipping through the other Realms like snapping bow strings. But as they passed through the Outer Darkness, they pulled some of the substance out with them, taking it into the bodies of the priests as the ropes snapped once more into their makers.

The song fell silent and the high priestess gasped, eyes

going wide with anger. "I will not have it! We cannot fail! I will have dominion—"

Her words cut off with a strangled cry. Her hands flew to her throat. The hub began to rotate, throwing out bursts of energy from the Outer Darkness. A hook-like tendril snagged each of the priests and hauled them toward the slowly spinning ball.

With wails of terror the priests struggled to free themselves. Each yelled words of power but they had no effect. They were dragged through the edge of the hub and into the dark band of the Outer Darkness, the Realm of Chaos. In seconds they were consumed.

The hub flared brightly then the whole image disappeared, leaving Maegwin and Rovann staring at an empty, silent room. Rovann looked around, forehead creased in thought. Maegwin could almost see the thoughts churning behind his eyes, making connections. She placed the heel of the staff on the floor and leaned on it, suddenly weak.

"Kandar suspects," he said almost to himself. "I should have guessed but I never made the connection."

"What connection? Rovann, what are you talking about?"

"The priests of Tyrvanan committed an atrocity that led to the destruction of the Shinnar civilization. We just witnessed it. They tried to shatter the Realms themselves. And now the Songmaker has built his fortress on a hub. Maegwin, he's trying to do the same thing!"

"Finally! How many clues do I have to give you? Call yourself a mage? Ha!"

A voice suddenly boomed through the chamber, so loud Maegwin put her hands over her ears. The room melted away before Maegwin's eyes. She cried out as she was hurled into sudden darkness.

Chapter Fourteen

Rovann threw out his arms and tried to grab something, anything to steady himself. His questing fingers met only air. Darkness enveloped him. He couldn't hear. Couldn't see. Then his fingers brushed against Maegwin's hand and clasped it tightly.

The voice boomed again. "So touching! So weak! You have betrayed your wife, King's Mage! Where are your vows now, betrayer? As fickle as water!"

"What do you know of Istra?" he shouted.

Laughter, harsh and biting echoed all around. "Everything. Is she here, do you think? Your dead wife? Does she exist in this void? Will you abandon her here now you've found another? Is that the extent of your loyalty?"

Maegwin tightened her fingers around his. Rovann couldn't see her but felt her close. He'd become so used to her presence. A familiar tightness suddenly closed his throat. Was the voice right? Had he abandoned his wife?

"Istra?" he whispered.

The darkness then dissipated like fog and he found

himself standing next to Maegwin in the room at the very top of Tyrvanan. But the room had changed. Tapestries hung on the walls and a huge red rug covered the flagstone floor. A fire crackled and popped in a large fireplace on one wall with two chairs lounging before it. In one, a man sat with his back to them, playing a lute and singing. The man's voice was clear and strong, filling the room with a haunting melody.

> *When will you come back to me?*
> *The road is long, the trail is cold,*
> *The sun has gone, the day grows old*
> *Oh, when will you come back to me?*

Prickles of unease crawled up Rovann's spine as recognition ran through him. In his memory he heard someone else singing those words, a slight, dark-haired woman strumming a harp. Istra. This had been their song.

The man fell silent. He took his time putting his lute back in its case then climbed slowly to his feet. Then he turned to face them.

Maegwin gasped. "Leo!"

The youth grinned and gave a flourishing bow. "Lady Maegwin! Lord Rovann! I knew you'd come! I never doubted you'd find me. It's good to see you, my friends!"

The young minstrel looked no worse the wear for his ordeal. His clothes were clean, his ginger hair washed and combed, his freckled cheeks rosy with good health.

"I don't believe it!" Maegwin said. "When you disappeared through that portal on the Sarth Road we thought you were dead!"

Leo tapped his nose conspiratorially. "It takes more than measly mage magic to get rid of the indestructible Leo

March!" He pursed his lips in thought. "Hmm, 'measly mage magic'. I like that. Sounds good. I might use it in a song."

Rovann narrowed his eyes at the young minstrel. "Maegwin," he said, voice low in warning.

Crossing the rug, she threw her arms around Leo, pulling him into an embrace. The youth yelped in delighted surprise then returned the hug.

"What happened?" she asked, placing her hands on his shoulders and looking him up and down as if checking he was in one piece. "How did you come to be here?"

"Maegwin," Rovann said again. "Step away from him."

She glanced over, a look of puzzlement on her face. "What? Why?" Turning back to Leo she asked, "Where's the Songmaker?"

Rovann's gaze never left the youth's face. "He's right here. Isn't he, Leo?"

A slow grin spread across the minstrel's boyish features. His eyes sparkled with merriment. Maegwin looked from Rovann to Leo and back again.

"What's going on?"

"Maegwin," Rovann growled. "Step away from him."

This time she seemed to hear the warning in his voice. Her gaze searched Leo's face then came to settle on the lute case propped against his chair. Her eyes widened in sudden comprehension. "No," she murmured, shaking her head. "No. I won't believe it." She backed away. "Leo?"

The youth cocked his head to one side. "Do you remember when we first met, Maegwin? It was in Angard. You rescued me from an angry mob of townsfolk who'd set on me. Do you remember why they'd done that?"

"They thought you were the Songmaker," Maegwin said

in a choking whisper. "They thought you'd called the mage storm to destroy their town."

"Full marks for remembering!" Leo replied jovially. "And do you know what? Turns out those townsfolk were right!"

Maegwin recoiled as if she'd been slapped. "No," she panted. "No. How could you? I trusted you. I thought you were my friend."

Leo spread his hands to either side. "Don't be too hard on yourself. We all make mistakes."

With a wordless cry of rage, she lunged at him. There was a flash of light and she was hurled across the room like a rag doll. Rovann threw out his hand and shouted a word of power, bringing Maegwin to a halt before she crashed into the hard stone of the wall then lowered her safely to the ground.

Leo, the Songmaker, or whoever he was, clapped slowly. "Very impressive."

Rovann grabbed Maegwin's arm, yanking her back. "Get behind me."

"I'll kill him!" she hissed.

"Do as I say!" he bellowed, thrusting her behind him with all his strength. "Where is Prince Owen?" he asked the Songmaker.

Leo grinned and the air in front of Rovann shimmered, revealing a small wooden chair. On it, Prince Owen lolled, head back, mouth hanging slack.

Rovann took a few wary steps then recoiled in horror. Prince Owen's eyes were open and staring even though he was clearly unconscious. Thick black wire showed through the swollen flesh where his eyelids had been sown open. The eyes themselves had become sightless balls of milky white tissue, full of fluid.

Rovann felt the prince's forehead. "Prince Owen? Your Highness?"

Owen roused at the sound. He gasped and moved his mouth wordlessly.

"Highness? It's me, Rovann. Owen?"

The prince shifted his head toward the sound of Rovann's voice, trying to pinpoint his location. "Rovann?" he croaked. "Lord First?"

Rovann took the prince's hand. Owen flinched, perhaps expecting a blow. "Yes, my lord. I've come to take you home."

The prince gulped. "I...I'm sorry."

Maegwin moved to stand on the other side of the prince. "He's blind," she whispered. "Leo blinded him." Her voice was full of revulsion but there was a strange look in her eyes that reminded Rovann of the night she'd attacked the man at the inn.

"Maegwin?"

She cocked her head, regarding the prince with fascination, then stuck out a finger and moved it toward the prince's left eye.

"Don't touch him!"

She startled, snatched her hand back.

"Don't touch him," he repeated more softly. "Move away."

"Who's with you?" asked the prince. "Is it her? Is it the one he's waiting for?"

Rovann placed his hand on the prince's forehead and channeled the Eorthe to send him into a deep sleep. Then he stepped forward, placing himself between the prince and Leo. And, for reasons he couldn't explain, placing himself between Maegwin and the prince as well.

The Songmaker laughed softly, a grating sound with no mirth. "Ah! At last he begins to suspect!"

Rovann faced the youth. He had trusted Leo. All this time, his enemy had been right under his nose. All this time. And he'd suspected nothing. What kind of power did this man wield? How was he able to escape Rovann's notice? How was he able to parade himself in Tyrlindon with nobody suspecting who he was? The implications left Rovann cold.

"Why?" he grated. "Why this charade? You could have killed me in Angard. Or on the road. Or in Tyrlindon. Why bring me all the way here?"

Leo stroked his chin in thought. "Sometimes the arrogance of mages astounds me. Why do you assume it's all about you? It isn't." His gaze swung to Maegwin. "It's about her."

"What do you mean?"

He waved a hand expansively. "Oh all right. It's not *all* about her. It's about both of you. Do you know what you are, King's Mage?"

Rovann remained silent, refusing to be drawn.

The Songmaker laughed, shaking his head in disbelief. "You really don't suspect? Honestly? Then I won't dispel your ignorance. Just ask yourself this: why have the angels of Aethyr chosen you to be their champion?"

"Answer my question, curse you," Rovann grated.

"Patience!" Leo admonished, waving a finger as if Rovann were a naughty school boy. "I'm getting to it. You say I could have killed you in Angard or Tyrlindon. Well, I'm not so sure of that. Here, on the hub of the Seven Realms is the only place I could ensure you wouldn't escape. I have power, King's Mage. But you..." He whistled under his breath. "What you did at Sandford Moor is like a grain of sand on a beach compared to what you are truly capable of."

"You lie. Poison drips from your forked tongue. You don't know me. You've hidden in the shadows for years, manipulating from the background. How can you know anything about me?"

Leo stared at him, unblinking. "Is that a fact? I was there, remember. At Sandford Moor. How many did you murder that day? Hundreds? Thousands? Did you enjoy it, King's Mage? Did it make you feel good?"

"Enough!" Rovann bellowed.

Around them, the tower suddenly shook, dust falling from the ceiling.

A look of smug satisfaction spread across the Songmaker's youthful features. "Ah. There it is. That rage you keep so expertly hidden. Feels good to release it, doesn't it, Slayer?"

"Shut your mouth!" Maegwin cried, stalking closer with both hands clasped on her staff. "Don't even speak to him, traitor!"

The Songmaker's gaze swung to her. "It's so sweet, the affection that's grown between you two. I must admit, I didn't see that coming. I'm afraid it will make what has to happen that extra bit poignant. Perhaps I'll write a song about it. *The Lay of Rovann and Maegwin*. Ah, maidens will weep at the sadness of it all!"

"What are you talking about?" she asked, edging closer.

"Ah, now we're getting to it. The second reason for bringing you both here." He smiled disarmingly as though he was no more than the boy he pretended to be. "You, my dear. I need you. I've brought you here to meet your destiny."

Maegwin went very still. She looked to Rovann like a rabbit that's just spotted the hawk circling above.

Rovann edged in front of her. "Explain yourself," he demanded.

"Didn't you know? She is to be my general."

"You're insane!" Maegwin yelled.

"Am I? Do you deny that you follow Shel-Masa? Do you deny that you've sworn yourself into Her service?"

"I follow Sho-La and none other!"

"You follow the Dark Goddess. Darkness runs through your veins. The power of Chaos has taken root in you."

Maegwin seemed to flinch as if struck. Rovann wanted to go to her but something stopped him. Something in the Songmaker's words made too much sense.

"Why are you doing this?" he growled.

"Oh, I can't take all the credit. I have my mentors to thank for showing me the way."

He waved his hand and four women flickered into existence around him. They were Shinnar, Rovann realized with a start. Each wore the trappings of a shaman, with bones and shells tied into their hair. Around them shimmered an aura of power that made the bile rise in Rovann's stomach. The very air seemed to bleed and distort in their presence.

Chaos. The power of the Outer Darkness made manifest.

Involuntarily, Rovann took a step back. He recognized these women and the realization made his heart thump against his ribs. He'd seen them in the room below, acting out the ritual of sundering all those centuries ago. These were the women who'd been devoured by the Outer Darkness. But they were here. Now.

"What is this?" he whispered.

But they ignored him completely. Instead, their hard black eyes fixed on Maegwin. One of them held out a bony hand.

"Come, child. It is time. You will join us. Together we will sunder the Realms and free our mistress."

———

This is insane, Maegwin thought. *Insane. Does the Songmaker really expect me to join him? After everything he's done?*

But it's Leo! A voice inside cried. *He's your friend!*

She'd come all this way to rescue him only to discover he'd deceived her from the start. She struggled to reconcile the grinning, cheerful minstrel with the ruthless killer of the stories.

The four Shinnar women stared at her. Their gazes were hard, insistent. *We know who you are*, those stares seemed to say. They expected something from her but Maegwin had no idea what it was. Well, they could go to the abyss for all she cared. Deliberately, she moved to stand by Rovann's side and pointed a shaking finger at Leo.

"You're a liar and a traitor. Why would you suppose I'd join you? You're responsible for the deaths of my sisters! You ruined my life! I'll never help you!"

As she said the words a cold rage lit inside her. Lord Cedric Hounsey had ordered the burning of her temple but he'd been working for the Songmaker. For Leo.

The youth frowned, narrowing his eyes in thought. "I am sorry for that, Maegwin. I truly am. It was never my intent to destroy your order. Hounsey overstepped his authority. I never sanctioned the destruction of your temple."

"How can I believe a word you say?" she replied. "Look

at you, Leo. Is that even your real name? You're the Song-maker. Holy Mother! How could I be so blind?"

Her thoughts suddenly sprang into crystalline focus. She'd sworn revenge and it was within her grasp. She must kill him. Kill Leo. Her friend.

"Maegwin," Rovann breathed in warning. "Don't."

His words had no effect. She barely heard him. Clasping the staff in both hands, she rocked onto the balls of her feet and tensed her muscles, ready to strike.

To her surprise Leo smiled and spread his hands wide, welcoming her attack. The Shinnar women remained as immobile as statues.

"I'm here, Maegwin," Leo breathed. "Do it. Take your revenge."

"Don't, Maegwin," Rovann said, reaching his hands toward her imploringly. "It's what they want."

"I'm right here," the Songmaker repeated. "Why do you hesitate? Are you going to pass up the chance for your revenge?"

An image flared suddenly in Maegwin's mind. A tree in flames. A man at an inn cowering in fear as she swung a sword at him.

The same exhilaration filled her veins now. It wiped away all thought. All concern. She was helpless in its grasp.

But suddenly Rovann was there, pulling her back, speaking in a low, insistent voice. "They're manipulating you. Don't give in to them. Remember who you are!"

Rovann's eyes were like balls of blue fire as he stared at her. In them she read his concern and determination. *They will not have you,* that stare said.

Other images filled her mind. The companionship of the soldiers on the road to the Highhold. The compassion of King William as he pardoned her. The friendship of the

Shinnar. The soft touch of Rovann's lips. The thump of his heartbeat next to hers.

And suddenly something else stirred inside her. A song. A golden song of peace and healing. The song of a Sentinel.

She blinked. Sucked a breath through her nose like a sob and sagged against him, dropping the staff with a thud onto the rug.

"No!" Leo hissed. "You will not deny me!"

His youthful features contorted into a twisted mask of fury and for the first time Maegwin saw the man beneath the boyish persona. The sight frightened her. Sorcery suddenly blazed around him.

Rovann thrust Maegwin behind him then raised his hands, energy crackling from them. But Leo didn't attack. Instead, he turned to the fireplace and threw a bolt of power into the flames. They exploded into a conflagration of deepest night and when they died down a face hung suspended in the flames. A woman's face of purest alabaster with midnight hair and blazing blue eyes without iris or pupil.

The Dark Goddess Herself.

Maegwin gasped. She collapsed onto her knees and bowed until her forehead touched the coarse weave of the rug.

"Mistress."

Do you think you can betray me? The Dark Goddess asked.

"Betray you? Never! I follow Sho-La. Always."

You follow me! she snarled. *You made a vow!*

Maegwin dared to look up, even though terror made her heart thump against her ribs. "I'm sorry, mistress." She gestured helplessly, trying to find the words to make the goddess understand. "I was broken when I swore that vow."

She glanced to Rovann who stood watching her. "But now I'm not. I'm not broken any more. When I made the promise to you I fully intended to keep it. Vengeance was all I wanted. But no longer. It's gone."

The Dark Goddess's lips parted and from her black hole of a mouth strange sounds escaped. It took a moment for Maegwin to realize she was laughing. Ice slid down her spine.

Oh, my daughter, the Dark Goddess said. *Do you imagine it's that easy? Do you think affection from some paltry human can turn you from my path? It is too late for that. Much too late. You are mine.*

Despite the bone deep terror that gripped her, defiance welled up inside. "No. I am not."

The Dark Goddess's blazing eyes narrowed and Her will enveloped Maegwin, almost crushing her flat. It squeezed and Maegwin clawed at her throat. Then suddenly the power eased and she gulped in a desperate breath.

I will not coerce you, the goddess said. *You will choose my path of your own free will.*

"I won't!" Maegwin gasped, massaging her neck.

The Dark Goddess's eyes flickered to Leo who stepped forward. His lips quirked in an expression of infinite amusement, as though this whole situation was somehow hilarious. He crouched in front of Maegwin and lifted her chin to force her to look at him.

"How did it feel to listen to the screaming as your sisters burned to death?" he asked in a conversational tone. "What was it like to smell burning flesh as they died? Do you remember, Maegwin?"

"Leave her be!" Rovann hissed, stepping forward but Leo flung out a hand to halt him.

"You will stay out of this, King's Mage! If you interfere I will kill your precious Prince Owen." He hummed a low note and the prince suddenly screamed in pain, his back arching and the chords in his neck standing out.

Rovann growled, power flaring around him. The Song-maker sang three higher notes and Owen convulsed, spittle frothing from his mouth.

"Damn you," Rovann whispered. "Damn you to the darkness." But he stepped back, sorcery winking out.

"A wise move, King's Mage," Leo said. "Perhaps the first wise decision you've made since you cut Maegwin from the noose in Mallyn."

The youth returned his attention to her. "That day seems so long ago now, doesn't it, Maegwin? The day you were hanged. The day you died. You were given a choice that day. Die, or live and take your vengeance. You chose the latter and it's too late to change your mind now. It's time to remind you who you really are."

Maegwin tried to look away but his fingers held her chin in a vise-like grip. Suddenly her memories went hurtling back to the clearing in the forest and the day that changed her life forever.

She is lying on her side. The smell of grass and earth fills her nose and at any other time she would have enjoyed it. But not today. Now she is struggling to breathe. There is blood in her nostrils, slurping and sucking whenever she tries to take a breath. Her throat feels crushed from where the men have grabbed her. In the distance, but horribly close, the temple is burning. Wooden planks have been nailed across the door, ensuring those inside cannot escape.

And the priestesses are screaming.

There is no other sound in the world. The fire consumes the temple hungrily but silently, the men laugh and jeer without making a noise. She struggles to get up but her hands slip every time she gets them under her. Her skull aches with the blow she received. Somehow she manages to pull herself to her feet.

Lord Meryk Hounsey is standing a few feet away, staring at her. His head is cocked to one side and he is looking at her with a quizzical expression as if wondering why she is still alive. There is no trace of guilt or shame about him. The self-possessed, wide-footed stance, the assured placement of fists on hips, the cool appraisal in his eyes; everything speaks of a lord who is confident of his actions. He has done no wrong. He has noble blood and has a right to mete out death as he sees fit. The lives of priestesses mean nothing to him.

And that's when Maegwin feels it.

It uncurls inside her like a flower. Hatred. In that instant she hates Lord Meryk Hounsey, despises him with a passion that fills her body like poison, right from the tips of her toes to the top of her head. She wants him to die. She wants him to feel pain and terror and despair. She wants to see his eyes go wide with shock as her sword punches into his flesh. She wants to see his blood spread on the green grass, wants to smell its sickly-sweet odor on the air. She wants to hear the gurgle of death in his throat and watch the final breath leave his body.

So she acts. As Meryk Hounsey takes a step toward her she grabs a sword and rams it into his heart with all the strength her battered body can muster.

She sees him die, tastes his blood as it splatters on her face, hears the breath rattle in his throat. But it is not enough. A berserker rage consumes her, all thought and emotion gone. There is only that black, burning hatred. She turns it on Lord Hounsey's men and soon three more of them lie dead. But it is still not enough, will never be enough. She fights until they club her to the ground; a pulpy mess barely holding onto consciousness.

And her sisters scream and scream and scream.

Maegwin's eyes widened as the scenes replayed in front of her. Her limbs shook uncontrollably. She wrapped her arms around herself and tried to swallow the bile rising in her throat.

"No," she whispered. "No."

Leo's voice spoke by her ear. "How would you like to take your revenge after all, Maegwin? How many died that day? Twenty? But you killed only four—hardly a fair bargain. No, to really redress the balance you must take your vengeance against the man who ordered the deaths of your sisters."

He waved his hands and the air shimmered to reveal a man standing there. He was beyond his middle years and had the grizzled look of a veteran. A fringe of iron-gray hair covered the back of his head and his hard black eyes glared from beneath shaggy eyebrows.

Maegwin's breath caught as she recognized the man. Lord Cedric Hounsey. Meryk's father.

The warlord looked around and a scowl twisted his features. "What are you doing bringing me here like this?" he demanded of the Songmaker. "I was in the middle of a briefing, curse you! My army has almost reached Tyrlindon. Send me back, now!"

Leo merely raised an eyebrow and then crossed his arms over his chest. He looked Hounsey up and down then waved languidly with one hand. "He's all yours."

The old warlord glanced at her and then sneered in disdain. "What is this?"

Maegwin clenched her fists. Something cold and hard was forming in the pit of her stomach. "You killed my sisters," she said softly.

Rovann shifted his weight, seemingly torn between rushing to her side and protecting the prince. "He's a revenant, remember," he warned. "He can't be killed. The Songmaker is manipulating you."

"*Was* a revenant," Leo corrected. "No longer. He lives and breathes just as we do. And that means he can die."

As if to emphasize his point he hummed a note and a

gash suddenly sliced its way down Hounsey's left cheek, spilling bright blood. Hounsey bellowed in pain and clamped his palm to his face.

"You promised me!" he howled. "You promised me immortality!"

Leo shrugged noncommittally. "I did, didn't I? Ah well. Looks like I've changed my mind."

Maegwin stared at the blood dripping down Hounsey's face. She couldn't seem to take her eyes off it. Her nostrils widened as she picked up its iron tang in the air. In response, all the hatred and anger she'd harbored since her sisters died erupted inside her. She thought she'd moved on, but as her pulse rocketed and her breathing deepened, she realized she'd been wrong. It was there all along, buried deep inside like a seed waiting to germinate.

And seeing Hounsey standing here before her, the man she'd hunted so long, was the catalyst that seed needed.

Leo moved to her side. The youth made one of his flourishing bows and held something out. With a start, Maegwin realized it was a naked sword. With trembling hands she curled her fingers around the hilt. Leo stepped back as she raised the blade. She saw Hounsey's puzzled reflection in the gleaming metal.

"At last," she breathed. "Hounsey, I'm going to kill you."

Rovann glanced down at a sudden sharp pain. Unwittingly he'd curled his hands into fists and clenched them so tight his fingernails had dug furrows into his palms. Deliberately he uncurled them and sucked a deep breath through his nose, trying to steady himself.

It didn't work. Rage boiled through him so hot he could

barely think. Rage at the Songmaker, at his own stupidity, at this whole situation. He longed to unleash his power against his enemies; to blast the whole cursed lot of them into oblivion. But he couldn't. If he did, Leo would kill Prince Owen. Rovann sensed a coil of Chaotic power curling around the prince's heart. One move from Rovann and Leo would snuff out the prince's life in an instant.

So he was forced to watch like a powerless bystander as Maegwin hefted the sword and dropped into a fighting crouch in front of Lord Cedric Hounsey.

His mind whirled with endless questions. Why had Leo tried to entice Maegwin to attack him? Why had he brought Hounsey here when she'd refused? And who was the dark entity hanging suspended in the flames?

Its essence roiled with Chaos and the stench of the Outer Darkness. Yet, Maegwin had called it mistress. Sho-La? Surely not. She was a goddess of patience and forgiveness. This creature was one of vengeance and anger. The Shinnar mages had referred to it as Shel-Masa and that was a name he recognized, a name from the deepest, darkest legends of the Seven Realms.

He shifted his weight, forced his hands to his sides and focused his attention on Maegwin. He suspected that everything somehow hinged on this moment and her confrontation with Lord Hounsey.

The old warlord glared at Leo and seemed to realize his master had abandoned him. He growled deep in his throat, the sound more animal than human. "So this is how you reward loyalty? When I've killed the bitch, I'll kill you."

He drew the sword strapped at his waist and threw himself at Maegwin in a series of lightning-fast strikes. Despite his age, the lord was an accomplished swordsman. Maegwin brought her own blade up in a sequence of deflections that somehow overbalanced Hounsey and sent him staggering behind her. She spun, blade hanging low to the ground, almost nonchalant in her stance. She raised her free hand and slowly beckoned him forward.

Lord Hounsey hawked up a gobbet of phlegm and spat it onto the floor. "Nice work, bitch. But it won't save you." He drew a second weapon, a short-sword this time, and attacked with both weapons, moving so quickly the two blades became a blur.

Maegwin stepped to meet him, deflecting his attack and again sending him staggering behind her. Hounsey's short-sword landed on the rug with a thud and Rovann saw blood flowing down Hounsey's arm where Maegwin had sliced through the tendons, rendering his arm useless.

This only seemed to make him angrier. He threw himself at her, sword held high in one meaty fist. Maegwin moved in a silent, graceful dance and this time Hounsey's longsword went thumping to the floor, his sword arm hanging by his side as Maegwin cut the tendons of this arm as well.

"Go on then!" he roared, arms dangling at his side, blood dripping onto the thick rug. "Do it, you faithless bitch!"

Maegwin stepped behind him and flicked her blade first across the back of his left knee and then his right. Hounsey's legs folded and he crashed to the floor, unable to move. His breath came in loud, ragged gasps, his chest heaving in and out. For some reason, Rovann found he couldn't look away. He'd seen that expression before: the realization of one's impending death when confidence suddenly gives way to terror.

He'd seen it at Sandford Moor and hoped he'd never see it again.

Glancing at Leo and the Shinnar mages he saw that their gazes had become fevered, expectant, and in a flash of awareness he realized that this had been orchestrated to push Maegwin into killing Hounsey. This execution served their purpose. With a sick jolt of understanding, he knew that if she killed the old lord, Maegwin would cross a threshold from which there was no returning. He couldn't let her do it.

As she raised her sword above the helpless man Rovann stepped forward, close enough to touch her although he didn't.

"Maegwin," he said low and urgently. "Listen to me. You don't have to kill him. He's already beaten. Put the sword down and come with me. Please."

She glanced at him and the ravaged expression of loss, horror, and despair that twisted her features almost made him cry out.

Ice and darkness swirling through her veins. Creeping into her heart. Shattering all emotion like shards of broken glass. Just one final push, one final stab of her blade into Cedric Hounsey's pumping heart and it would be over.

But she hesitated. Rovann's voice cut through the wall of ice and gave her pause. It was quiet, soothing, familiar. It spoke of another path she could walk. Another life she might lead.

Part of her wanted to take that path but she knew with a cold finality that it was too late. The hatred inside her was too strong. As she looked down at the cowering figure of Lord Cedric Hounsey and saw the fear flooding into his eyes, she realized that she *wanted* to kill him. She *wanted* to feel the blade of her sword slice into the thick muscle of his heart just as she had done to his son all those months ago.

It had been her choice all along. The Dark Goddess had merely shown her the path to her true self.

She turned away from Rovann, raised the sword two-handed over her head, then thrust it into Hounsey's chest with such force it erupted from his back, sliced through the rug and slammed into the hard flagstones of the floor beneath.

Hounsey convulsed, a great gout of dark red blood exploding from his mouth.

"My debt is paid," she said. "A life for a life. Now die."

She knelt by his side, placed one palm flat against his chest and with the other gently stroked his sweat-soaked hair like a mother comforting a frightened child. His gaze found hers and he opened his mouth to gasp out one last curse but the effort was too much. His head fell back, eyes staring sightlessly.

It was such a beautiful sight. How could she have ever doubted herself? This was what she'd wanted. What she had promised herself, her sisters, and her mistress. It was *right*.

"No," Rovann whispered by her side. "Maegwin, what have you done?"

She glanced at him. His face had gone slack with horror, one hand held out as if to deny what he'd just seen. His sparkling blue eyes and handsome face were the same as she remembered. His voice was as smooth as it ever was. Her memories of his kiss, his touch, his laughter were as bright as ever. And yet... and yet when she regarded Rovann she felt... nothing. Nothing at all.

"Ha!" The Songmaker cried. "I never doubted you, Maegwin, my dear! Oh, all right, you had me worried for a minute there but you came through for us in the end, just like I knew you would! Now join me."

She nodded and walked the ten steps across the room to where he waited, feeling Rovann's gaze boring into her back the whole time. When she reached the Songmaker's side she turned to face Rovann and saw his emotions written plainly across his face. It didn't matter. Rovann had been nothing more than a distraction, she realized. In service to her mistress she felt more complete, more alive than she could ever have done by choosing a life with him.

In the black flames the Dark Goddess smiled and then slowly faded from view. When She had gone, the four Shinnar women rushed forward, each of them touching Maegwin as if to check she was real.

"Welcome home, my child," they said. "Welcome home."

Chapter Fifteen

Rovann felt dislocated from reality, as though he was watching a dream. A shiver slid down his spine as Maegwin walked to stand by the Songmaker's side.

He could not be seeing this. He couldn't.

"Maegwin?" he said. "What are you doing?"

The Songmaker's teeth flashed as he grinned. His eyes shone with triumph and amusement. "Told you, didn't I? Told you! Too trusting, that's your problem, King's Mage! Didn't I warn you it would end badly? Oh, how sad *The Lay of Rovann and Maegwin* has turned out to be! Maidens will weep to hear it!"

"How can you do this?" he rasped at her. "How can you?"

Maegwin's green eyes flicked to his face and he was shocked to see how cold they'd become, like chips of ice. "I can only be what I am, Rovann."

"You speak as though there's no other choice."

"There is no choice for me. There never was."

Rovann shook his head, struggling to understand. "No.

You've been manipulated. Coerced. This isn't you. It isn't. What do you want with her?" he demanded of the Songmaker.

This time the smile that cracked Leo's face held no warmth. "Haven't you figured it out yet? Maegwin is special. In her two powers have been fused: Chaos and that of a Sentinel. It gives her...unique abilities. She is to be my general. Together we will destroy Amaury."

"No, you won't. I will stop you."

Leo laughed, throwing back his head and howling at the ceiling as if this was the best joke he'd ever heard. "Really?" he asked, wiping his eyes. "Look around you, King's Mage. You are alone. Abandoned. How will you stop me?"

"I'll find a way," Rovann growled.

The Songmaker waved his hand irritably. "Right, I'm bored with your prattle. Time to do what I brought you here for. Kill you."

He took up his lute and began plucking a slow, haunting melody. He started singing in tones so low Rovann couldn't make out the words although their power rumbled in the stones beneath his feet.

The Shinnar women clasped their hands and bowed their heads. They launched into a deep, staccato chanting that worked in counterpoint to Leo's song.

The hairs on Rovann's neck rose. He moved to stand before the prince, shielding him from whatever the Songmaker was summoning.

Gray smoke began seeping up through the floor, coalescing into the shapes of men and women. In a heartbeat, insubstantial specters surrounded Rovann and the prince.

Involuntarily, he took a step back, eyes going wide. Ghosts, he realized. The Songmaker had resurrected

Tyrvanan's dead. The spectral figures stared at Rovann with eyes full of desperation.

Help us.

The Songmaker's song changed, becoming a deep chant that seemed to come straight up from the earth. In response, the ghostly forms solidified before Rovann's eyes. Color returned to their pale cheeks, the sound of their frightened breathing whispered through the room.

"What is this?" he asked, even as the awful truth dawned on him.

Lord Cedric Hounsey all over again. The dead, given life. And compelled to fight.

In unison the dead raised their hands and gleaming blades flickered into existence in their grasp. Rovann's heart thumped. These people were not his enemies. Yet he'd be forced to kill them all the same.

He opened his senses to the Realms and wove a blade of light from the Eorthe. He grasped the weapon two-handed and dropped into a crouch.

The dead rushed forward in a silent wave. He ducked under the swing of the first blade and brought his sword round in an arc, slicing through a woman's stomach. The woman, once a Shinnar warrior by the look of her, opened her mouth in a mute scream. Her eyes flooded with fear before she collapsed backward and lay still.

Memories of Sandford Moor flashed through Rovann's mind. On that blood-soaked battlefield he'd faced innocent camp-followers. And he'd slaughtered them all.

Now here in Tyrvanan, at the heart of the Songmaker's power, he was being made to do the same again.

"Curse you!" he howled, spinning to parry a blade. "Leo, you traitorous bastard! Curse you to the Burning for all eternity! Are you too frightened to face me yourself?"

There was no response. The strange chant continued unbroken.

The dead doubled their assault. They attacked from all sides, swinging their blades at his abdomen, his neck, his throat. Rovann spun and jumped, parrying and dodging as best he could.

"I won't do it!" he bellowed. "I won't kill these people!"

Suddenly his attackers backed away and stood in a ring. Rovann halted, watching them. The atmosphere in the room felt heavy, punctuated only by the chanting of the Songmaker and his Shinnar.

Jerkily, the figures lurched into motion once more and Rovann brought his sword up, ready. But instead of striking him, they turned on the unconscious prince.

With a yell, Rovann threw himself forward. Just in time he caught a blade, deflecting it from the prince's exposed throat. Howling his rage and frustration, Rovann swung, severing the man's head from his shoulders. Even as the man collapsed in a shower of blood, a howl of torment rocketed through Rovann's soul.

You bastards! he raged silently at the Shinnar shamans and the Songmaker. *I will kill you for this!*

A large man wrapped in shaggy yellow furs lumbered up on the prince's left, swinging his sword with the clumsiness of a man who had never handled the weapon before. Rovann turned to meet him, knocking his blade aside, but not before a shallow cut was opened along the prince's cheek.

Rovann punched his sword into the man's chest then spun, snarling. There were so many of them. How could he defeat them all? How could he bring himself to destroy so many?

I can't do this, he thought. *Not again.*

Who else is there? he answered himself. *You are the King's Mage.*

He straightened and let his sword drop from his fingers. Closed his eyes, sucked in a deep breath and opened them again.

Yes. I am the King's Mage. So be it.

He cleared his mind, emptied himself of thought and emotion. And then relaxed all restraint.

Incandescent power erupted from him in a shockwave that ripped through his attackers as if they were made of paper. Bodies exploded, limbs tore away, blood and viscera spilled onto the carpet.

But more smoke rose up through the floor and solidified into new waves of assailants. Rovann howled in anguish as he ripped them apart. He collapsed to his knees but the ranks of his opponents didn't thin.

And as Rovann fought, he discovered he could reach deeper, further than he ever had before. The power of Aethyr filled him. The power of the Eorthe filled him. And now it was joined by the rage of Fire, by the slippery vitality of Water, the ephemeral touch of Air. And yes, finally even Chaos itself answered to his will.

He became a being of pure energy burning so bright he must surely be devoured. He felt the Realms groan around him, recoiling against this unleashing of power.

Then a presence drew close. An ancient, wise being just beyond the border of Fire. Rovann recognized the dragon, Tanyaka. "Careful, Warrior of the Realms," her voice said in his mind. "It is beginning. The Sluargh are awakening."

Rovann sent Chaos whipping into the Outer Darkness and sensed a wave of creatures flinch behind the veil at his touch.

"No," he said. "The way is closed."

And he laid about him, destroying everything in his path.

It took a while for him to realize that all sound had ceased. Slowly he came back to an awareness of his body. He knelt in the middle of the blood-soaked rug, surrounded by the bodies of the slain. There were so many. The space around him had become a mass of reaching limbs, glassy eyes and faces frozen in the last rictus smile of death. To any who looked upon him he must appear like some kind of demon, his Shinnar disguise washing off and covered in blood not his own.

Footsteps approached. He glanced up and saw Maegwin standing before him. He sighed, exhaustion sweeping through his body. He struggled to hold his head up as Maegwin stared down at him.

"The slayer of Sandford Moor," she breathed. "I can see why you earned that nickname. But it's just you and me now, Rovann, and I don't think you'll find me such an easy opponent."

He shook his head. "I won't fight you, Maegwin."

"Really? We'll see."

A wave of Chaos enveloped him. Its touch on his skin was like being stung by thousands of tiny insects. His essence began to unravel. He felt bits of him being torn away to go spinning into the void. A scream of pain and utter horror erupted from his lungs. In response he sent a pulse of Aetheric power exploding from his body. The Chaos was ripped to shreds and Maegwin backed away, watching him.

Bracing his hands on the blood-soaked floor, Rovann staggered to his feet. "Stop this, Maegwin. I won't fight you."

Her nostrils flared in anger. She made a tiny gesture and

a sliver of energy as cold as ice plunged straight through his shoulder. Blood sprayed and with a wail, Rovann doubled over in agony.

"Defend yourself!" Maegwin hissed. "Fight me!"

Rovann staggered a few steps then steadied himself on the back of one of the plush chairs. "I won't."

Something sliced into his side, reopening the old stab wound he'd received in the woods near the Highhold. He clamped his hand to the puncture and suddenly coughed blood that sprayed over the chair.

With a cry of pain he yanked himself around to face her. She strode toward him and the look of cold detachment on her face made her barely recognizable. Her eyes, which were normally such a brilliant green, had changed to the hue of deepest midnight. The mark of the Dark Goddess.

He couldn't save her. He couldn't save her because she didn't want to be saved. At times on the long journey he'd glimpsed the darkness within her but had never imagined that this would be the outcome. A stab of betrayal pierced his heart and twisted. He doubled over, clenching his teeth against despair that almost made him blackout.

She was going to kill him. Maegwin, his friend, his lover, was going to kill him.

Is this it? he asked himself. *Is this how it's going to end? Betrayed by Leo. Betrayed by Maegwin. Will you leave Amaury unprotected? Will you leave Prince Owen to become the Songmaker's tortured puppet? Will you abandon your duty all because you've been betrayed by a woman?*

Tanyaka, he whispered in his mind. *Help me.*

But the dragon's presence had faded and he was alone.

A snarl escaped his throat and his fingers curled into fists. *No*, he thought. *I am the King's Mage. I will do my duty.*

Duty? That word again. A word Istra had always hated.

And now his duty was to kill the woman who'd replaced her.

Oh, Istra! he wailed silently. *I'm sorry!*

He straightened, flung out his hand and a blast of force shook the tower. It tore into Maegwin, lifting her from her feet and tossing her across the room. Her eyes widened in shock and anger and a wordless cry of rage escaped her lips. She crashed into the wall with a sickening crunch and slid to the floor where she lay in a heap.

Rovann strode forward, sorcery lashing around him. He grasped the oily power of Chaos and fashioned it into a sword point. The Songmaker and Shinnar mages threw waves of sizzling energy at him, enough to tear him to shreds should it reach his body. With a nonchalant flick of his wrist he sent shields of Air and Aethyr to deflect them whilst he stood over Maegwin.

She rolled over groggily and opened her eyes. They were unfocused and had once again turned back to the green Rovann remembered. Gone from her face was the emotionless mask and now she looked up at him with a mixture of incomprehension and concern.

"Rovann?"

Something like a sob escaped him as he held the blade of Chaos above her. Tears tracked their way through the grime on his cheeks. What would he become if he did this? Certainly not Rovann anymore but another kind of King's Mage. One devoid of emotion. Of conscience. The Slayer of Sandford Moor.

He blinked, steeling himself. *So be it.*

He raised the blade.

"I'm sorry," he whispered.

A silent concussion rocked the stones beneath his feet. The tower lurched, throwing Rovann from his feet. He scrambled up in time to see the entire west wall explode in a shower of rocks and dust.

A huge creature burst through the gap.

Leo backed away, screaming at his Shinnar, "Kill it! Kill it now! Don't let it take him!"

Rovann shook his head, ears ringing. Through the dust the beast emerged. Massive reptilian body, wings tucked to its sides, wedge-shaped head on a long scaled neck, golden eyes as large as cartwheels and teeth as long as Rovann's forearm.

"Warrior!" the creature cried, her piercing gaze fixing on him. "Come quickly! There is no time!"

Rovann gaped, barely able to register what he was seeing.

"Tanyaka?"

The dragon lumbered toward him. "Yes, now come on!"

Waves of Chaos tore at the dragon and with a snarl that seemed to shake the ground she whipped her tail out like a scythe only to have it rebound from the wards Leo and his Shinnar had set around themselves. With a howl of rage Fire erupted around her instead, sweeping through the room in a howling inferno. But it didn't touch the mages.

"How dare you?" Tanyaka roared. "How dare you touch me with that tainted stench? I am a dragon of Fire! I will not tolerate it!"

Rovann threw himself across the room, grabbed Prince Owen by the armpits and dragged him toward Tanyaka just as the chairs, table and even the stone seemed to burst into flame. Smoke and heat filled the room.

He glanced to where Maegwin had been lying and saw that she was gone. He spun around, searching, but could see nothing through the raging fires and cloying smoke.

"Ready?" Tanyaka boomed at him.

The dragon scooped him and Owen up in her massive claws and then reared onto her hind legs. She beat her enormous wings and they lifted off the floor and through the destroyed west wall of the tower. Rovann searched the smoke, trying to spot Maegwin, Leo and his Shinnar mages. But there was no sign. The raging inferno obscured everything.

They rose into the air. A clean, cold wind was blowing. It sliced through Rovann like glass. The prairie stretched below them, a vast empty sea of grass. Behind, the tower of Tyrvanan burned like a giant beacon.

Rovann breathed against the tightness in his chest. The dragon held him firmly, her claws digging painfully into his sides. He welcomed the pain.

"Tanyaka," he gasped. "How can you be here? In this Realm?"

Her golden eyes swiveled toward him. "The angels asked me to intervene. The borders are shredding. Chaos is bleeding through. We need you, Warrior. We need you whole and unbroken."

"Need me? Why?"

She snorted a laugh but didn't answer.

Something moving on the plains caught Rovann's eye. Ponies and a cart with two people riding on the seat. Kandar and Preyen.

Rovann closed his eyes and sent a message winging toward the shaman. *Kandar! I failed. The Lord Shaman will come for you now. You must take your clan and flee!*

The old shaman glanced up, eyes widening at the sight of the huge dragon sailing overhead.

Flee? he answered. *I don't think so. We will fight. Gather your armies, King's Mage. When the time comes, call on us. The Shinnar will fight for you!*

Rovann nodded.

A dark stain on the horizon marked where Roamsford Edge met the plain. It grew larger, spreading like a pool of ink. A tall hill rose above the trees. On the hill's summit, Rovann saw a massive silver wolf looking up at them.

"Fenris!" bellowed Tanyaka, "You saw?"

"I saw," the elemental shouted. "Warrior! It is beginning! The Realms are fraying and it is time to choose sides. I go to gather the wights of Roamsford Edge. We will fight for you!"

And then they were leaving the forest behind and crossing the border into Amaury.

"Tyrlindon," Rovann croaked. "We need to get to Tyrlindon."

Something was digging into his thigh. He reached into his pocket and pulled out a piece of wood. It was the carving he'd been working on all through his long journey. He squinted at it. A woman's face stared back at him. She had high cheekbones, a straight nose and long, flowing hair.

Istra. His dead wife.

He frowned suddenly and peered closer. No, not Istra at all, he realized. The long hair, the wide eyes. Maegwin. He'd been carving her all along.

He growled suddenly, deep in his throat. His hand clenched and the carving exploded into dust.

Tanyaka looked down at him. "The Unraveling is beginning, Warrior. What will you do?"

A chill seeped into his heart. He bared his teeth. "I'm going to kill them," he answered. "I'm going to kill them all."

Next in The Songmaker Series

vinci-books.com/traitorssong

Trust is a weapon—and it cuts both ways.

Rovann and Maegwin's failed quest has left them trapped by their
choices. With the rebel forces closing in, Rovann must choose
between saving thousands or exacting vengeance. As Maegwin
confronts the emptiness of her path, the fate of the realm hangs in
the balance.

Turn the page for a free preview…

The Traitor's Song: Chapter One

Maegwin de Romily pinched the bridge of her nose, fighting back a headache that was slowly drilling through her skull.

The wind on the hilltop swirled, sending her hair whipping out behind her and squeezing tears from the corners of her eyes. She squinted into the biting breeze at the darkening landscape below. By the light of the setting sun she saw grassland spreading out in an undulating map all the way to the horizon.

This was the land of the Shinnar, a prairie bordered by the forest of Roamsford Edge on one side and the distant Sunbiter Sea on the other. A landscape of gullies and hidden valleys, of a million different places that might hide an enemy.

Oh, how she hated it.

Footsteps thumped to a halt behind her. After a moment, General Shallon, the commander Leo had assigned to her, cleared his throat.

"High priestess, the scout has returned. We're ready."

Ready? she thought. *Do you think so?*

Maegwin turned to stare at the general. Somewhere in his middle years, he had the physique of a blacksmith and blunt, almost homely features. He wore a black uniform with a silver breastplate over the top and a helmet tucked under one arm. Although his tone was always carefully respectful, Maegwin knew he didn't like her one bit. That was fine with her. She didn't like him either. Shallon was Leo's man and served Maegwin only because Leo had ordered him to. Shallon wasn't the only one in the army who resented Maegwin's sudden rise.

Her eyes flicked to the Shinnar scout kneeling at General Shallon's side. A dark tattoo on his shoulder marked him as a member of the Bison Clan, the only Shinnar clan to have gone over to Leo's side.

"Tratek. I hope you bring me good news."

A quick look of triumph flashed in the young man's eyes. "Yes, mistress. We've found them. There's a small ravine about five miles east where they've made camp. We can take them now if we move quickly."

Maegwin's heart thumped. At last. After all these weeks of tracking, after all the failed missions, she might be able to capture Leo's prize and redeem herself in his eyes.

"General Shallon, ready your men. Tratek, lead the way."

They moved quietly and swiftly through the gathering dusk. Maegwin walked up front with Tratek and the general whilst their troops, a strike force of thirty elite soldiers, spread out around them. Nobody spoke.

The grass was so high it came almost to Maegwin's waist. In the breeze the grass shimmered and hissed.

Traitor, the voice of the prairie seemed to whisper. *You are not welcome here.*

Gritting her teeth, Maegwin strode on. It was not the first time she had heard such voices in her mind and she doubted it would be the last. But they were not important, only figments of her past coming to haunt her. If she achieved her goal tonight she hoped those voices would be silenced forever.

General Shallon suddenly paused and dropped onto his haunches, signaling for Maegwin and the other soldiers to do the same. Maegwin went to her knees in the long grass and waited. There was no sound except the whisper of the wind. The smell of grass and the pungent yellow wild-flowers that dotted the prairie filled her nostrils. A large black beetle crawled over her knee. Maegwin sat motionless.

A whisper ran through the soldiers and they pressed themselves flat into the grass. Carried on the wind, Maegwin thought she heard a drum of hooves. They approached her hiding place and then receded into the distance. General Shallon let out a long slow breath.

"That was close," he muttered. "Too close."

"The Eagle Clan?" Maegwin asked.

Shallon shook his head. "Impossible to say. Whoever they were, they were traveling in a hurry, messengers possibly. They didn't see us, luckily, otherwise we could kiss goodbye to any hope of completing our mission tonight."

He poked his head above the tall grass and turned his head slowly to right and left, trying to locate their scouts. He nodded. "It's clear. Safe to move on."

When he paused, Maegwin realized he was waiting for her command. Even after all these weeks of having the soldiers do her bidding, it still felt alien to be the one in charge. Well, she'd better get used to it.

"Very good, general. Lead the way."

They moved more slowly as they approached the Eagle

camp, pausing regularly to flatten themselves into the grass whilst the scouts checked for any enemy pickets. Maegwin bit back her impatience. She'd waited weeks to get this opportunity, a few more minutes would make no difference. She chewed her lip.

A damned book, she thought. *All of this for one damned book.*

After the fall of Tyrvanan, in flame and smoke, Leo had gone a little crazy. He'd disappeared for days and left Maegwin in charge of securing the ruins of Tyrvanan and marshaling their forces. He left a company of a hundred soldiers with her, an excessive force to Maegwin's mind, as the only things left behind were Leo's instruments, some old documents, and his library. These Maegwin had collected into a series of wooden chests, locked them in one of Tyrvanan's remaining cellars and set a guard on the door, all in line with Leo's instructions.

So she'd been utterly unprepared when she was woken in the middle of the night by the bellowing and shrieking of soldiers. A Shinnar raiding party had approached in the dark hours before sunrise and caught Maegwin's force unawares.

At first Maegwin assumed they'd come for her, to take revenge against the woman who'd betrayed them. Or perhaps they had merely seen an opportunity for a quick strike with Leo gone. But it wasn't until Maegwin's men had fought off their attackers that the dawn light had revealed the Shinnar's true goal.

The door to the cellar had been broken open, the guards killed, the chests scattered across the floor and one of Leo's precious books stolen.

The raid had been a feint, a diversion, yet Maegwin didn't understand it. Why risk lives to steal a journal? What could possibly interest the Shinnar in that book? From what she remembered, it had been filled with Leo's ramblings. Why did the Shinnar want it?

Leo had returned the next day and been incandescent with rage at the theft. He wanted that book recovered at all costs. At all costs.

And that's why she was here, crawling through the grass toward the camp of the Eagle Clan. To steal back what they had stolen.

A book. All this for a damned book!

Ahead, the ground began to rise until she saw a sharp escarpment cutting through the landscape. Shallon ordered the soldiers to take cover behind a large rock outcropping. Maegwin pressed herself against the hard stone and carefully peered out. The escarpment had been scoured by the wind until all the covering vegetation had been removed. It stood out of the grassland like a backbone. Cut through it, almost invisible unless you knew what to look for, Maegwin saw the deeper shadow of a defile.

"This is as far as stealth will take us, my lady," said Shallon. "I recommend we attack quickly, take out the guard at the entrance and then pour through the defile in force, sweeping away any of their defenders, and if the Lady is with us, catching them unprepared."

Maegwin peered at the defile. From her position it looked like a dark tunnel leading to who knows what. "How do we know this isn't a trap?"

The general shrugged. "We don't. It's a risk we have to take. The Songmaker's instructions were clear. He said to retrieve what they stole—"

"Yes, I remember," Maegwin snapped. She sighed. "Fine. Order the attack."

The general nodded tightly then gave silent orders to his men through a series of curt hand gestures. They burst from their hiding places and sprinted toward the defile, keeping low to the ground and into the shadows. Maegwin was swept along in their rushing advance. As she ran, heart pumping, breath laboring, exhilaration washed through her. Action! At last!

Tonight there would be bloodshed. Tonight her mistress would be pleased.

Close to the entrance, two Shinnar warriors suddenly stood up from the grass. They took one look at the force pelting toward them and then turned tail and sprinted back through the defile. Maegwin's men saw them and, like hounds spotting their quarry, increased their pace, swords clutched in their fists.

Maegwin passed into the defile. Darkness flashed by on either side. Her skin prickled. This was the perfect place for an ambush. Up ahead, a tumult ran through her soldiers as they reached the end of the defile. Maegwin tensed, expecting to hear the clash of weapons, the cries of struggling men. There was nothing but the pounding of her feet and the labor of her breathing.

With Shallon beside her, she burst from the ravine, holding her knife high, and dropping into a fighting crouch, anticipating attack. But what she found was a broad basin ringed on all sides by sheer walls. A fire burned in a pit in the center of the basin, surrounded by several sleeping figures. Of the fleeing guards, there was no sign.

What was this? Frowning, she straightened then nodded to Shallon. He and four others crept toward the fire, weapons ready. When they were only a few feet away they paused for a moment and then rushed forward, stabbing at the slumbering forms.

Who didn't even flinch.

"Hold!" Shallon cried and his men froze, blades held

high. The general crouched and pulled away the blanket of the nearest figure. "Curse it!"

Maegwin stared. A tumbled heap of sacks lay beneath, arranged carefully to appear like a sleeping person. As the rest of the blankets were removed, they revealed the same.

"Quickly," Maegwin barked, "five of you go back through the defile and guard the entrance. Give warning if you see anyone approaching. The rest of you spread out and check every inch of this place. I want to know who was here and what direction they took."

And why they went to the trouble of this ruse, she thought uneasily.

"We won't find anything," General Shallon said, sheathing his sword as he returned to her side. "They're long gone."

"Really? Then who were the guards we saw? And where did they go?"

The old soldier frowned but didn't answer. Maegwin stalked toward the fire and kicked the embers over the grass in a fit of rage. Sparks flew into the sacking which began to burn steadily. Good. Let it. The whole prairie could burn for all she cared.

Fury and frustration made her giddy. The goddess-damned Eagle Clan had thwarted her again. Curse them. Curse every last one of them. She would have to return to Leo's camp empty handed. Again. She glanced around the shadow-filled bowl and wondered. Why would the Shinnar dupe her so? Why not just attack? What were they up to?

Rovann flinched as Maegwin's gaze passed over his hiding

place and moved on. Beside him, Kandar whistled under his breath.

"By the World Mother's sagging tits, it worked. She can't see us."

"No," Rovann agreed. "She can't."

He went to his haunches, placing one palm flat against the stony ground. He and the Eagle shaman crouched atop the high cliffs surrounding the basin, both cocooned in a shield of Aethyr. Below, Maegwin's soldiers were milling in confusion.

"Dranvey and Preyen escaped?" Rovann asked, thinking of the two warriors who had volunteered to act as lures.

The old man snorted then grabbed one of the bones tied in his hair and yanked it savagely. "Yes. We left a rope ladder attached to the far side of the cliff. They pulled it up after them." He cackled suddenly. "Curse my behind but it feels good to pull one over on the bitch, doesn't it?"

Rovann didn't answer. This was the first time he'd seen Maegwin since she'd betrayed him in Tyrvanan. During the intervening weeks he'd returned to Tyrlindon and mobilized its defense. He'd rallied the Council of Mages, visited Silverport, Mandrake and Mallyn to oversee their garrisons. He'd deployed a circle of mages to each of the major cities to guard against a surprise attack by the Songmaker.

Together with Prince Owen, Mage Syrie and Captain Tyan, he'd set up an elite strike force whose job was to gather intelligence and hunt down any rebel mages at large in the countryside. He'd talked Tanyaka, a Dragon of Fire, into helping with the defense of Tyrlindon and right now she was patrolling the skies above the capital, keeping Lord Cedric Hounsey's besieging army at bay.

The last few weeks were a blur, a haze of activity that bled one day into the next and as he'd worked, done his duty as King's Mage of Amaury, Maegwin had grown and grown and grown in his mind until she'd become some kind of monster. A cruel, dark-hearted woman who couldn't possibly bear any resemblance to the Maegwin he had known. But now, as he watched her quietly talking to her men, he realized she looked no different. No different at all.

Rovann startled at a sudden cracking noise and glanced down to see that he had inadvertently curled his hand into a fist and in that fist was a rock that he had squeezed so tightly it had shattered into dust.

Kandar crouched beside him. The old shaman rested his elbows on his bony knees and watched Rovann with hard black eyes as keen as a hawk's. That knowing gaze flicked toward Maegwin and back again.

"We should kill her now and be done with it."

He said it casually, with no emotion. To Kandar she was now merely an enemy, just like any other enemy of the Eagle Clan. For Kandar, it was as simple as that. Rovann wished it were as simple for him.

He shook his head. "No. We must discover where the Songmaker is and what he's planning. We might not get another chance to follow her. Besides," he added dropping the shattered remains of the rock onto the ground by his foot, "I'm not sure we would find killing Maegwin so easy. She's the Songmaker's creature now, remember? She's protected by his powers as well as her own."

The old man's tanned face scrunched up into a frown and he spat out a stream of brown phlegm. "That's what I think of the Songmaker's powers! Haven't we been beating the bastard? If it wasn't for the Shinnar he'd be halfway to Tyrlindon by now!"

Angry pride flared in the old man's eyes and Rovann placed a hand on his shoulder.

"Peace, friend. Your people have done more than I could ever have wished but the fact remains: we must discover the Songmaker's plans. Both he and Maegwin have eluded our scouting parties until now."

He didn't bother to add that the only reason the Songmaker had not yet swept aside the Shinnar resistance and marched into Amaury was because of his desperation to recover the book Rovann had stolen from him. Right now that book lay under close guard in the Shinnar camp miles away, far away from where it might fall into Maegwin's hands.

It was another reason why he had to follow through with this plan. The book was a mystery that must be solved. To Rovann it appeared to be nothing more than a logbook of Leo's travels as a minstrel. It was full of maps, poetry, diary entries. None of which seemed overly important despite all the hours Rovann had spent poring over them.

It had been Prince Owen who had alerted him to the importance of the book. He had been Leo's prisoner for many weeks in the tower at the top of Tyrvanan. During that time, before he'd been tortured into blindness, he'd seen Leo sitting by the fire reading this book hour after hour and having his servants bring in other books and maps that he would cross reference with his own before tossing them away in anger.

Yes, definitely a mystery.

Dusting off his hands, Rovann rose. Down in the bowl, Maegwin's soldiers had finished checking the perimeter and had found no trace of anyone. Even from this distance Rovann could see the fury in Maegwin from the harsh set of her shoulders. She snapped something at her soldiers who sheathed their weapons and marched toward the defile.

"Kandar, it's time. Is everything ready?"

The old shaman nodded. Although I can't say if this will work. Pluck my eyes out, but I've never heard of any human surviving such a thing. I would tell you you're insane, but I'm sure you know that already.

Rovann smiled wryly. "I must be, Kandar. Who but a madman would put up with you and your ridiculous sense of humor?"

"Ha! Charming!" He straightened, leaning forward to get a better look into the valley. "She's moving. Ready yourself. It will be any moment now."

Rovann nodded. Maegwin had sent soldiers on ahead of her and now, alone in the valley, she spread her arms wide and began to walk forward. On the edges of his perception Rovann sensed her power flare and something draw close in response. The air around her began to rip as though a set of claws had raked through a sheet of fabric. Through the tear, darkness bled. And into that darkness, Maegwin stepped.

Something tugged, deep in his belly, as the trace that he and Kandar had placed on Maegwin took effect. Around him the air shimmered as if reality was beginning to melt. Then he was yanked violently forward. Kandar, the bowl, the prairie, all disappeared as Rovann was pulled into the realm of Chaos.

Rallack, the college's resident mage of Chaos, had postulated that traveling through Chaos would be much like traveling through the Eorthe. It wasn't. There was no sense of movement or the passage of time. Instead there was an infinite moment where Rovann's mind and body were stretched and mangled beyond all recognition. He felt as though he was being flayed. An alien, violent force took him and shook him, trying to find its way into his very soul.

When he opened his eyes he was surprised to find the night sky above him. Surprised to find that his body was still whole. Surprised to find that he was still alive.

Every bit of him hurt. Blinding pain twisted his muscles, forcing him onto his side where he retched into the dirt. He lay insensate, feeling as though he'd been turned inside out and put back together incorrectly. Finally, he opened his eyes and forced his screaming body to its knees.

Rows of neat white tents surrounded him. Guards patrolled between the rows, weapons gleaming at their hips. Rovann gulped and reached for Aethyr then choked out a gasp of relief when he realized the shield he and Kandar had woven had held, even through the fury of Chaos.

Thank you, angels, he thought. *Thank you.*

Nevertheless, he went as still as a statue as a pair of guards strolled by. They were arguing in loud voices about a dice game. They walked right by without seeing him.

He blew out a breath and scrubbed a hand through his hair. Directly before him rose the pristine white walls of a large pavilion. The trace Kandar had woven was locked onto Maegwin so he guessed she must be inside.

Get up, he told himself. *Get moving.*

With a groan, he clambered to his feet. He was going to kill Rallack. Next time anyone needed to travel through Chaos, *he* would to be the one to do it.

Bracing his legs wide to steady himself, Rovann closed his eyes and sent his senses questing outward. He detected thousands of lives, clustered together within two square miles. The space where he stood was at the center of the camp.

He allowed himself a small smile of satisfaction. So far,

so good. The trace had brought him to the Songmaker's camp. Closing his eyes, Rovann slowed his breathing and heart rate then focused his consciousness inside. He floated out of his body and up onto the astral plane. He moved warily, cautious that there might be enemy mages patrolling the astral plane. Until now, the danger of discovery should he walk the astral had been too great. Now he'd found the Songmaker's camp, the risk was worth taking. The Shinnar needed all the intelligence they could get. Floating gently on the astral tides, he looked down on the landscape below.

The Songmaker's army sprawled in a natural enclosure made by a line of low hills. It lay within Shinnar lands but close to the border with Amaury. A couple of miles to the east of the encampment spread the dark, brooding mass of the great forest of Roamsford Edge.

Rovann turned slowly, fixing every detail of the enemy's deployment in his mind. Brennan, the chief of the Eagle Clan, would want every scrap of information he could gather.

Satisfied, he dropped back into his body and opened his eyes. After a quick glance to left and right to check for guards, he pulled out his belt knife and silently slit a hole in the tent wall. Slipping through, he found himself in a large space, sectioned into smaller rooms by canvas hangings. He went very still, listening, but no sound came to him.

He stepped noiselessly forward, weaving his way between the hangings until he reached the center of the tent and crouched out of sight behind a chest. Carefully, he peered around the chest into the large, circular space beyond. This was unadorned but for a large rug covering the floor. A figure sat cross-legged in the middle of the rug, murmuring in a low voice.

In the dim light it took Rovann a moment to recognize

Maegwin. He tensed, his hands balling into fists. She was only a few meters away and completely unaware of his presence.

I will kill them all, he had promised Tanyaka. He should start with Maegwin right here, right now. After all, he owed her precisely nothing. Not anymore.

But before he could complete the thought, Maegwin glanced up suddenly and her hair billowed in a wind that gusted through the tent, strong enough to send the walls sagging outwards. When it subsided, it revealed a person seated opposite Maegwin. A gangly young man with red hair, green eyes and freckled skin.

Leo March. The Songmaker.

The youth grinned at Maegwin. "Ah! You are a sight for sore eyes! It was very cruel of you to leave me with our Shinnar friends. Not an ounce of humor among them. I've seen more life in a bowl of withered prunes!"

Maegwin didn't bother with greetings. "Leo, you are the one who left, remember? How go our plans?"

Leo's grin faded. "Oh, don't tell me you're going to be as bad as they are! All business and no pleasure will turn us all into bores! Tell you what, I'll sing us a song, shall I? I've been working on it for weeks. I call it, "The fall of Tyrvanan." Ah! It will make you weep!"

"Why have you been gone so long?" Maegwin asked, ignoring his question. "And why didn't you answer my messages? The Eagle Clan has been causing problems."

Leo tapped his nose and winked conspiratorially. "Ah yes! Very vicious fighters, the Shinnar! Now can you understand why I had so much trouble taming them? Even when I was their Lord Shaman the buggers would thwart me at every turn. Yes, certainly an entertaining contest!"

"This isn't funny," Maegwin grated. "They've killed many of my soldiers and made me look a complete fool!"

"Oh, I wouldn't worry about that," Leo waved a hand graciously, "if I worried every time someone thought me a fool, I'd never have left my house. And where would I be now? Well, still in my house, obviously. But you see my point."

Maegwin shifted uncomfortably. "Leo, I—"

The minstrel held up a finger. "I know what you're going to say."

"You do?"

"Of course. You're going to tell me you failed to retrieve my book from the Eagle Clan. Again."

The blood drained from Maegwin's face. "How did you know?"

Leo stared at her and suddenly his sharp gaze seemed full of menace. "I'm the Songmaker, Maegwin. I have my ways. You would do well to remember that."

"I've never forgotten!"

Leo raised a hand and scratched his arm pit. "Yes, I was right. You are in quite the crabby mood today, Maegwin, my dear. Are you sure you don't want to hear a song? It might cheer you up."

Maegwin placed her hands in her lap. She looked ready to throttle him. When she spoke, her words were barely above a whisper. "Leo. You have been gone for weeks. In your absence I have fought the Eagle, Wolf and Lynx clans at every turn. I have done my best to protect our supplies and baggage train from their guerrilla attacks. I have led raids on Eagle Clan camps to try to recover your cursed book and now you sit there grinning like it's all some damned game!" Her last words ended in a shriek.

Leo flinched, ducking as if she would hit him. "Whoa! Remind me never to get on your bad side, Maegwin! All right, all right. Calm down. I'll tell you everything."

She crossed her arms. "Go on."

A wide grin split Leo's face. "I'm not concerned with the book anymore. Oh, my life would be easier if we recovered it, but it no longer matters. Let Rovann have it. He'll never understand it, anyway. You see, I've found it."

"Found it? Found what? The book?"

"Not the book. Something better. Something I thought I couldn't find without the book. But I did. All on my own. Aren't I clever?"

Maegwin shook her head, exasperation making her voice sharp. "What are you talking about?"

"I've been scouting. That's why I've been absent. I've been searching for what I need to complete my plans and give us a way to topple Tyrlindon. And I've found it."

In his hiding place behind the chest, Rovann tensed. What was this? He leaned forward, determined to memorize every word.

Leo rubbed his hands together. "A place. A very special place. Called Near Point. It's close to the mountain passes in the north, just within the border of Amaury. This is where we will gather our forces, Maegwin. It is from this place that we'll launch our attack."

"Why Near Point? I've never heard of it."

Leo nodded, a smug grin on his face. "Not many have. My mages wait for us there and their ranks grow by the day. When we're ready we'll move swiftly on Tyrlindon from the north and hit them so quickly they won't have time to prepare. Hounsey's army is already besieging the capital from the south. We'll have the city surrounded."

Maegwin said nothing for a moment. Finally, she asked, "And what of Rovann?"

Leo's eyes flashed. "What of him?"

"You're sure he doesn't suspect your plans?"

"He doesn't suspect. Why would he? With Hounsey's forces marching on Tyrlindon and your attacks on the Shinnar here, his attention must be consumed. He's already fighting a war on two fronts. He won't expect us to bring a third."

Maegwin nodded although she appeared distracted. Leo leaned forward, peering at her.

"What is it?"

"Nothing."

"You've got that look on your face again."

"What look?"

"The look you get whenever you think about him."

She straightened. "I don't know what you're talking about."

Leo rested nonchalantly on one elbow. "Really? Shall I tell you what's going through your head right now? You're wondering if he hates you. You're wondering if he'll ever forgive you. You're hoping that you'll never have to face him in battle because you're not sure what you'll do. Am I right?"

Maegwin glared at him.

Leo sighed. "How many times must we go through this? We gave him a choice didn't we? He could have joined us. He could have served Sho-La, but he walked away. He left you with no choice. You couldn't abandon your goddess for him."

Leo's voice was smooth and charming. Utterly reasonable. How could anyone argue with such slick persuasion? He made it all sound so simple.

"From the start, you were my creature, never forget that."

He leaned forward suddenly and gripped her chin, forcing her to look at him. "You have darkness in you, Maegwin de Romily. You may have played at being the good little girl for a while but you have been walking my path since the day you were born."

An unreadable expression passed across Maegwin's face. Rage? Horror? Or was it acceptance?

"Have you practiced the Song Spell I taught you?" Leo asked.

"Yes," she sighed, throwing up her hands. "But I still haven't mastered it."

Leo nodded. "I'd be surprised if you had. It took me months to get it right. Let's try it now."

Rovann tensed as Leo reached behind him to pull his lute from where it had been strapped against his back. The minstrel set it into the crook of his arm and began to play. A bawdy, cheerful tune rang out. It was a tavern song you might hear anywhere. Nothing special. Nothing out of the ordinary.

Except, at the sound, the hairs on the back of Rovann's neck stood on end. Power bled out from those notes, charging the air like lightning. After a moment Maegwin began to sing.

> Long years and memories,
> A life of sweat and toil,
> I am the one who waits for you,
> A seed growing in the soil.

Energy rippled out in a warm wave, stirring the curtains. Maegwin's words seemed to gather the notes from

Leo's lute and weave them together into something new. Something *other*.

"I can't do it!" she cried suddenly, slumping forward as if exhausted.

Leo stopped playing and the manifestation evaporated. He seemed frustrated, annoyed and something else. Worried?

"It doesn't matter," he said eventually. "It will come in time. This is how it should go."

Plucking the string of his lute forcefully, Leo sent the tune spiraling into the air once more and now he sang as well, the same words that Maegwin had. Only this time the words and the notes melded together seamlessly, forming a complex Song Spell that made Rovann's stomach twist with dread.

Somewhere deep within the Realms, Rovann sensed something stir. Something with a vast regard turned its attention on the tent.

"Sho-La," Maegwin murmured.

Aethyr suddenly flowered in Rovann's mind. The voices of angels cried, *we cannot protect you from Her! Flee now! Before She sees you!*

Rovann spun, making no sound as he wove through the tent to the hole he'd cut. He ducked through it and ran. He felt tendrils of a dark presence following him, reaching out like tentacles.

Run! She is almost upon you!

Rovann fled, pelting through the camp as fast as his shaking legs could carry him. He reached the camp's edge, burst through the pickets and out into the dark prairie. Gradually the presence faded. Finally, miles from the Song-maker's camp, he came to a halt, heart laboring, breath a ragged saw burning his lungs. He threw himself into the grass to catch his breath.

What was that? he thought.

He was surprised when a voice answered him from the Aethyr. *That, Warrior of the Realms, was Shel-Masa the Destroyer.*

The Traitor's Song: Chapter Two

Maegwin sucked in a deep breath. With it came…peace. Contentment. The song of Sho-La shimmered in the air like mist, rocking her as though she were a sleepy child. She'd been frustrated at her lack of progress with Leo's Song Spell but now that dissipated. She swayed gently, humming softly along with Leo's music.

But he suddenly fell silent and Sho-La's presence vanished abruptly. Maegwin opened her eyes, gasping at the sudden absence. Leo's eyes were narrowed, staring at something behind her.

"What is it?" She twisted, scanning the tent.

Leo shook his head. "Nothing. It's nothing." He grinned suddenly and gripped her hands. His touch was like ice. It was all she could do to stop herself flinching. "Things are coming together nicely, my dear, don't you think? Things are falling into place. Soon we'll have everything we've been fighting for! I can feel it in my bones!"

Maegwin pursed her lips. "So you say. But we haven't

yet achieved our aims here, Leo. The Shinnar are still a problem."

Leo waved a hand dismissively. "Oh, forget the Eagle Clan! General Shallon can take care of them."

Maegwin stared at him. "What? After all they've done to me? Are you mad?"

Leo shrugged. "That depends on your point of view, doesn't it? Does a madman see that he's mad? If he realized, it would prove he wasn't mad, wouldn't it? Only someone who believes he's sane can be truly mad."

Maegwin crossed her arms and arched an eyebrow at Leo. The youth frowned as though confused by his own words then threw up his hands.

"Anyway, that's beside the point. What I mean, my dear, is that I have a different task for you."

"Which is?"

He stared at her for a long time and Maegwin got the uneasy impression that he was assessing her. At last he nodded. "I know you think I overreacted about the theft of my journal. And I know you reckon I wasted too many of our resources guarding my library in Tyrvanan. But, as I hope you'll soon agree, there can be huge power in the written word."

Somewhere outside a coyote barked. The tramp of guards moved past the tent. Maegwin waited, saying nothing. She had learned that silence was often the best way to get Leo to come to the point.

"I have a gift for you, Maegwin."

He sang a note and she sensed an emanation of Air. The space before Leo shimmered and when it cleared, he was holding a book in his hands. He held out the thick, leather-bound tome toward her. "Here."

Maegwin took the book hesitantly. It was much heavier than she expected. "What is it?"

"Take a look."

Maegwin unclasped the two golden locks that kept the book shut and carefully opened the cover. As she read the title she gasped and glanced at Leo sharply.

"Where did you get this?"

He grinned, enormously pleased with himself. "What did I tell you? Books, my dear, are far mightier than any blade. It is in knowledge that we find true power."

With trembling fingers, Maegwin lightly touched the page, hardly daring to believe it was real. The pages were brittle and yellow with age. The faded script was written in a language that had been dead for centuries. Even so, Maegwin could read it. Any priestess of Sho-La could read it. Four words. That was all.

The Canticle of Darkness.

The lost chapter of the Book of Sho-La. The chapter that had been banned, along with worship of the Dark Goddess. As far as she knew, nobody within living memory had ever read what she was holding in her hands now. Except Leo, it seemed.

"Why didn't you tell me you had this?" she asked, breathless and a little fearful.

"I'm telling you now," he shrugged. "You weren't ready. But now? Now it's rightfully yours. Read it. Study it. You're going to need it."

"Need it? For what?"

Leo tapped his nose and winked. "All in good time, Maegwin. All in good time." He stood abruptly and brushed down his garish shirt. "Now, I'll leave you to get acquainted with my gift. We'll leave for Near Point in the morning. I think you'll like it there." A huge smile showed his big square teeth. "In fact, I'm sure you'll love it there."

He was being evasive again, dropping hints that he wouldn't explain. There was more to this, Maegwin suspected. There was something he wasn't telling her.

"I'll be ready," she murmured.

"Excellent!" Leo clapped his hands together. "Well, until the morrow, my dear!" He turned with a flourish, flinging his cloak over his shoulder in a swirl of yellow material, and strode from the tent.

Maegwin was left alone. The sounds of the camp reached her: people talking, the braying of horses, the tramp of many booted feet. Yet it seemed distant, unimportant. She gazed down at the *Canticle*. Slowly, hesitantly, she reached out and ran her fingers along the title. A shiver slid down her back. In sudden fear, she dropped the book on the floor and scooted backward a few paces. She stared at the book as though it was a viper that might bite her.

"Fool," she muttered to herself. "What do you think will happen? It's just words."

But she didn't approach. Instead, she rose and made her way over to her traveling trunk. She took out another book and returned to the rug, seating herself cross-legged once more. This book was smaller, less grand. Opening it, she read the words on the title.

The Canticle of Healing.

This was the most studied of the chapters of the Book of Sho-La, a goddess of peace and forgiveness. It was the chapter closest to Maegwin's heart. She opened the book to the page she needed and set it on the rug in front of her.

With her left hand she reached up, grabbed the collar of her tunic and yanked it over her head. Sudden pain shot through her shoulder and she grunted, biting her lip to keep from crying out. She set aside the tunic and sat only in her under-vest. The cool air sent goose bumps riding up her skin.

Squinting, she studied her right arm. There had been no improvement. The skin from hand to elbow was blackened and burned. Her fingers were useless and curled in on themselves so that her hand appeared more like some shriveled claw. She may have survived the fall of Tyrvanan but she hadn't survived unscathed. Nothing helped. She had tried every potion Leo's people could offer her. She had tried every healing trick she knew. It made no difference.

Pulling the *Canticle of Healing* closer, she scanned the words on the page and softly began to sing. As usual, nothing happened. Once, long ago it seemed now, she had been healed by a Sentinel. In turn, she had used that power to heal Rovann. But something had changed. She suspected that the *Canticle of Healing* used the energy of Aethyr, the Realm of the angels.

And they no longer answered her.

Sudden tears pricked her eyes and she blinked them away ruthlessly. With a cry of exasperation she snapped shut the *Canticle of Healing*.

Instead, she reached for the *Canticle of Darkness*.

———

Rovann walked all night. When he judged he was a safe distance from the Songmaker's camp, he let the cloak of Aethyr slip and was grateful for the sudden burst of energy. Holding a cloak of Aethyr was exhausting. He marched roughly south, hoping he was heading in the right direction.

Even though he'd spent the last few weeks living with the Shinnar, Rovann was still surprised at how silently they could move. One moment he was treading warily through the darkened prairie, the next he was surrounded by armed men who rose from the grassland like dark, silent ghosts.

He recognized Dranvey, the Eagle warrior who had apprehended him and Maegwin the first time they'd entered Shinnar lands. Realms, it seemed like a life-time ago. The young man approached Rovann, shaking his head and grinning.

"I don't believe it. You're still alive!"

Rovann frowned. "I'm not sure whether to be pleased or offended by that statement. Clearly, you didn't think I had it in me."

Dranvey's eyes widened. "Oh no, I didn't doubt you. It's just that... well...Kandar says..."

"Kandar says a lot of things. Sometimes I think the old man's made of nothing but piss and wind." He slapped the young man on the shoulder. "Although we'll keep that last remark to ourselves, eh?"

Dranvey snorted then clasped Rovann's hand, forearm to forearm. "It's good to see you whole, Lord First. This will make a fine tale!"

"I hope so," Rovann agreed, grinning. "Let's get back and start telling it, shall we?"

Dranvey nodded to his men who melted into the darkness to scout the way. Rovann walked by Dranvey's side. Before long they reached a deep gully that had once been a river bed. Dropping down into its dusty base, they walked along its course for what seemed like hours until the ground began to rise and they began passing through low hills.

They were challenged by Shinnar guards at the entrance to a fissure that cut through the hill. At a shout from Dranvey, they stood quickly aside. Rovann followed

Dranvey gratefully through the cleft until he emerged into a shallow valley.

A sea of conical tents filled the valley's slopes and at this late hour a few campfires were still burning. Rovann paused for a moment, taking it in. The fighting might of the Shinnar people lay spread out before him. Or at least, those who refused to follow the Songmaker. The Eagle Clan, led by Chief Brennan and shaman Kandar and also the Lynx, the Bear, the Wolf.

As Dranvey's warriors walked into the valley, people hurried over. A barrage of questions was fired at Dranvey which he waved away with a few choice curses. The warrior led Rovann to the north side of the vale where the Eagle Clan had set up camp. Here a group of people were on their feet, waiting.

Brennan, chief of the Eagle Clan, stood with his arms crossed and Kandar by his side. Perala, chief of the powerful Lynx Clan fingered her weapons as she always did, a fierce expression on her face. Halan, chief of the Bear Clan, was chewing on something and as they approached, he turned and spat a stream of brown into the grass.

"Look at this!" barked Kandar. "A bloody welcoming party! Kiss my hairy arse, I bet you didn't realize you were so popular!"

"I never doubted it," Rovann answered with a tired smile.

Kandar was silent for a moment, yanking on a bone in his hair. Then he shook his head. "You did well, boy," he said. "You did well."

"Perhaps you should hear what I have to say before you make that judgment."

Chief Brennan issued instructions. "Bring food and drink for the King's Mage." He turned to Rovann. "Sit down before you fall down, friend. Rest, eat, and then we'll talk."

Rovann wearily seated himself on the grass by the campfire. He felt so tired. Pinching the bridge of his nose, he closed his eyes for a moment, gathering strength, then opened them again, stifling a yawn.

The other clan chiefs folded onto the ground around the fire and, with a rattle of bones, Kandar settled not two paces from his side. A short time later three Shinnar youths brought a big pot of stew and ladled it into bowls for everyone.

Rovann ate mechanically then squeezed his eyes shut, desperately searching for that quiet space inside that would allow him to gather his thoughts. But images of Maegwin and Leo floated on the back of his eyelids like ghosts.

It seemed only moments before the meal was finished and tidied away. One by one, Rovann felt the eyes of the Shinnar leaders fall on him. He sighed. Realms, he just wanted to sleep.

Chief Brennan cleared his throat. He was a big man with thick arms and a long braid hanging over one shoulder. "So. Tell."

Rovann pursed his lips, gathering his thoughts. After a moment he began to speak. "Kandar's trace worked. It took me straight to the Songmaker's hidden base."

There was a murmur of approval and the old shaman looked smug.

"Their numbers are more than we anticipated and they seem to be growing. I risked Walking the astral and saw many thousands in that camp. Trained, disciplined soldiers for the most part."

"So give us their location and we'll go wipe them out!"

growled Perala of the Lynx Clan. "Their presence here is an insult to the World Mother!"

"No, Perala. You must not face them."

The woman bristled. "Are you questioning the strength of the Shinnar?"

"I'm not," Rovann said soothingly. "Only your numbers. The enemy are too many. So far your tactics have worked because you have attacked in small parties, hitting their supply lines and scouting parties. You know this terrain. You can attack quickly and get out again before they can regroup. But an all-out assault? They would dig in and wear you down gradually."

Perala opened her mouth to speak but Kandar barked, "He's right, woman! What good are our horse-archers against heavy infantry?" He turned his raptor's gaze on Rovann. "So what do you suggest? We just let them sit there?"

"Yes, that's exactly what you do. I have a feeling they won't be bothering you for much longer. Leo has a second force, one made up of mages, gathering in a place called Near Point. He and Maegwin are leaving to rally the forces there. I suspect the Songmaker was only tarrying in Shinnar lands until his forces in Near Point were ready."

"And now?" Perala asked.

"Now he will march out of Shinnar lands and begin his assault on Amaury."

Silence met his words. He wondered what they were thinking. Pleased that the hostile force was leaving their lands? Angry at how the Songmaker had used the Shinnar people?

A low muttering broke out. Several fingered weapons as though itching to use them. Chief Brennan rubbed his chin and said, "Has it all been for nothing? We have fought, we have died, all to halt the Songmaker's advance. If what you say is true, we have failed."

There was a rumble of agreement.

"Failed?" Rovann asked incredulously. "That's not a word I'd ascribe to the Shinnar people. Each life given has bought us valuable time. Time to decipher the Songmaker's plans. Time to mount a defense. Without your efforts the Songmaker would be rampaging unchecked through both Amaury and Shinnar lands. So no, Brennan, it has not been for nothing."

The chief nodded, conceding the point. "So what now?"

"Isn't it obvious?" snapped Perala. "We divide our forces. Some stay here. Some go north to this Near Point and attack his forces there. The bastard is making fools of us and we cannot allow it!"

Halan of the Bear Clan, a stocky man with a ring through one nostril turned to the fiery woman. "We should let them go. The Songmaker wants to leave our lands? Why don't we let them do it? Once they're gone we can go back to our lives."

Kandar drew himself up and waved a bony finger at the man. "I might have guessed that whiny voice belonged to you, Halan. Are you an idiot as well as a bloody coward?"

The man bristled and one hand moved to the ax hanging at his side. This didn't deter Kandar.

"Scratch my arse with a pointy stick! Have you learned nothing?" the old shaman barked. The Unraveling has begun. The World Mother's final battle is coming. We fight for Her! Do you think the Songmaker will be content with destroying Amaury! Fool! He will wipe us out like insects! By the World Mother's sagging teats, am I surrounded by utter idiots?" He glared around at the gathering, scorching them with his dark gaze.

For a moment the leader of the Bear Clan glared back, but when he received no support from the others, he crossed his arms over his chest and pointedly looked away.

Rovann spoke. "Halan has a right to his doubts. If I could, I would keep the Shinnar out of this. But I can't. You know this. You've seen what the Songmaker is capable of. So Kandar is right: the fight doesn't stop at Amaury's border. Curse it all, it doesn't even stop at the border of our Realm. If the Songmaker isn't stopped, soon there will *be* no borders. The Realms will unravel and Chaos will take us all."

He glanced at each of the faces before him in turn, trying to decipher their expressions. Most looked resigned to the fight, some even eager. "But you still have a choice. There is no shame in giving up the fight. Should you choose to leave and join your kin sheltering at the coast, none here will say a word against you."

He fell silent, allowing his words to sink into the dense atmosphere between them like a stone into a pond. A long, heavy silence stretched out, punctuated only by the crackle of the fire and the scrape of someone sharpening a sword in the distance.

Then finally, Chief Brennan barked a laugh. "A pretty speech! I can see why they made you Lord First, Rovann. Yes, we could run. We have done all you asked of us. No shame in admitting that. But you won't find the Eagle Clan abandoning its friends. We fight on. Who's with us?"

Instantly, Perala of the Lynx Clan said, "The Lynx stand with the Eagle."

A moment later Halan rumbled, "And the Bear."

Jojen, spokesman for the injured leader of the Wolf

Clan added, "The Wolf stand with the Eagle. My chief has spoken."

Kandar threw his head back and cackled. "We're all bloody in it! Did you really think it would be otherwise?"

There was a roar of agreement from every throat around the fire and its sound reverberated deep in Rovann's stomach. They thumped their chests with their right fists and began a deep, throbbing chant.

"Shinnar! Shinnar! Shinnar!"

At a campfire nearby, the warriors took up the chant. The sound spread until a sea of men and women were rising to their feet throughout the valley, thumping their chests.

"Shinnar! Shinnar!"

Slowly, deliberately, he bowed to each of the war leaders around the fire. They responded in kind, faces grave.

"Take no risks," he said. "Hold them here for as long as you can but do not spend lives needlessly. Should Amaury fall, the task of opposing the Songmaker will pass to you."

Kandar pulled a bone in his hair. "The World Mother will look after us. She's annoyed at what that goat-faced bastard is doing in Her name. I can feel it in here." He rubbed his belly with one spindly hand. "What about you?"

"As soon as Lady and Tallo get back we're going to Near Point."

"I thought you'd say that."

"Well, I'd hate to disappoint."

The old shaman stared at him for a moment. "You can't take them all on by yourself."

I made a promise, he thought. *I will kill them all.*

"I can try."

Kandar looked about to speak but then thought better

of it. "Come. We've set up a tent for you. You can rest there until you're ready to leave."

Rovann allowed himself to be led away to a small conical tent in pride of place next to Brennan's own. He ducked through the flap to discover that his meager belongings had been placed inside.

With a sigh he threw himself down on the pile of furs in one corner. Exhaustion washed through him. His limbs felt weighed down with stones. His thoughts were becoming foggy and slow. But he couldn't let himself sleep. Not yet.

Forcing his aching body into a seated position, he pulled over a faded hessian sack sitting by the door and placed it in his lap. With a sigh he reached inside and took out a small, leather-bound book. Its pages were empty. It was nothing more than a blank notebook but he set it down with reverence on the floor in front of him. Then, closing his eyes, he opened a gate to the Realm of Aethyr. Reaching through the gate, he snagged the item he'd hidden there and pulled it through.

When he opened his eyes the book still sat there. But now, instead of empty pages, a scrawl of scribbled diary entries, snippets of song and rough sketches met his eye.

Turning the pages carefully, Rovann began to read, searching for any reference to the village of Near Point. There was none.

What had Leo been referring to when he'd spoken to Maegwin? What was contained in this book that he'd needed so much? Rovann ground his teeth in frustration. For all he knew, the book was meaningless drivel and this whole charade was just another of Leo's elaborate games. He studied the maps and diagrams, hoping to find a clue there. Still nothing. The pictures seemed to be stylized diagrams that bore no resemblance to anything Rovann recognized. One showed a circle with tall pillars placed at intervals around it. Some sort of pattern of power radiated out from the circle but Rovann had no idea what it was. Another seemed to show a grid of some sort that reminded Rovann of a castle portcullis with a place name scrawled next to it that he didn't recognize.

"Curse him," Rovann growled under his breath. "Curse them both."

Tucking the book protectively beneath his body, Rovann closed his eyes. He would rest his eyes. Just for a while. Perhaps things would make better sense when he was rested.

"My Lord First!" a woman's cry startled him from a deep and dreamless sleep.

He shot upright, already reaching for his power, before he recognized the two familiar faces grinning at him from the tent flap. The first was a dark-haired woman with ringlets piled on top of her head and a gleaming gold torc around her neck. The second was a man with a huge, drooping mustache oiled into points.

"Lady, Tallo," he greeted them, indicating for them to sit then clasping their hands in turn.

The two soldiers had been assigned to him by Captain Tyan back in Tyrlindon. Both were elite fighters and, despite his protestations to the contrary, seemed to consider themselves his body guards. No doubt they'd been apoplectic when he'd left them behind whilst he went after Maegwin.

Absently, Lady took out one of the many knives she kept about her person and began twirling it. Light flashed from the spinning blade.

"You and I need to have a little talk, Lord First," she said with a dangerous edge to her voice. "About how you ran off and left us." Rovann opened his mouth to speak but she talked over him. "However, that can wait. We've been trying to contact Tyrlindon, just as you ordered. We've checked the cotes in this valley and the next. None of our birds have returned. Somehow all our messages are being intercepted although I don't know how."

"Don't know?" Tallo snorted, stroking his mustache nervously. "Of course we know! Someone's betrayed us, that's what!"

"Shut up, Tallo." Lady snapped.

"It's true, I tell you. Everyone is against us!"

"You and your bloody conspiracy theories!"

Tallo shook his head. "What if I'm right? The cursed Songmaker has done a thorough job of severing our lines of communication, the shitty little bastard."

Rovann took this news in silence. It was over a week since he'd last had word from Amaury's capital. Due to the risk of being overheard if they communicated by sorcery, Rovann had instructed the Council to communicate by messenger bird only.

"Perhaps I should Walk the astral," Rovann muttered.

Lady narrowed her eyes, thin eyebrows pulling down. "Captain Tyan said none of you mages were to do that."

"I know what he said," Rovann snapped. "I was the one who gave him that order. But what choice do we have?" He sighed. "I'm sorry. I shouldn't snap at you."

"We're used to it, eh, Tallo?" she nudged the soldier. "With Tyan as your captain, you get immune to outbursts of temper."

Tallo narrowed his eyes at Rovann. "So, where've you been? What's so important you had to go running off without us? The Shinnar are rushing around like an ant's nest that someone's just poked a stick into. I'm guessing that's your doing, Lord First?"

Rovann sighed. "I'm afraid so. How do you fancy a bit of scouting?"

Lady raised an eyebrow and Tallo frowned. "What kind of scouting?"

Rovann told them of everything he'd overheard in the Songmaker's tent. When he finished his story Lady let out a stream of colorful curses that any dockworker would have been proud of.

Tallo looked thoughtful. "Near Point, eh? Never heard of the place. So when do we leave?"

"As soon as we can get word to Tyrlindon."

Tallo pulled on his mustache and then leaned back on one hand. "The way I see it is this. This is a war, right? All wars carry risks. It's a damned risk contacting Tyrlindon, that's for sure. But on the other hand, knowledge is power. Or at least, that's what Sergeant Hannel is always saying. So we need knowledge, right? We need to know what's happening back home and they need to know what the Songmaker is planning."

"Thank you for that insight," Lady said. "It's really helpful."

Tallo frowned at her. "What I mean is we have to contact Tyrlindon but can't do so using the Lord First's normal, um, means. Neither can we use message birds. So, we need an alternative."

There was silence for a moment. Then Lady prompted, "And?"

"And what?"

"What do you suggest?"

Tallo shrugged. "I dunno."

Lady rolled her eyes.

Rovann chewed his lip, thinking. "Wait, you may have a point."

Tallo brightened. "I do?"

"Perhaps I'm going about this the wrong way. I don't need to contact the mages in Tyrlindon directly. There's somebody I can contact who can pass a message on for me. Tanyaka."

Rovann had often communicated with the dragon whilst she still dwelt in the Realm of Fire by using Fire as a conduit. Would such methods work now she was in the Realm of Earth? There was only one way to find out.

"Tallo, give me your tinder pouch."

Wearing a puzzled look Tallo handed it over then scrambled after Rovann as he made his way through the flap and sat down a few feet from the tent. He scraped together a few twigs and used Tallo's tinder pouch to make a spark. Soon a small blaze was burning.

Fire. That was the key.

He stared, unblinking into the blaze until its image was burned into his eyes. Gradually, the fabric of the flames began to separate, becoming the whirling lines of energy that made up the living fire. He formed these into a conduit and sent out a summons.

Tanyaka! Hear me!

Grab your copy…
vinci-books.com/traitorssong

About the Author

Elizabeth Baxter spent most of her childhood wandering the paths of the Shire, the trails of Narnia, and the sun-speckled glades of the Hundred Acre Wood. She wrote her first book when she was six years old and plans to continue until they nail shut her coffin. When she's not sipping a latte and dreaming up fantastical places for her readers to visit, she enjoys reading, hiking, watching cricket, and cramming as much world travel as she can into one lifetime.